GW01445006

THE P
for Walter Irwin
all the latest spe
the many worlds of Star Trek. And the latest
Trek #18 is chock-full of such fascinating articles as:

"How Many Sulus?"—Which is the real Sulu, scientist, swashbuckler, helmsman, commander?

"Humor in Uniform—Starfleet Issue"—From the
overt comedy of "The Squire of Gothos" to the
far more subtle humor in "The Search for
Spock," a close look at the comedy-drama mix
that makes Star Trek work.

"Star Trek: Three Faces, Same Mirror"—From
the original series to *The Next Generation* to
Deep Space Nine, how Star Trek continues to reflect the changing beliefs and problems of our
own time.

These are just a few of the provocative, thought-
ful, and original explorations of the many universes of Star Trek that await you in—

THE BEST OF TREK
#18

"A fine job ... a balanced account of the creation of *Star Trek* that even dedicated Trekkers will find informative."
—*Washington Post Book World*

STAR TREK CREATOR

The Authorized Biography of Gene Roddenberry
by
David Alexander

With a Foreword by Ray Bradbury

Every time you watch an episode of Star Trek, you see a piece of Gene Roddenberry. Now this fascinating book lets you see this many-sided man and his multifaceted life and mind in their enthralling entirety—and in so doing, gives you new focus and fresh feeling for the show that has soared beyond its time to reach the realm of legend and myth. Even the most fervent fan will find startling new illumination about: Gene Roddenberry's real life inspiration for Mr. Spock; how Roddenberry's background put its subtle but significant stamp on *Star Trek*; the strange, dramatic actual genesis of the *Star Trek* series that was to take Roddenberry and so many others to popularity and a place in TV history beyond anyone's wildest dreams; and the inside stories of how some of the most unforgettable *Star Trek* episodes came into being.

With an Introduction by Majel Barrett Roddenberry

"Comprehensive ... Roddenberry was a complex, creative, controversial and versatile individual."—*Chicago Sun-Times*

"Provides fascinating insights ... contributes worthily to the understanding of an enigmatic man and his creations."—*Booklist*

from ROC

*Prices slightly higher in Canada.   (0-451-454405—$6.99)

THE BEST OF TREK®

#18

EDITED BY
WALTER IRWIN & G. B. LOVE

RoC

A ROC BOOK

ROC
Published by the Penguin Group
Penguin Books USA Inc., 375 Hudson Street,
New York, New York 10014, U.S.A.
Penguin Books Ltd, 27 Wrights Lane,
London W8 5TZ, England
Penguin Books Australia Ltd, Ringwood,
Victoria, Australia
Penguin Books Canada Ltd, 10 Alcorn Avenue,
Toronto, Ontario, Canada M4V 3B2
Penguin Books (N.Z.) Ltd, 182–190 Wairau Road,
Auckland 10, New Zealand

Penguin Books Ltd, Registered Offices:
Harmondsworth, Middlesex, England

First published by Roc, an imprint of Dutton Signet,
a division of Penguin Books USA Inc.

First Printing, February, 1996
10 9 8 7 6 5 4 3 2 1

ROC REGISTERED TRADEMARK—MARCA REGISTRADA

Printed in the United States of America

CONTENTS

INTRODUCTION

Thank you for your overwhelming response to our previous volume! It is gratifying to know we were missed, and you have welcomed us back with open arms and open hearts. Even more gratifying is the number of letters we've received from old friends and former contributors; it is wonderful to hear from each and every one of you again. We're also thrilled to hear from new readers from all over the United States and from the far corners of the world. Welcome aboard!

As this introduction is written, the latest chapter in the Human Adventure is just beginning. The *fourth* Star Trek series, *Star Trek: Voyager* has just premiered on the new Paramount network. The quality of the show has already reached, and will undoubtedly maintain, the high standards set by the late (and very lamented) *Star Trek: The Next Generation,* and continued in *Star Trek: Deep Space Nine.* But what is important and ultimately so exciting about the appearance of *Voyager* is that it represents an ultimate continuity of Star Trek.

Yes, *The Next Generation* succeeded wildly, beyond the expectations of anyone involved with the program (with the possible exception of Gene Roddenberry), and proved that the Star Trek "franchise" could provide a loyal weekly audience beyond the core group of "Trekkies" and do so without the original cast. Had

Next Generation failed, even slightly, it would have meant the end of Star Trek for many years, perhaps permanently.

Deep Space Nine, while a solid performer in every market and an excellent series, has not matched *Next Generation's* critical or ratings successes. This is not the time or place to debate why (although you can be sure we'll be featuring an article doing so very soon), but the fact remains that many people feel that *Deep Space Nine* "slipped up" in some vague, undefined way. Unfortunately, some of those people were in the Paramount hierarchy, and they were quick to say "I told you so."

Nay-sayers to the contrary, Paramount decided to launch its new network with a proven winner in the lead spot: a new Star Trek show. We fans watched in something akin to open-mouthed amazement as the hype for the new series grew and grew and grew. How could any show measure up?

Voyager, we are happy to say, more than measured up. So far, it is a stunning critical and ratings success (its premiere episode beat out *two* of the major networks in many markets and finished first overall in the evenings' ratings). Time will tell if it continues to be a critical success; it is already evident that it will be a success as Star Trek and is a hit with fans. In fact, our initial polling of fans indicates that *Voyager's* premiere episode is considered by a vast majority to be the finest of all three "new" series.

Voyager's future seems assured, as does that of *Deep Space Nine* and the rest of the Paramount network. There is even talk of another Star Trek series. We've heard two ideas bandied about: One would be a "Tales of the Enterprise" anthology show, featuring stories of past and present captains and crews of the various vessels bearing the name *Enterprise*. Another would feature the adventures of Captain Sulu and the crew of the *Excelsior* (a scenario which many fans wanted to see in the last movie). And there are others, we're sure.

Plans for yet another Star Trek film proceed nicely; a script is being written and preproduction will be beginning later this year. Patrick Stewart and the rest of the *Next Generation* cast will be appearing, as well as a *new* ship and some surprises.

The point is, *everyone* now automatically assumes that there will *always* be a Star Trek series of some kind appearing on television and movie screens. That's *everyone,* friends. . . . Not just us, the fans, the eternal optimists and keepers of the faith, but *everyone*. Your parents, your best friend, your barber, your local dogcatcher . . . *everyone*. And that includes—oh, so most importantly—the powers that be at Paramount. Finally, finally, after so many long years, they are nurturing that little goose, giving it love and care and, yes, *respect* in return for the many golden eggs it has given them over the past twenty-nine years. The respect is the important and thrilling part, friends. The respect for what Star Trek is and what it represents to millions upon millions of people is long overdue and hard earned and even harder won.

That respect is the final validation of Gene Roddenberry and Gene L. Coon and Robert Justman and all the other wonderful people who shaped the original series. That respect is the thank you to Michael Piller and Rick Berman and the hundreds of other hardworking people who took up the torch and lifted it even higher than before. That respect is the best reward we fans could ever have for our love and our loyalty.

In these *Best of Trek* volumes, we do our best to continue with the tradition of respect for our readers and for Star Trek in all its incarnations. We believe we have some really interesting and perhaps even controversial articles for you in this collection, and we hope you'll enjoy reading them.

As always, if you have any comments on the contents of this volume or any of our proceeding ones, please drop us a line. We'd love to hear from you. And if you feel you'd like to write an article yourself, please do so and send it to us. Every article included in this collection was sent in by one of our readers who was introduced to us by purchasing an earlier volume. They made it to print; you can, too!

Please address your articles and correspondence to:

Trek
1415 Graysville Rd.
Ringgold, GA 30736

Remember, please don't send us fiction; we can't and won't publish Star Trek stories or novels.

Again, thank you for the many warm letters and greetings; we only wish we had the time to respond personally to everyone that wrote. Rest assured, we read all your letters and enjoyed each and every one of them! Thanks again and "Keep on Trekkin'!"

Walter Irwin
G. B. Love

FANDOM, WHAT A CONCEPT

By Miriam Ruff

I was walking down the street the other day wearing one of my many different Star Trek T-shirts, when I noticed that people were looking at the shirt, and me, strangely. This was not the first time that such an event had occurred, to be sure, but it prompted me to think anew about how we Star Trek fans are viewed by the general public and, more importantly, about our responsibilities as fans, not only to ourselves and to the show, but to the rest of society.

Perhaps the best way to start is to define "a fan." In the case of most television series, movies, or musical groups, a fan is someone who likes it or them, and eagerly watches or listens. The fan may also collect memorabilia or information about his or her favorite.

In the case of Star Trek, fans can be split into two discrete groups: "Trekkers" and "Trekkies." A Trekker is one who adheres to the ideals of the show and watches it for what it has to say about us and the society in which we live. A Trekker may also have interest in the production values of the episodes, such as writing, direction, acting, music, etc. A Trekkie is more likely to be running around a convention with a phaser in hand, and may corner you into a debate about the code Kirk used to open his safe in episode 63. (In the famous *Saturday Night Live* skit featuring William Shatner, the people he told to "get a life" were most definitely Trekkies.)

Please, don't get me wrong. I am not saying that these people don't have the right to express their support for the show as they wish, but because of their generally overzealous and persistent natures, they are the type of fan best known to outsiders. It is unfortunate, because Star Trek and its fans have so much more to offer than zap guns and trivia questions.

Aside from personal interaction at conventions, where outsiders can be startled by Trekkie behavior, the media is mostly to blame for the distorted image of Star Trek fans. At any convention I have attended where the media is present, they have always sought out the fans with strange costumes or obvious props to film or interview. Face it, they feel that image looks better on the eleven o'clock news than a bunch of people standing around discussing the impact of the show on modern society. But in their eagerness to get a sound bite, the reporters and producers forget they have ignored the greater percentage of the population, and their coverage is slanted and far from complete.

The *Arsenio Hall Show* was an example of media distortion. Though guests such as Patrick Stewart were common, Mr. Hall continually commented on how strange and almost rabid the "Trekkies" are (all fans are obviously considered the same by Mr. Hall). He degraded the aliens on the show, claiming that Klingons look like "butt heads," and that the makeup of other aliens was "bizarre." Mr. Hall is funny and people laughed, but his comments only served to reinforce what is shown by the rest of the media. It was disheartening to see someone who worked so hard to overcome "black" stereotypes, and gain acceptance for blacks as a whole, set up an entire new set of stereotypes for people who enjoy Star Trek without trying to understand fans or what fandom is all about.

On a more personal note, I was invited several years ago to introduce a Star Trek film festival on a local cable station. I was told to wear a uniform, pointed ears if I had them, and to bring all my "Trekkie" stuff, like books and dolls and whatever else was in my collection. I consented to do the show, but absolutely refused to play the Trekkie. As I was running a local space-exploration group at the time, I opted to discuss the influence Star Trek had on the development of manned and unmanned space flight, and what the future is likely to bring in the way of space stations and colonies. Despite my position, I was still asked when I walked in why I couldn't have just put on a uniform and brought my stuff anyway.

The show itself went fairly well, but I really haven't stopped smarting since that time. The people at the station didn't have and didn't want any knowledge of what Star Trek was all about, despite the fact that they were running a film festival about it. They simply assumed that anyone speaking about the subject would naturally conform to the stereotype they knew, and didn't know what to do with me when I didn't. Needless to say, intelligent conversation about any aspect of the show was almost impossible.

It is this type of reinforcement which gives rise to the stares on the street for anyone wearing a Star Trek T-shirt or carrying a bag or reading a book. It is this type of reinforcement which gives any associated with Star Trek fandom a bad name. And the sad part is, there is almost nowhere (outside of fandom itself) where Star Trek fans are portrayed in any but the most superficial or unflattering of lights. In the eyes of the general public, we are all "obsessed."

Well, if we are "obsessed," what is it that we are obsessed about? Many fans enjoy the action/adventure format of the show. Others like the futuristic elements and the idea that one day we will travel out into the galaxy. But for most fans, judging from what I have heard and read and the hundreds of fans that I have met and spoken to, it is the underlying messages in each of the shows, and the series themselves, which attracts them and brings them back not only week after week, but year after year.

Perhaps the most important message in both the original show and *The Next Generation* is the philosophy of IDIC (Infinite Diversity in Infinite Combination). This idea—that all people can and will live together in peace, regardless of their differences, and together will become greater than the sum of their parts—was first formally mentioned in the original series episode "Is There in Truth No Beauty?", but it can be said that it was the central philosophy of Star Trek.

IDIC was an inspirational, though radical, concept for the time during which Star Trek originally aired. Unfortunately, it looks as if we still have a long way to go before we achieve it. But it is a worthy goal, something to which we as individuals and as a people should aspire. It is through IDIC that we will be able to stop wars and decimation of the planet and work as a species toward creating and utilizing resources to benefit us as a whole. It seems a little "Trekkie-ish" to say that Star Trek is a way of life, but when we consider the fantastic implications of adopting IDIC in the here and now, it hardly seems we can afford to *not* make it a part of our daily lives.

Another important message, one which goes along with IDIC, can be found in the Prime Directive. Also known as General Order One, the Prime Directive is a policy of noninterference in the affairs of developing societies, regardless of the consequences. Each society is to be given the freedom to develop naturally, without artificial inducements to upset the balance. In fact, each Starfleet officer swears an oath that he or she would rather die than violate this most important mandate.

The Prime Directive is instrumental in preventing an outbreak of moral superiority, preventing Federation personnel from assuming that their way of life is somehow better or more just than others simply because it is one they know and understand.

Our history is littered with every possible instance

of the destruction of indigenous societies, from the English and French invasions of Africa to the American pioneers' near-genocide of the Native Americans. "Good interference" and "bad interference" are meaningless terms; to interfere and impose one's own set of rules upon another society inevitably leads to that society's destruction. Like IDIC, the Prime Directive tells us that difference is acceptable and even good, and we must learn not to destroy something just because it's different.

Another central message in Star Trek is the value of friendship: real friendship, where one person is always there to help the other, no matter what the cost. We are shown not only how difficult real friendship can often be, and how demanding on both parties, but how precious it is, as well. No matter what the danger, no matter how great the cost, friends in Star Trek can count on each other for help, or advice, or simply being there when it means the most. It presents to us an ideal of how we would like our own relationships to be. While few people achieve more than one such friendship in their lives, and while many may never achieve it, it is a goal to work toward. A relationship that gives purpose and meaning to our lives and our actions makes us better and greater than we could ever be alone.

So this is what we fans are "obesessed" about: friendship, loyalty, hope for a better world, and striving to create a common, brighter future. We see in Star Trek a glimpse of ourselves, or of who we aspire to be, and a world that has managed not only to survive the crises we now encounter, but expand and thrive beyond them. Hardly as bizarre or threatening as some would have you imagine, but some people won't, or can't, see beyond what is right in front of their faces. What can we as fans do about this?

First, we can and should indulge our obsession and continue to watch and support the show, but with that indulgence does come responsibility. We have to participate in a more active way than simply watching in order to keep the momentum going, to keep the series alive and help bring in new fans. Our responsibilities, therefore, are not only to ourselves as fans, but also to the show as television and to outsiders, those who have no knowledge of or experience with fandom.

The responsibilities to ourselves are fairly obvious. We are entitled to enjoy the show and help keep our "passion" going, no matter what others say, through conventions, get-togethers, discussions about the episodes, costume-making, and story-writing. Fanzines and periodicals such as *The Best of Trek* are excellent for giving us the opportunity to discuss, in written form, almost any aspect of Star Trek; it gives us new ideas about the shows and movies and ourselves to think about. Without our participation fandom dies, and with it an environment that enriches and entertains. Fandom is necessary for us to more completely embrace a show and an idea that is so important to us.

That is why it is so distressing to me to see such divisive and destructive actions taking place among a small section of fandom. The group to which I am referring is known informally as the "Classic Trekkers." While they have a right to express their views, it seems to me that they have forgotten their responsibility to not only keep fandom going, but to keep Star Trek alive. Basically this group feels that the only Star Trek which is acceptable is that derived from the original series and movies. While considering *The Next Generation* an entertaining show, they don't think it is really Star Trek, as it does not feature the original cast members.

These fans will loudly argue with any supporter of the new series; I know this well, because in addition to hearing stories from many others, I have been the "victim" of such behavior myself. I was speaking with someone whom I did not know at a convention. When I mentioned I was a big fan of *The Next Generation*, he let loose, telling me in no uncertain terms that "if it didn't come from the original show, it couldn't be Star Trek," and that the new series and my opinions were nothing more than "junk."

Now, as I have said, he is entitled to his opinion just as I am to mine, but to be told outright that my opinion is worthless is ludicrous. What happened to IDIC? How can anyone say that they support the ideals of Star Trek while blatantly discarding them?

Star Trek, as we have seen, is more than a show, it's an idea and an ideal, and both can be expressed in many different ways. Exploration and IDIC and adventure and friendship can be found on both the original and the new series, as well as in the novels, the fanzines, the homemade videos, the crews and shows yet to come, and even in some parts of life around us here in the twentieth century. Why should they be the exclusive domain of one three-season TV show? Part of the responsibility to ourselves is that we are allowed to *be* ourselves, to express our views and know that we have the freedom to do so. We are allowed to enjoy what we want without fear of recriminations. When a group of fans takes the attitude that only they are right, it can only serve to sever the ties we have built with each other and drive the show and the multifaceted expression of fandom into the dust.

Our responsibility to the show follows from that to ourselves. Through fandom we keep the show alive, by demonstrating to the television stations and these ever-vigilant Nielsen executives that we are there and watching, by writing letters to the actors and producers, and by holding conventions so that we can publicly display our interest and affection. Letter-writing campaigns, such as the one aimed at NBC to prevent the premature cancellation of the original series, or those to support the careers of actors we like, are ways to tell the general public that *this* series is something worth watching, *these* people are quality craftspeople worth hiring again.

Responsibility also extends to writing critical letters when we see something we find offensive or questionable and speaking out when there is something we think is wrong. Star Trek is not infallible, nor should it be, for that would only serve to distance it from its viewers, who could no longer relate to what it has to say, being fallible themselves. While we don't have the right, not being on the production staff, to dictate creative choices to them, we do, as the "keepers of the flame," so to speak, have the right to be heard, and we need to let them know what we think. It is only through communication that our opinions and our support can be ascertained; it is only through communication that the positive interaction between the show and its followers can continue.

Of equal importance to these responsibilities, however, is our responsibility to the non-Trek fan. IDIC tells us they, too, have a right to their opinions. The Prime Directive tells us that we shouldn't impose our views on people who don't want to hear them. That is all well and good, and sets the guidelines by which we should function, but the responsibility goes beyond this, extending to the point of education. Nowhere does it say we have to sit by and listen to lies told by people who are too lazy or too uncaring to learn the truth. As Picard told Worf in "Redemption," you have to challenge the lies. Allowing them to continue is the same as saying people are correct in their erroneous assessment of us, and this is not acceptable. We will not and should not accomplish the challenge by brute force, but rather by subtlety, by disseminating information to people who want to hear it.

Oftentimes at conventions outsiders will come up to a fan and ask what's going on, and sometimes even want to get involved. Speaking with them about why we're there is a great way to get the point across; after all, word of mouth is a very powerful tool. Refusing to play along with the stereotypes, such as on that cable show I helped introduce, lets people know in no uncertain terms that there are those of us who do not like being classified as something we are not. Discussing Star Trek as literature or as cinema, rather than just talking about the plots or playing trivia games, helps to broaden the spectrum of most people's knowledge of Star Trek. There will always be people who have no interest in the subject, and it is imprudent to try to change their minds; after all, that just reinforces the stereotype of the overzealous fan. But there are many people who simply don't know what it's all about, and comments to them may indeed prove helpful.

We, the Star Trek fans, are a strange lot. We have a collective obsession with a show that has been out of production since 1969. We have hope in the future and a plan for getting there. We travel in spaceships across light years and meet strange new civilizations every week. We are dreamers. We are doers. We are optimists. With our futuristic outlook and our humanistic concern, we can be a powerful force for positive change. That is an awe-inspiring concept and a tremendous responsibility. Part of the price we pay for that is to be perceived differently than others who aren't sure how to relate to such commitment. But there is no reason why that has to be translated into negative treatment, and no reason why others can't join us; we are not part of an exclusive club. By being patient with other people, and showing them that our hopes and dreams are not really so strange or different from theirs, we move that much closer to achieving acceptance. And by refusing to force others to join us if they don't wish, we move that much closer to establishing a real-life version of IDIC and a global society. The responsibilities of being a Star Trek fan and being a member of the society in which we live are huge, but if we accept them, there is no limit to what we, as a species, can accomplish.

A CRITICAL OVERVIEW OF STAR TREK: THE NEXT GENERATION— SEASON ONE

By Roberta G. Carpenter

This article is not about the characters or the ship or the twenty-fourth-century universe of *Star Trek: The Next Generation*. I may do reviews on those later. This article is about the episodes from Season One—a fan's look at each and every one of them.

To start with, we have to go way back to "Encounter at Farpoint." That may seem like ancient history, but it was a major milestone in Star Trek lore. All the other *Next Generation* episodes were just episodes in comparison—this one was special. It even won a Hugo for best dramatic presentation.

Besides that, it was a good show. In fact, I think that "Encounter at Farpoint" was one of the best episodes in the first season.

Let's start with Q. Q is an interesting character. They couldn't have picked a better actor than John DeLancie. He simply looks the part. The story gave us very few clues as to what kind of science the Q use. Obviously they have the power to suspend a person or group of people in an instant of time, and then interact with other creatures for a while, which would probably create a whole new time continuum. In fact, the Q seem to be experts at manipulating time and space. Time is their speciality.

"Encounter at Farpoint" leaves a great deal of room for thought about the Q. What kind of creatures are they? We know that Q can assume different forms—is he something altogether different from humanoid? Obviously he has a sense of humor. Why does he need to wear costumes all the time? Why does Q refer to himself as an individual, Q, and also to his entire race as "the Q"?

Q wasn't the only focal point of the episode. "Encounter at Farpoint" might, indeed, have been two episodes. The crew's other problem was the mystery of Farpoint Station. The answer proved to be surprisingly simple—but difficult to come by. It was a classic Star Trek episode, introducing a strange, new world, orbiting the distant Deneb on the outskirts of the known galaxy, strange new life—the beautiful space creatures—and new civilizations—the Bandi and the Q. Besides all that, the writers did an exceptional job of introducing the new crew and displaying twenty-fourth-century technology without flaunting everything.

On a scale of one to ten, I'd give "Encounter at Farpoint" an 8.5.

"The Naked Now" was essentially a remake of the original series episode, "The Naked Time." This did not mean it was lacking in originality. For one thing, the crew had the increasing threat of an unstable star nearby. The reactions of the crew to the disease were as comical and unfamiliar as before. The acting was superb. I think at this point, writers were still trying to get the audience more familiar with the series. Data explains his physiology, and we get in-depth looks at the characters' personalities: Crusher's affection for Picard, Tasha's wish to be more feminine, Geordi's longing for real eyes.

The characters all handled their situations well. One thing puzzles me: Why didn't Worf get the disease? And if he had, what would he have done? That leaves plenty of room for imagination! "The Naked Now" gets an 8.

The next episode was fairly interesting, but not as good as the first two. "Code of Honor" was also a typical episode of Star Trek, but not as well done. It gave Picard a difficult task, it presented a problem in diplomacy, and it offered a situation where a crew member was threatened. This is a fast-moving and dramatic episode, with a realistic conclusion, but there were certain things about it I didn't like.

First, these people are supposedly so devoted to honor that they make the Romulans look like liars. Yet Lutan first deceives Picard, then kidnaps Yar, then refuses to keep his promise for her return. He tries to cheat in the fight. Are these the actions of a man of principles?

Another thing: Hagon was terribly surprised at Tasha's defensive abilities. Yet it was obviously common for Ligonian women to be trained in self-defense should they be challenged the right of succession.

Lastly, why didn't Picard simply beam Tasha up to the ship? This would not have violated the Prime Directive, because taking her would not interfere with the Ligonian's culture and her life was endangered.

I give "Code of Honor" a 7.

The next episode was one of the worst. Or, at any rate, one of the least interesting. Partly, I was disgusted because it introduced the Ferengi, and it is well-known that Ferengi are much hated by the majority of Trekkers. They are puny. They are clowns. Not to mention stupid. They're laughable. How can the Federation call these people its adversary?

I didn't really mind the concept behind "The Last Outpost"—it reminded me a little of "Requiem for Methuselah." What I minded were the Ferengi. Disgusting. I give this show no more than a 4.

The next week: Wow! "Where No One Has Gone Before" was *the* best episode of the first season. I liked it, other fans liked it: it was truly Star Trek.

Instead of taking the ship to Warp 14 as planned, the episode takes them far beyond that, to the edge of the universe. Here, thought seems to be reality. The ship is saved with the aid of a Traveler, an alien from another place (dimension? time? universe?), journeying through this reality.

I liked the show. I liked the concept. One of the best things about Star Trek is that Gene Roddenberry seemed to come up with ideas which I believe we might discover, far in the future, to be true. The special effects were superb. So was the acting. And we all loved the scene where Wesley was given the rank of Acting Ensign.

"Where No One Has Gone Before" instantly became my favorite. It was nearly topped by five other episodes, but only one of them really came close. It gets a 10.

Next came a few fairly ordinary episodes. There was nothing wrong with them, but they certainly weren't exemplary. "Lonely Among Us" concerned an energy being (a common and unfortunately repetitive idea in Star Trek) invading the ship. The special effects for this one were okay. So was the element of mystery and intrigue, and the climax was great. But it only gets a 7, the score I give to all episodes that are only average.

The next one only got a 6.5. "Justice" was a typical psychological interplay. What I didn't like about it is that we all knew Wesley wasn't going to be executed. What was the point? At least we expected Picard to have to fight for him or something. All he did was give a typical Kirk speech and beam them up. 6.5 is being lenient.

I'm resentful toward Paramount for even airing "The Battle." Guess who popped back up? The Ferengi. Blaahh. There was no point to the episode; I think they probably did this one because they had run out of good scripts. If anything, this episode could be called a psychodrama, and Star Trek is not a psychodrama show. I expect I'm not alone in my contempt for this episode. I give it a 2.

Fortunately, for every bad episode, Paramount seems to do at least two good ones. In this case, the next one was again exemplary. It was the long-awaited sequel to "Encounter at Farpoint," and was even better than the two-hour premiere. In "Hide and Q," Q was back, up to his old tricks, this time trying to brainwash Riker into joining him.

It's a humorous episode. Q acts like Trelane, but you don't feel like you're watching a pathetic temper tantrum; you feel like laughing at Q's feeble underestimation of the humans. This was my third favorite episode of the first season. It was a true Star Trek show, placing people in alien settings, impossible situations, and featuring the funny and interesting Q. It rates a 9.25.

Next week came another good episode. The first few had followed a general pattern which most fans didn't like, trying to give all the major characters the same things to do and say. Ultimately, we began to see episodes with individual problems for the characters. "Haven" was the first Troi episode.

In the end, Troi doesn't get married (which we all knew was what was going to happen), but there was a logical reason behind it, and during the show there were enough instances when we thought she might go through with it to keep it interesting. It also was a funny episode, thanks to Troi's eccentric mother. I give it an 8; certainly better than average.

"The Big Goodbye" was another good episode. This took us into the depths of twenty-fourth-century technology, especially the holodecks. And it made you wonder—when a computer can create a soul, does that mean we have created a god? "The Big Goodbye" didn't seem to be as much a Star Trek episode as something you might find on *The Twilight Zone*. Interesting enough to be a 7.5.

"Datalore" was perfectly indicative of the Star Trek

that Gene Roddenberry imagined years ago. Everything about this episode was perfect. We had no idea where it was going for quite a while; because of the similarity between Data and Lore, it was shocking to see Lore give the ship over to the hungry alien. Lore's cunning was disgusting—just as it was supposed to be. I'm not a naturally violent person, but I liked the big smash-'em-up fight between the two androids. I think an occasional brawl is in order for Star Trek—something it has lacked until now. And it was fun to see Wesley make a fool out of Picard.

I would give "Datalore" a 10, but it somehow didn't quite come up to the standard of "Where No One Has Gone Before." I give it a 9.999999.

The following week we saw a sort of average episode. "Angel One" was thought to be very good by some fans, very poor by others. I thought it was ordinary. It seemed that it wasn't worth giving less than a 7, but there wasn't really much point to the show. They had a concept with the flip-side of male chauvinism, but the plot they came up with didn't quite cut the mustard.

Another pretty average show was the rather complicated "11001001," about little aliens called Binars (who think and speak in binary language) stealing the *Enterprise* because the computer on their world is breaking down. They are not bad, only interested in self-preservation.

I didn't go crazy over it, but it was a reasonable plot. I did think that it was slow-moving; half the episode takes place in the holodeck, where Riker falls in love with a woman called Minuet who was created by the computer. There was a big action scene where Data and Geordi evacuated the ship's crew onto a space station. It was certainly no worse than average, so I'll give it a 7.25.

The next episode was a little worse than normal. The story was pretty weak; just how do you make a youth pill, anyway? This show illustrated that you can't recapture youth.

In "Too Short a Season," an aging admiral became young in order to confront an old enemy who is holding many hostages. But the drug has deadly side effects and the admiral dies.

It was an interesting enough episode, but it was ordinary. It just wasn't terribly compelling. I believe that we can expand our lifetimes, and that an eighty-year-old man in the twenty-fourth century might only be middle-aged, but I don't believe that one can genetically turn back the clock. Note that they never explained how the drug works. This one gets 6.75—a tad less than average.

The following show, "When the Bough Breaks," was a sentimental story, but also realistic. The acting, story, plot, and technology were all good, but not superb. I think that "When the Bough Breaks" overdid it just slightly. The suspense is bogus—we know for a fact that they are going to get the kids back—but it was well done and fairly interesting. It rates a 7.25.

"Home Soil" was excellent. It was about a totally new form of life—microscopic crystal—which is far more intelligent than humans. We don't learn what kind of brain or manipulative limbs the creatures have; one wonders how they evolved to their present intellect without them.

The acting was wonderful. Data has an opportunity to once again demonstrate his superhuman strength. The special effects were good and the action and suspense were great—I found myself sweating once. It is a good and touching episode which leaves room for a sequel. "Home Soil" gets an 8.25 from me.

For a long time, we seemed to be getting some pretty good episodes, and the next one was no exception. "Heart of Glory" was a Worf episode. It gave us a great deal of insight into the Klinzai society, and the desire of some of them to live life "as Klingons should live it."

Worf gets into big trouble by learning to like and respect the renegades. He is torn between his loyalty to Starfleet and the feelings in his heart. His problem solves itself when the two Klingons try to escape and Worf proves his loyalty to his ship.

"Heart of Glory" is an exemplary show. Besides good special effects, plot, and acting, it really made me *feel*. It takes a strong episode to do that. I give it a 9.

"Coming of Age," the following episode, was okay—an average show. I liked the part with Wesley being tested for Starfleet Academy; it gave us lots of insight into Starfleet procedure. Not exceptional, but not a bad show: a 7.5.

The next show is one of my personal top five favorites: "The Arsenal of Freedom." This was definitely an action show. There was an intriguing concept behind it all, of course, but the main thing was action. I like the way Picard solved the problem. I give it a 9.25; I like action.

"Symbiosis" was one of the best shows in terms of plot, but I thought the acting left just a bit to be desired. Although the Prime Directive won't let Picard interfere in the drug addiction problem, he manages to solve the problem in a fascinating, ingenious, and mutually beneficial way. It is a good, moral story, and a fine example of the way Gene Roddenberry uses the Star Trek setting to comment on our present-day problems. I give it an 8.5.

Several months of perfectly good and somewhat exemplary episodes had to end sometime. But we were all in for a surprise when Paramount cruelly aired "Skin of Evil." That's the one where they killed Tasha Yar!

I hate it. I hate everything about it. I hate Denise Crosby for leaving the show. I hate the script writer for writing a stupid script that served no purpose except to provide a plot around which Tasha's death could occur. Sure, the acting was reasonable. Sure, the special effects were good. That's no excuse for an inexcusable episode.

Tasha Yar was my favorite character. I thought it was awful that she died. And I have to reflect on an irony: In all of Star Trek history, the only permanently dead characters have been security guards. Tasha was also a security guard.

Maybe I'm not being fair, but this is a personal opinion article and I'm angry just writing about this. I give "Skin of Evil" a .25.

You'd think that after the shocking "Skin of Evil" they'd do a good episode. Not so. "We'll Always Have Paris" was less than average. They started with a very good science fiction concept concerning time and other dimensions. Now only if they had presented this theory with a better plot. Everything was too easy and there was no suitable climax. And we get pretty sick of Picard's old romances. Somehow it's hard to imagine Picard at an age when he'd attract any women. "We'll Always Have Paris" gets a 6.5 from me.

The next episode was even worse. "Conspiracy" really left me feeling very cheated. It was the first horror plot introduced on *The Next Generation*, and Star Trek has never been much of a horror show. Yes, it was good suspense and reasonably interesting, if only they didn't have the exploding head and the creature coming out of Remok's stomach. A purely horrid sight, matched by Data's chilling statement at the end that the creature sent off a homing beacon to an unknown galaxy. I give "Conspiracy" a 5.

I thought "The Neutral Zone" was good. Not excellent, but good enough. I was very pleased that the Romulans came back; now, at last, we'd have some good enemies! Their threat, matched with the problem of the three twentieth-century people who had been frozen, made for an interesting episode. It gets a 7.75.

I am looking forward to reviewing the second season of *Star Trek: The Next Generation* and another twenty-four exciting adventures. I'm assuming the Ferengi will be kind enough to stay out of things.

ROBIN CURTIS—A SAVVY SAAVIK

By M. S. Uram

No tribute to the twenty-fifth anniversary of Star Trek could be complete without including an interview with Robin Curtis, who played Lieutenant Saavik in two Star Trek movie installments: *Star Trek III: The Search for Spock,* and *Star Trek IV: The Voyage Home.*

Curtis describes the first days on the set as exciting, nerve-racking, and intense.

"I was not exactly sure, interestingly enough, way back when a few months prior to being cast, which part I was being considered for. I had not met Leonard Nimoy. During the first few hours we spent together, we spoke a great deal about my background."

She continues, "Nimoy was very interested to know all about me and made references to my resume, especially to my musical theater background and so forth. He seemed genuinely to want to get to know me."

At one point Nimoy offered her sides, which are pages that represent scenes from the film. As Paramount and Nimoy had been very secretive about the movie, Curtis felt privileged to be able to read the sides.

"Nimoy gave me a few minutes to study the sides in his outer office and then I went back in," she says. "We then went back and forth with the lines of the side where he would read the character in whatever scene it might have been, and then I read the part of Saavik."

After some guidance and direction from Nimoy, he seemed to think she knew what she was doing with the part. They left on a handshake and the rest is history.

"Nimoy said, 'I have no doubt you can do the part. And now, it is merely a question of the powers that be,' " Curtis said.

There were many other stages beyond that one, according to Curtis, in which she had to prove herself. Interestingly enough, Nimoy taped the audition, so she did not have to show up in person. Nimoy merely ran the tape for the upper echelon at Paramount.

Her first day on the set of *The Search for Spock* was admittedly exciting.

"Here was this man, Nimoy, who thinks I know what I am doing, and I am not certain *I* know what I am doing," Curtis comments. "I was not a Trekker, as it were. So, I did not know a great deal about the Vulcan/Romulan folklore. But, Nimoy put images in my mind about this. For example, things like having the impression of one thousand years of wisdom behind my eyes. I was very concerned about revealing too much emotion and betraying the character in that way."

Curtis continues: "I remember in preparation, I would practice looking into a mirror and delivering lines and saying just about anything without all the normal facial expression that I was used to doing from my theater background of being lively and animated."

She adds, "It has always been difficult for me to tone down all that emotion, much less eliminate it all together, to play a part such as Saavik. But, that was Nimoy's bent on the character. He wanted her to be primarily Vulcan. And, so, I went with that."

After the first couple of days, Nimoy approached Curtis and said he would never leave her out on a limb by herself and would guide her every step of the way. "And he did."

"The first few days on the movie were very tense," Curtis continues. "And although I was very excited, I tried to give off this serious, 'I am here to do my work and I have done my homework—I think!—and I am not sure what I am doing, but you are going to help me' kind of impression."

The rest of the cast was warm and welcoming to Curtis. "They had been doing their stuff for a long time, so they did not have the same hurdles to jump that I did. Jimmy, Nichelle, Walter, and George all knew who their characters were supposed to be. I had to sort of establish a character and find my way. They were relaxed enough to extend themselves to me, the new cast member, and made me welcome."

For example, Curtis mentions one incident where she did not understand what was going on during a scene. Nichelle Nichols promptly placed her at ease by joking that no one knew what was going on, but they would just do it and it would eventually make sense.

As the role of Saavik was originated by Kirstie Alley, Curtis had to make some character adjustments to make the role her own.

"I had not seen *Star Trek: The Motion Picture* or *The Wrath of Khan* prior to my interview with Leonard Nimoy," she said. "I think it behooved me at the time not to have seen the films because I am fairly impressionable and might have had a tendency to mimic or glean from her [Alley's] performance. I might have tried to include it in my own portrayal of what I thought the character should be instead of just starting from scratch. So, I think it was a good thing for me not to have had exposure to either of the first two films. And I have not seen them since, except for bits and pieces."

Curtis adds, "It really helped for me not to have any preconceived ideas whatsoever and just to let Nimoy put the ideas into my head of what he wanted from the character. Then, I could just go from there."

Regarding Nimoy's transition from actor to director, Curtis had this to say:

"I saw no difficulty in this transition during the filming of the Star Trek movies. I think that if there had been any uncertainty on his part as to which shoes he was wearing when he was talking to me as a director or talking to me as an actor, I might have sensed it. But it was never a problem at all.

"At least not for me," she continued. "I cannot speak for the other cast members because they had all worked together for so long. It must have been odd on some level to suddenly have someone who was a teammate of yours, and working side by side with you, getting on the other side of the camera and telling you what to do. But for me, it was the perfect situation."

But her fondest memory of *The Search for Spock* had nothing to do with the actual shoot.

"My father was battling cancer at the time. When I got the part, it was the most wonderful news and a marvelous event to have taken place during a sort of touch-and-go time in our lives. This was a very emotionally charged time period.

"It was so wonderful to have something outside the family to get excited about and turn our attention to. It tickled me no end that my dad made it to the premiere back at the mall in Utica. I come from a small town in upper New York where the mayor pumps gas! Anyway, the theater owner would not cooperate with us and save seats for my family. So we had people waiting in line all day to save the seats for them. My father made it and saw the movie and that was just like a gift from God to have that happen. Although we lost him soon after, he was the biggest fan that I could ever hope for.

"So on a personal, intimate level," she adds, "that is what made Star Trek special to me at that time. At least my father saw me succeed and I will always be grateful to Star Trek for that."

In response to fan speculation on the relationship of Saavik and Spock in *The Search for Spock,* Curtis says, "I think the fans are pretty much responsible for this because Paramount led me to believe that Saavik was being groomed for more participation. Many people were excited about a pregnancy storyline and that sort of romantic thing."

Paramount's intent, Curtis feels, was to include some new, perhaps younger, characters into the films, but plans changed and Saavik was dropped.

"It would be fun to form and go further with the character again," Curtis agrees. "But until the writers and others at Paramount choose to include Saavik, she does not exist at the time being, except through the eyes of the fans. To be honest with you, in order for my own peace of mind, I have put Saavik to rest for the time being."

Curtis explains, "Because I am not a science fiction fan, it is difficult for me to jump into that world and imagine what would happen with the Saavik character if I did."

She laughs, "The fans would probably call me on it left and right on how I was contradicting what would be happening at that time in the future, and so forth. When I have taken a chance and speculated on the future, people have debated with me on the topic. So I keep my hands off the speculation end of it. I think, for the most part, that the Saavik character is taking a permanent break . . . for a while."

Rumor has it that Saavik was to appear in *Star Trek VI: The Undiscovered Country.* Curtis comments, "There was a question at one time of my participation in *The Undiscovered Country,* but I am not in the movie. The Saavik character, at least as I performed her, did not appear. There was some confusion because they did include a character [Valeris] that might have been Saavik, but due to creative differences, she was renamed.

"From what I understand," says Curtis, "they had

the character doing things that Saavik might not have done. They decided to opt for an entirely different character, as she would be involved in an assassination plot against the Klingons and so on."

Curtis was never contacted about playing the role, either as Saavik or Valeris. The situation was far too emotional for her to pursue the role; she could not bring herself to be aggressive enough to call and question why she was not considered. She was deeply hurt by the oversight, but remains pragmatic. "That is the nature of the business—it gives a little and it takes it away. The lesson I learned is that life can be disappointing sometimes. You pick yourself up and keep going." She laughs. "I should have a T-shirt printed saying, 'I Survived Star Trek'!"

(One report said that the original script for *The Undiscovered Country* featured Valeris as the daughter of Spock and Saavik. Her rapid aging would be explained by her conception on the Genesis Planet. Curtis thinks that this rumor is not true.

"It would be terribly confusing to fans," she says. "I think the character was originally supposed to be Saavik, and not her daughter named after her.")

The introduction and subsequent deletion of strong female leads in the Star Trek movies and series has always been a subject of debate among fans. If a female lead such as Saavik was included in the cast, a reason would be found to facilitate her demise.

Of this, Curtis says, "I really don't know to what to attribute that. Majel Barrett-Roddenberry commented that Gene Roddenberry's original concept for Star Trek was to have a crew complement consisting of fifty percent female and fifty percent male. Paramount [actually NBC] would not have it and preferred a thirty percent female to seventy percent male ratio for the crew.

"Perhaps this reflects the overall state of the business. Men are paid more and work more, and it is difficult for women to get leads. But I cannot knowledgeably comment on Star Trek when I am not as familiar with it as I perhaps should be."

About the introduction of new characters, Curtis said, "I do not know the reasons for introducing characters and then disposing of them. We lead the fans to think they will see more of them and suddenly they are gone. There is one realistic aspect to it that I can see. First, it is a large cast, an ensemble cast. I was particularly delighted with *The Voyage Home,* because it seemed to include everyone so beautifully into the plot.

"When you concentrate on one character," she continues, "I think the whole thing goes out of whack. I think, personally, the better stories are those which involve everyone equally. I guess what I am trying to say is you have a lot of prominent people all vying for a part in the storyline. But, there does seem to be a majority of male characters."

Curtis does not consider herself a Star Trek fan despite her involvement in the genre. "I do consider myself a fan of the fans. I have a great deal of admiration and respect for the people interested in Star Trek, and who are able to express their passions in constructive or artistic ways. This has endeared me to all Star Trek and science fiction fans."

She adds thoughtfully, "It is quite something to be the object of such loving devotion. The fans are not narrow-minded. Once you are in the family, it seems that they will be a follower of your career whether it has to do with Star Trek or not."

For example, Curtis cites her ten-week stint on the daytime series *General Hospital.* "I am a 'soap-opera' fan, but it is hard work. I knew they did one show a day. But, the enormity of it, the pressure of it . . . I do not think you can know until you are involved in it." She says, "The workload for me was not all that intense. I worked, at the most, three days per week. But for some of the actors, it was every day, with voluminous dialogue, and it is shocking how quickly it all goes down.

"For example, you barely block in a scene and then, four hours later, after all of the scenes have been blocked and you have a lunch break, you come back, dress, and walk through it one more time, perhaps twice. You might receive intense direction, and then they shoot it. And that is it.

"It is very confusing, especially for someone who is a fringe character like I was. It is hard to know where a story is going. Every time you get your weekly script, it is a frantic search to see what your character will be doing next." Curtis' character was abruptly derailed from the series, and she thought she was done with it. But, "I was told by the producers, just like in science fiction where Spock returned from the dead, anything is possible." She laughs.

Curtis felt that her time on the soap opera, while certainly not all there is to an actor's education, was excellent training and experience. "It keeps you thinking on your feet. You do not have a lot of time to weigh your options and work through a scene as you would if you did a play, for instance, where you have weeks of rehearsal. You are forced to fly by the seat of your pants and make quick decisions.

"That is a lovely tool to have, because, as an actor, you are often in audition situations where you have very little time to see the material. It shows the director that you are willing to take the risk."

Even so, Curtis feels the swiftness of daytime television production tends to mislead an actor. "Perhaps superficially you are developing a character," she says, "but you have to ask yourself if you are really getting something meaningful and long-term going. I think that it can be a little confusing. But it can certainly teach you valuable acting tools."

The threat of typecasting has caused many actors to fear taking a role in Star Trek. Curtis feels otherwise. "I do not have that fear, and let me explain why.

It has a lot to do with my naiveté. Knowing that about myself is really important. It is similar to what I said earlier about Leonard Nimoy's ability to be an actor one moment and a director the next. He was very clear about that, so I got the point.

"I think it just depends on the actor and how he or she chooses to be seen. I just refuse to think that from two films I could become typecast. Particularly given the strong components of my personality, which are the direct opposite of Lieutenant Saavik. Besides, I think typecasting tends to take place more often in television than in the movies."

Curtis elaborates: "I am only going into your consciousness for one hour and forty minutes; my actual screen time is perhaps fifteen minutes of that. So, you are only getting fifteen minutes of this character going into your subconscious. The arena of the theater tends to remind you that this is just a movie.

"But television comes into your home," she points out. "That is why people seem to feel they *know* these characters. They automatically assume that the actor *is* the character they are playing. For example, the original *Star Trek* series came into your home week after week and then it went into syndication. It was as if these people were actually in your house and you could talk to them. It is a much more 'real' type of situation than a movie theater. Movies do not occur inside your home. Television has a difficult time suspending reality in that respect, whereas in the film medium, it is clear that it is *not* real. So you really do not get typecast from films."

Based on this belief, Curtis still wishes to remain in the world of Star Trek.

"I have auditioned for a role in *The Next Generation*, but I have not gotten the job," she says. "They could alter my appearance enough so I would not resemble Saavik. I would like to keep playing an alien rather than a human, however. I liked the Vulcan/Romulan mix in Saavik. But I am open to anything."

She grins. "I'm not really familiar enough with *The Next Generation* to choose an outrageous alien. I would like to be outrageous, because that is more akin to me. I did logic and—oh, God!—you would not believe how difficult that was! I struggled for days with the line, 'David is dead.' And, even as we shot it, I allowed a little breath in between the words which sort of came naturally. Nimoy said, 'I want nothing—no emotion, no pause, not even a breath, no inflection whatsoever in your voice.' I had to literally robotically say that line, and it was so hard for me not to convey the loss and the sadness of it. So, I think I would prefer to be a character who is a little more in tune with her feelings and willing to reveal her emotions."

(Editor's Note: Ironically enough, Curtis was subsequently cast as the Vulcan Ta'syl in "Gambit". Ta'syl was, however, rather demonstrative for a Vulcan, so a little of Ms. Curtis' personality won through.)

As for future goals, Curtis feels she is not like other actresses. "I do not have lofty goals where I want to win an Academy Award and be well known. I do not want a grand lifestyle but just to live comfortably. I am an ordinary person from a small town. So, when I do act, it is like someone else doing it and not me. I still get a big charge out of it."

Curtis is currently working in commercials and with a small theater group of about twenty actors, which was formed about two years ago.

"It was my way to feel I had some voice and could get some joy without someone else telling me when I could and could not get it," she explains.

Curtis visits Star Trek conventions in an attempt to raise funds to allow the group to produce a play based on its own experiences. She has also co-written a screenplay. While she awaits word on these projects, she resides in Los Angeles, where she spends time gardening and socializing with friends.

"I audition quite a lot, too," she says, "which feels more like the 'job' aspect of this career rather than the work itself. I find the work is always fun and thrilling, and always new and different. The 'job' seems to be going out and looking for the work!"

She concludes, "That can take its toll. Sometimes you come close and you let a project get inside of you, so losing it can hurt."

She remains philosophical, however. "That's part and parcel of what I do. So, I keep going. I think perseverance is an important key to trying to make it in a business where the odds are against you. You just have to stick with it."

A CRUCIBLE OF STARS

By Sherry Hopper

An android serving with biological life forms on the bridge of a twenty-fourth-century Federation ship is *at least* as remarkable as a Vulcan among humans on a starship bridge a century earlier—especially when the vessels in question share a celebrated name: *Enterprise.*

Perhaps because fate or the Great Bird has appeared to play the same galactic prank on two intriguing individuals, Star Trek fans have persisted in their speculations about the similarities between the android Data and the half-Vulcan Mr. Spock. These two share a distinctly logical outlook on life, but the most important role each has held is that of observer. Through the Vulcan's eyes, viewers discovered a new way of looking at their universe. Through the eyes of an android, they found a new way of looking at themselves.

When *Star Trek: The Next Generation* began its fifth season with the episode "Redemption II," some of the speculations were resolved. In this episode, *The Next Generation* illustrated that both Spock and Data have singular identities and unique roles to play in the Star Trek Universe.

A portion of "Redemption" echoes the classic *Star Trek* first-season episode "The Galileo Seven," in that each presents a vessel with a pivotal test for an officer in the *Enterprise*'s chain of command. Lieutenant

Commander Data and Commander Spock face crucial tests of their command abilities. The results provide a crucial step in the development of each character.

Although not the focus of "Redemption II," Data's command assignment to the starship USS *Sutherland* was integral to the resolution of the storyline (exposing Romulan interference in the Klingon civil war). Spock's command ability, however, was definitely the focus of "The Galileo Seven," where the shuttlecraft carrying the Vulcan and a handful of crew members crashlands on a hostile world. While there are direct similarities in their circumstances—both Data and Spock were placed in command of wholly human crews, and each was subjected to immediate personal prejudice—Spock's test was the most severe because of its isolated scenario and life-or-death consequences.

The Vulcan and a crew of seven that included Dr. McCoy and Engineer Scott were dispatched to study the Murasaki 312, a giant quasarlike phenomenon. As science officer, this was a normal role for Spock. When the shuttle crashed on Taurus II, he assumed command, which was his duty in Spock's dual role of first officer. And, being Vulcan, Spock began by submerging his personal anxiety beneath a veneer of logic. He may not seek command, but he will take charge when that duty is thrust upon him. He was uncompromising regarding his absolute authority in this situation. No, they will not draw lots to see who will be left behind so that some will have a chance at rescue. No, they can't afford the time or risk the danger to perform a burial for three dead crewmen. Both McCoy and Lieutenant Boma openly berated Spock and rebelled at his cold, unfeeling leadership.

As crew members died and the monstrous natives continued to menace them, Spock became overly analytical. Aloud, he wondered why his precisely logical, correct steps failed to gain the desired results. Why did the humans not understand his position or his goal to get as many as possible away from the planet safely? Spock exhibited confusion, uncertainty, indecision.

At the climax of his test, surrounded by his companions' fear and in a decaying orbit, Spock chose to commit what McCoy described as a very human act of desperation. Unable to contact the *Enterprise,* they were facing death without rescue. Therefore, without telling anyone what he planned, Spock jettisoned the shuttle's remaining fuel and ignited it, hoping the flare effect would alert the *Enterprise* to their location.

When it seemed that nothing more could be done, and all aboard would die, Dr. McCoy appeared pleased that the Vulcan's last act should be a human one. Even Scott expressed admiration for Spock's last gamble.

Before the shuttle burned up in the planet's atmosphere, the gamble paid off. The *Enterprise* found and retrieved them.

In *The Next Generation*'s "Redemption II," Data was not immediately considered a viable candidate for a command role. When personnel were desperately needed to lead Picard's armada to blockade the Klingon border, Data was passed over for a captaincy. With the android's background experience, and bridge position, he was right to question that decision. And faced with Data's legitimate question, Picard did not debate his officer; he told the android to report aboard the USS *Sutherland* as captain. Therefore, unlike Spock, who at least found himself among his shipmates, Data was assigned away from the *Enterprise* to command officers and crew to whom he was known only as what he was—an artificial life form.

Once aboard the *Sutherland,* Data faced similar, direct prejudice as the Vulcan experienced decades earlier. Upon Data's formal assumption of command, the first act of Lieutenant Commander Hobson, second-in-command, was to request an immediate transfer. He was honest about his reason for this request: "I

don't believe in your ability to command this ship."
And Data's first act as Captain was to summarily deny
that request, without explanation.

Throughout the episode, Hobson continued to fill
the role of antagonist, much like Boma in "The Galileo Seven." As Hobson made spontaneous decisions
and took action regarding the ship's weapons systems
and crew safety, he was told quite firmly by his new
captain that *all* strategic and shipwide decisions must
be presented to command—to Data—even when they
were the right actions. As Hobson, argumentative and
resentful, continued questioning Data's every action,
the android grew even more firm. Facial expressions,
stance, tone of voice . . . everything about him radiated
conviction and assurance. Data never questioned the
correctness of his actions, although he offered some
explanations when asked. It was obvious Data had
been very observant on the *Enterprise* bridge; he effectively incorporated the traits he witnessed in Picard
and Riker into a personal command style. He doesn't
have long to develop or exhibit that style, but if asked
to describe his actions and comportment in one word,
that word would be "confidence."

Just as Spock acted outside his own predictable nature in jettisoning the *Galileo*'s fuel, Data acted beyond what was considered normal android behavior.
At a crucial point, Data blatantly disobeyed Picard's
order to fall back and did not answer his hail. Instead,
Data was guilty of what, for a human, would be described as "initiative." He enacted a maneuver designed to defuse the Romulan cloaking devices and
expose their positions, and he succeeded. The Romulan stalemate was concluded, without bloodshed, when
they retreated back to the Neutral Zone.

With the mission concluded, as Data left the *Sutherland*'s bridge, for the first time Hobson addressed him
with respect as "Captain." And when Data submitted
himself for disciplinary action for disobeying orders,

Picard told him Starfleet didn't need officers who blindly follow orders. In other words, "Nicely done."

What remains at the close of each episode is a valued Starfleet officer, tested under fire, who must now analyze the results . . . and himself.

Spock is well-known for the statement, "I have never sought command." After "The Galileo Seven," the character of Spock progresses steadily away from the command structure; the Vulcan settles more securely into a life's work that he will describe often as both purposeful and logical. He is, first and foremost, a scientist and an observer. He is also a teacher. When he was, ultimately, promoted to command the *Enterprise* (*The Wrath of Khan*), Spock accepted because the capacity in which he served was to train cadets in shipboard matters. The moment the *Enterprise*'s training cruise became an investigation into matters at the space lab orbiting Regula One, Captain Spock easily deferred command to James Kirk. The trial that Spock faced on Taurus II, among his shipmates, showed him that his "best destiny" lay somewhere beyond the captain's chair.

Although Data completed his command test without casualties, he was no less dramatically tested. His accomplishments were significant. Beyond a doubt, he led the crew of a starship with command strength. Further, he acted in the best interest of his ship and his crew, to safeguard human life whenever possible. He also accomplished the larger mission objective of the Fleet against the Romulans, even though this last achievement came as a result of disobeying orders. Yet he illustrated, to both crew and command officers, that he could use his intelligence and observations to be an effective leader.

Vulcans have served as effective starship captains and crew; the USS *Intrepid* (referred to in "The Immunity Syndrome") was an all-Vulcan vessel of which the Federation was justifiably proud. But, ultimately, command is a personal thing. Spock succeeded in bringing almost all of his crew back alive, but the crucible of his trial burned away questions about command ambition. Though he stubbornly insisted his action was "logical," Spock accepted the truth of his trial and did not pursue command options.

We are not sure how Data viewed his first command. Did he take success for granted? Did he analyze the experience, as Spock must have done, to determine what he did right and what he could have done better? Will, one day, a Starfleet vessel find an android serving as captain for more than one short mission?

The purpose behind their separate trials was similar: to set patterns for tomorrow, and to lead or step back and let others take that role. Spock found satisfaction in following another whose destiny was to lead him to all of those "strange new worlds." Data continued to show his determination to participate in all of the opportunities that life in Starfleet—and in the universe—would offer him.

"Redemption II" effectively ended some of the speculation that Data is the Spock-clone of the twenty-fourth century. They may both be logical, intelligent characters who are our best observers of humankind in their respective centuries, but they are also individuals.

And, at least in the role of commanding a crew and a vessel, Data surpassed Spock's abilities and ambitions.

A HISTORY OF SPOCK'S PROBLEM

By Tom Lalli

What would have happened if Sarek had raised his son to accept and express his emotions whenever he felt them? Would Spock have been a better adjusted individual? Perhaps Spock's only problem is that he can't fit in; he is too emotional for Vulcan tastes, and too cold for humans . . . but closer examination shows there may be more to it than this simple explanation.

In several episodes, notably "The Enemy Within," Spock refers to a constant battle *inside himself.* This battle is between his two halves, and not necessarily just his Vulcan half striving to extinguish his human half. Spock says he must use his intellect to win out over *both* halves, Vulcan and human. He must force them to live together. This implies a certain inevitability to Spock's internal torment. Spock was the first surviving Vulcan/human hybrid, and even the most understanding of parents would have found it difficult, if not impossible, to guide such a unique child toward a life of internal peace and contentment. If Sarek had been more logical with his half-human son and tried to help him work out his emotions, perhaps Spock would have had it easier (though we can certainly understand why Sarek, a product of Vulcan culture, could not do this). However, Spock's problem is partly *physiological,* and thus is something he must deal with himself.

There are physical differences between the brains of

Vulcans and those of humans—there must be. Vulcans were once savage and barbaric as a race, and their passions almost destroyed them. They eschewed emotions and embraced logic as a means of self-preservation. It is erroneous to infer from this that humans could do the same if they chose to. No human being could ever completely quench his or her emotions, or even come close to doing so; the mere thought of such an effort is unpleasant to us. The proof of this is Dr. Miranda Jones. Even though she is an exceptional woman who has studied on Vulcan for years and finds emotion distasteful, she is, as Spock says, "still quite human in some ways; particularly in the depth of her jealousy."

Thus, there must be some characteristics of Vulcan physiology which allowed the Vulcans to become more logical (just as their physiology allows them to be telepathic). Spock, since he is physically predominantly Vulcan, finds it *almost* natural to be unemotional and logical (he is not simply a human who is repressing his emotions—and would find a character like that very disturbing and not at all admirable). However, there is a human influence which refuses to be ignored, and which prevents Spock from achieving psychological stability. It is this physiological contradiction (reflected in his lack of certainty over his own *pon farr*) which, along with the mixed signals he received as a child, causes Spock's internal battle.

Spock's human half is ever apparent, such as in "The Paradise Syndrome," when he holds Miramanee gently in his arms; in "Mudd's Women," when he stares appreciatively at the chemically enhanced ladies; in "The Empath," when Gem touches him, reads his thoughts/feelings, and smiles. She immediately feels affection for him. Spock also prides himself on his knowledge of Earth history and human behavior ("Spectre of the Gun"). His background in these areas is often more extensive than that of his human crewmates. Though this is due in part to Spock's intelligence and professionalism (he wants to understand his fellow crew members), it also indicates that Spock *likes* humans, is curious about them, and has a secret fascination with his human heritage. (Spock has even worked on Earth—with Leila Kalomi—for six years before the five-year mission of the *Enterprise*.)

Spock's problem remained the same throughout the televised episodes. The reason is that a television series exists in a kind of limbo. Though it may run for years, it remains in a closed loop—each episode must end at the point where it began. The characters usually do not change, except superficially (though we may learn new things about them). Also, Spock's value as a projection of our fears, hopes, and ideals was dependent on his remaining the same. If Spock were to resolve his conflict, the impact of the character would be defused or, at least, changed greatly. This is why the ending of "This Side of Paradise" must be an unhappy one for Spock; it is the price we pay for seeing him happy.

When it was decided to make a Star Trek movie, Spock's character had to be developed further, for several reasons. Obviously, the actors had aged over the years, and the character has to reflect this maturation. And movies, unlike television, are open-ended; we expect the characters to grow in a film, not to end up in the same place at the end. (The Star Trek films try to change this, however, by having Kirk at the same point at the beginning of each picture: unhappy and in need of a ship.) Another reason Spock had to change was the fact that he was the most typically 1960s-era character in *Star Trek*. Both Kirk and McCoy are basically old-fashioned character types— Kirk a futuristic Horatio Hornblower and McCoy the crusty cynic—and both are classically heroic and moral. Spock was a more timely character: alienated from his peers, torn by philosophical anxiety and emotional turmoil. Spock's IDIC philosophy, his vegetarianism, pacifism, meditation, and inscrutable, Oriental nature reflect the values and interests of a 1960s audience. Even if it were not done consciously, the character of Spock required a 1980s incarnation. Most important, for us to respect Spock, and for him to respect himself, he had to at least attempt to break free from his "self-made purgatory." After all, his problems are really our problems, and no one can bear stress and turmoil indefinitely, or at least they shouldn't have to. For all these reasons, it was essential that the first Star Trek film portray Spock as actively seeking, if not achieving, an answer.

This is why Spock is on Vulcan at the beginning of *Star Trek: The Motion Picture*. He has come to a turning point. He believes he is nearing a solution, trying to purge himself of emotion and reach *Kolinahr* (sort of a Vulcan variant of nirvana). Despite all of Spock's knowledge and intelligence, he is something of a blockhead when it comes to realizing the inevitability of and the value of his emotions. Even after living with humans for years, and after the experiences of "The Naked Time," "This Side of Paradise," "All Our Yesterdays," etc., he refuses to do the logical thing: accept his emotions and try to deal with them. In Gene Roddenberry's novelization of *Star Trek: The Motion Picture,* Spock remembers something Kirk once said to him: "Why fight so hard to be part of only one world? Why not fight instead to be the best of both?" *(STTMP,* novelization by Gene Roddenberry, p. 24).

This is far from easy for Spock, given his socialization on Vulcan, which taught that logic was good and emotion bad. Here is an example of the thinking he must overcome: "Spock knew ... that the human half of him was far from extinguished. That half had simply been capable of human guile and had learned to hide itself even from his own notice. He had foolishly and carelessly underestimated it and believed it gone. But like the enemy it had always been, his human half had merely lain in wait in order to assault him while he was defenseless" (p. 25). Given this attitude toward his humanity, it is obvious that accepting emotions is a monumentally difficult thing for Spock to do (as it sometimes is for humans). We can understand why he would delude himself by thinking he could extinguish his human half; he *had* to believe this in order to remain sane.

The only solution to Spock's internal battle is that he accept his emotions and value them as he does logic. At some level of consciousness, Spock must have always known this, but he was never able to use this knowledge because he feared insanity. We can see this in several episodes: In "This Side of Paradise," the spores, which are supposed to give contentment and pleasure, at first give Spock pain and mental anguish. His emotions are being wrenched violently from his subconscious; the same thing happens in "The Naked Time" and "Plato's Stepchildren." Dr. McCoy claims that forcing emotion out of Spock will kill him. And, in "All Our Yesterdays," Spock, realizing he has felt and indulged human desires, says, "This is impossible. I've lost myself. I do not know who I am." These and other instances make it clear that Spock's self-identity and sanity, however precarious, are based on a denial of his emotions and a pursuit of total Vulcan logic.

Contact with Vejur, however, forces the Vulcan to reexamine his choices: "Spock was startled . . . in all those tumults of thought and consciousness there had been a sense of puzzlement—and a strange hint of desperation in that puzzlement . . . he had sensed not only logic, but awesome knowledge. What was there that could still puzzle knowledge and logic of that greatness? What could all that be seeking, almost desperately? Spock was certain that he had not erred in searching for his own answer here. Was it possible that this immensity could have some need which might be fulfilled by an insignificance called Spock?" (p. 128-9).

Yes, it was possible. Spock's search parallels Vejur's search exactly, and not until Spock mind melds with Vejur (and is almost killed) does he realize that total logic is empty and childish: "Vejur is everything that Spock had ever dreamed of becoming. And yet Vejur was barren! It would never feel pain. Or joy. Or challenge. It was so completely and magnificently logical that its accumulation of knowledge was totally useless" (p. 218). When Spock melds with Vejur, he sees the question in all its clarity—"Is this all that I am?" It is an epiphany, a transcendent conversion, bypassing all the defense mechanisms and thought patterns that Spock had built up over the years to deny and deflect his emotions. It is an occurrence of such great effect that it allows Spock to conquer his fear of insanity and to acknowledge the answer to the physio-psychological schism which has tormented him all his life. Not until his contact with Vejur can Spock finally admit that "logic without need is sterile" and that "simple feeling" is essential to a meaningful life (p. 219). Spock has, to a great extent, resolved his internal battle— Spock has changed.

The subtexts of *Star Trek: The Motion Picture,* that emotions are necessary for a meaningful existence, and that man's destiny lies in outer space, are not very original, though they are nicely expressed. The root of the story—the story that *had* to be told—is that Spock confronts his fear of his humanity and accepts his emotions. The fans, sensing that this was the real importance of the film, were disappointed that the focus strayed so wildly to special effects and the Decker-Ilia relationship. Too much was cut from the release print of the film, and the character relations were more often implied than shown; the film is strewn with intriguing but dormant ideas. Still, we are left with an updated group of characters, especially Spock, who has changed greatly, though he is not a central character in the film.

Neither was Spock a major character in *Star Trek*

II: The Wrath of Khan, despite the fact that he dies in the film. We did see that he is more relaxed and at ease with humans, but still is not openly emotional; he does not cry or laugh or shout. In *Star Trek III: The Search for Spock,* of course, Spock is absent from much of the story. In *Star Trek IV: The Voyage Home,* Spock seems to have lost, or forgotten, the tenuous acceptance of emotion which we saw in *Wrath of Khan.* Spock is mellower now than in the first film, a more integrated being, but he is as reticent as ever to engage in emotionalism or betray his humanity, despite his "extraordinary" admission that he is guessing during the film's climax—this exchange is the film's only comment on Spock's condition, and it is nothing we haven't seen before, going back to "The Galileo Seven."

In *Star Trek: The Motion Picture,* Spock changed ... but into what? The post-Roddenberry Star Trek has not shown much concern for Spock's internal progress. Much has happened *to* Spock—death and rebirth—but he remains essentially the same character we have known since the television series. The novelization of *The Voyage Home* by Vonda McIntyre suggests that McCoy and Spock have each retained remnants of the other's psyche as a result of their extended mind meld in *The Search for Spock.* In the film, however, there is no real evidence of this.

Spock's character has always been defined by his inner turmoil, but the legend of Mr. Spock now looms larger than the character himself. While Kirk and McCoy are just as real two decades after their conception, Spock carries baggage which makes him a writer's dilemma. The issues which the character originally addressed are out of place now. What is left but to simply spend time with our "old friend" Spock? Ironically, now that Star Trek is a motion picture property (and one influenced greatly by Leonard Nimoy), the character of Spock seems destined, more than ever, to remain the same. *The Voyage Home* proves that gloss-

ing over Spock's problems does not impair the show
as entertainment. However, the cohesiveness of the
Star Trek universe is not aided by Spock's blithe trans-
formation from an unhappy misfit to a deadpan middle age.

A STAR TREK HOW-TO

By Kiel Stuart

Since many people who enjoy Star Trek also enjoy writing, we feel this is a splendid opportunity to discuss some important elements of dramatic writing.

The key element in dramatic writing of all kinds, whether fiction, screenplay, or stage play, is conflict.

The late, great fiction master Paul Darcy Boles (author of *Storycrafting,* a highly recommended book) liked to refer to conflict as "wrestling." Why he did so should be obvious to anyone who's ever watched Saturday morning wrestling on television. Good struggles against evil, and sometimes evil looks like it's winning. When good finally prevails, that's dramatic satisfaction in spades.

Here's a useful skill to help polish your own writing. Take a published piece that you enjoyed and try to analyze the "wrestling" within. Putting it into sort of a flow chart, try to see how the author handled character and situation to arrive at dramatic conflict. And what better example to use in a Star Trek anthology than the vastly popular *Star Trek IV: The Voyage Home?*

Star Trek IV: The Voyage Home

THE SETUP: Kirk and gang are staring at court-martial for the naughty things they did like stealing the *Enter-*

prise and blowing it up. But this probe thingy pops up, sucking the energy out of everything in its path by using some force that no one has ever seen before.

SITUATION: Kirk and gang have polished up their Klingon ship and are headed toward Earth to face the music.

COMPLICATION: They get the message that Earth's dignity is being raped by this unknown probe sucking up the ocean and eating everyone's energy while it makes weird noises.

SOLUTION: They figure out what language the probe is speaking because Mr. Spock is so smart.

LEADS TO:

SITUATION: The probe's looking for humpback whales.

COMPLICATION: There ain't none left.

SOLUTION: The gang sees *Back to the Future,* and says, hey, that looks real rad, let's try it.

LEADS TO:

SITUATION: They go back to 1986 and sell Kirk's glasses.

COMPLICATION: They need some whales and magic aluminum and photons from plutonium because *Back to the Future* was so bitchin', man, but they don't know where to get any.

SOLUTION: Kirk sees some whales on a bus and they get on it and beat up a punker; Scotty pretends to be Doc in the neat movie; and Chekov asks where the nuclear subs are kept.

LEADS TO:

SITUATION: They're at Marineland, where they meet Mary Sue and see some whales.

COMPLICATION: Mr. Spock goes for a swim, and the whales are going to be flown to Alaska, and one of 'em's pregnant. He says "hell" and "damn" a lot.

SOLUTION: Kirk tells Mr. Spock not to curse, and Mary Sue buys them a pizza.

LEADS TO:

SITUATION: Doc Scotty bullshits his way into some magic aluminum to put the whales away in; Sulu steals a chopper by being nice; Chekov and Uhura find some photons on the *Enterprise*.

COMPLICATION: "Captain, ma transporter!" Before it can get fixed, Chekov gets interrogated by security guards who are just as good as the ones on the other *Enterprise*, runs away, and takes a bump over the top rope. Then the whales get shipped early so Mary Sue hits her boyfriend and goes running to Kirk.

SOLUTION: They ask Mary Sue to take them to the hospital so McCoy can paste Chekov together again.

LEADS TO:

SITUATION: They're at the hospital and looking for Chekov.

COMPLICATION: They're not real doctors.

SOLUTION: They act silly, so everyone thinks they're real doctors, and they get to fix Chekov up and an old lady's kidney, too.

LEADS TO:

SITUATION: Mary Sue tells them the radio frequency for the whales, jumps on Kirk, and they all fly to Alaska in their invisible Klingon ship.

COMPLICATION: A whaling ship just happens to be shooting at George and Gracie, of all the whales available in the ocean.

SOLUTION: Kirk's invisible ship blocks the harpoon, and then appears and scares the whale boat away, and they get the whales.

LEADS TO:

SITUATION: The whales are on board, and they start to go back to the future.

COMPLICATION: Mr. Spock has to guess, and they have trouble when the DeLorean, I mean Klingon ship, sort of stalls.

SOLUTION: Mr. Spock figures out what to do because he's so smart.

LEADS TO:

SITUATION: They're back in the future.

COMPLICATION: The probe sucks their energy and they crash and the ship floods and the whales are trapped.

SOLUTION: Kirk puts Krazy Glue on his rug and swims underwater and lets the whales out.

LEADS TO:

SITUATION: The whales swim around San Francisco Bay.

COMPLICATION: Everyone wonders why they're not talking to the probe thingy, which is still sucking up water and energy.

SOLUTION: George and Gracie get over their jet lag and sing to the probe, which makes it go away.

LEADS TO:

SITUATION: Everyone dries off and gets court-martialed.

COMPLICATION: For ripping off and blowing up Federation property and being a rulebreaker, they bust Kirk to captain again.

SOLUTION: But because he saved the Earth and got some whales, too, they build a new *Enterprise* and give it to Kirk, and all his old crew again.

LEADS TO:

"Star Trek Five: Back in the Saddle Again."

HUMOR IN UNIFORM—STARFLEET ISSUE

By E. B. Friar

The other day I was at my local bookstore and I came across one of those books titled something like *The Encyclopedia of Television*. I picked it up and looked for "Star Trek," but I couldn't find it. For some reason it wasn't listed with all the other "comedy" shows. Why not? There's more humor (and most of it intentional) in Star Trek than in most sit-coms.

I don't want to insult *Star Trek* by comparing it to the average situation comedy. If all of television is indeed made to appeal to the lowest common denominator in entertainment, then we certainly want to consider *Star Trek* in a category all by itself. True, you may call it an action-adventure program, but that description, while accurate, is imprecise. Action is only one aspect. *Star Trek* is founded on many deeper levels, not the least of which is humor. (Ask any fan: He or she will have you by the ear for hours.) *Star Trek* is the first series, in my video memory, that dared to mix real drama with truly funny stuff, and the humor always advances the story.

You rarely got the feeling *Star Trek* did something just for a laugh. (If you did get suspicious, you didn't care.) The Genes (Roddenberry and Coon) succeeded in giving us everything from slapstick to the subtlety of one raised eyebrow accompanied by an all-knowing "fascinating."

The humor worked and no joke ever jerked me out of the carefully constructed world of the Federation. It worked because there was a purpose behind every witticism, subtle or obvious. Comedy in drama relieves tension, as the Genes knew so well, but they also understood that we humans are sometimes more secure with a chuckle aimed at our gut than a direct assault. Character flaws were presented to us gently and then underlined through humor. Satire was used to make statements about the real world that gave us a universe where no man had gone before. The humor adds another dimension to the characters and helps us to believe in the reality of what we are seeing.

It is also used to enlarge personalities. We know we are seeing real heroes at work when our *Enterprise* guys can save the Federation or even the whole galaxy and manage to have a good time doing it. They are not like you and me. If we ordinary mortals were forced to face an apparent omnipotent alien (Balok or the Squire), or a planet killer, or worse yet, the prospect of being marooned on a desolate planet with vicious savages and the obnoxious Mr. Boma, we'd like to think we'd survive, but we know we couldn't do it with style. During the entire affair, we would cry out for Mama and call on every deity we could think of. Not so with Starfleet Academy's finest. They could carry it off with aplomb, sometimes dignity, and not a few laughs.

Frankly, I can't help wondering if Starfleet Command assigned the *Enterprise*'s command personnel on the basis of humor type. Perhaps it is regulation to require a certain mix. I wonder if they have some sort of humor quotient that they have made into a mathematical formula: ". . . so much dry wit multiplied by a certain amount of sarcasm is equal to or greater than an infinite amount of shtick and/or satire." This "factor of prime humor," when divided by an indeterminate amount of drama, equals one well-rounded plot line (and a heck of a television series, too).

"A little old lady from Leningrad inwented it." It is not accident that Ensign Chekov insists everything important in Earth history originated in Russia. There is also something basically funny in the idea that gentle Mr. Sulu harbors a secret desire to emulate Errol Flynn. I know he'd look great in the tights, but what about a pencil-thin mustache? And then there's Uhura's answer to "a fair maiden": "Sorry, neither." It is one of the best lines I've heard in a long time. Too bad they didn't give Uhura (and Nichelle Nichols) more opportunity to deliver lines like that.

Mr. Scott was given more opportunity to be developed into a complete dramatic character, but he has a most definite comedic side. Except for when he's in love, he is mostly relegated to the background, fixing something, but there are times he hits the limelight of high comedy. In "By Any Other Name," we get to see him drink a Kelvan under the table (and we get the idea he could drink even a Klingon under it, too). But what is so precious here is that although he captures the Kelvan's device, poor Scotty never makes it back to the captain. We see him slide down the wall and pass out wearing one happy grin. Imagine tomorrow's headache.

Scotty in his cups is a *Star Trek* tradition. In "The Tholian Web," McCoy whips up an antidote to the space madness using a derivative of Klingon nerve gas. Scotty is delighted to learn it works best when mixed with alcohol. I bet they had quite a party in the crewmen's lounge. In "The Trouble With Tribbles," Mr. Scott gets a chance to shine. Not only is he given the punchline for the entire episode, but we will never forget how he abstains from fighting the Klingons in the bar—even though they insult Captain Kirk—until they call the *Enterprise* a garbage scow. We will never forget Kirk's face when Scotty tells him about it, either.

McCoy is at his best when making the kind of comments most of us can think of only when the opportunity has passed. McCoy, a master of the one-liner, calls them as he sees them. He has the uncanny knack for stating the embarrassingly obvious at just the right psychological moment. In *Star Trek: The Motion Picture:*, he says "Why is any object we don't understand always called 'a thing'?" In *The Wrath of Khan,* as Kirk and McCoy are preparing to beam down, Spock admonishes the captain to be careful. "*We* will!" McCoy replies, in true cantankerous form. Toward the end of "The Galileo Seven," Scotty says, "Mister Spock, a while ago you said there were always alternatives." Spock replies, "Did I? I may have been mistaken." The situation is desperate, destruction is imminent, but McCoy has one last, irascible comment to make before he's willing to go to the great beyond. "At least I've lived long enough to hear *that*!" (Kinda makes it all worthwhile, huh?)

McCoy's humor may be obvious, but as McCoy himself tells us, Mr. Spock, a master of deadpan delivery, has the gift of understatement. He also has a sense of timing that must be Vulcan in its accuracy. He can say the kind of things that may or may not make me laugh out loud, but they do leave me with a great feeling of satisfaction. In "The Mark of Gideon," Mr. Spock is forced into verbal fencing with Gideon's ambassador, who uses Starfleet regulations as his weapon. Mr. Spock, looking rather put upon for a Vulcan, remarks with much wisdom, "A bureaucrat is the opposite of a diplomat, but they manage to achieve the same results." Another example of Spockian wisdom from the same episode: ". . . the purpose of diplomacy is to prolong the crisis." In "Bread and Circuses," when McCoy tells Spock that all medical men are trained in logic, Mr. Spock responds that, until now, he ". . . wasn't aware that McCoy was trained in anything."

But Mr. Spock never jokes. At least that's what he tells a Roman guard (in "Bread and Circuses") and us. When the guard pulls off the cap that hides Spock's ears, he asks, "What do you call those?" Mr. Spock's logical reply: "Ears." "Are you trying to be funny?" demands the Roman. "Never," Spock reassures him. I'd be tempted to call Spock a liar here, but perhaps he meant that he doesn't have to try.

No discussion of McCoy or Spock's humor would be complete without a few references to their verbal dueling. It's always funny, but it stops just short of being actually vicious, as if they are in silent agreement that their arguing is not to be taken too seriously. Perhaps that's why Captain Kirk doesn't seem to hesitate to stir up trouble. Captain's prerogative, or what? Be on the lookout for this the next time you watch "The Tholian Web." Notice how Kirk gets a gleam in his eye just before he asks Spock and McCoy about his last orders. Then watch closely as Kirk leans back comfortably in his chair to enjoy the spectacle of his two top officers squirming. "Orders? What orders?" Kirk knows good and darn well what went on in his absence.

I've noticed, too, that our good captain likes to remind people of things they'd rather forget. In "This Side of Paradise," after Kirk communicates with an uncooperative Spock, he turns to the puzzled McCoy and says, "I thought you might like him if he acted more human." McCoy, astonished, replies, "Did I say that?" "You said it," Kirk assures him. "I never said that!" McCoy insists.

During the first season, it seems to have been Kirk's job to take Spock to task, before that duty was passed along to the efficient McCoy. Kirk is no slouch himself, though. In the tag to "The Galileo Seven," Kirk questions Spock about his "emotional outburst" and concludes that Spock is "a very stubborn man." Spock, logical as always, must agree.

It's not only the characters who have their individual humor quirks. Whole episodes exist that display their own brand of humor. Several of them are based on nothing more than very broad comedy. At least two are famous for it: "A Piece of the Action" and "The Trouble With Tribbles."

"Tribbles" has been discussed at length by its author, David Gerrold, in his book about the making of the episode, so I will not try to repeat his comments, except to remind you of a couple of choice incidents. I've always thought Spock looked deliciously uncomfortable at being caught stroking one of the miserable (Klingon adjective) creatures. Remember the tribble with command potential—the one who kept taking Kirk's seat away from him? No other villain in the series managed to capture that chair as many times.

In "A Piece of the Action," there is just something inherently funny about anyone in a zoot suit. Add pointed ears, and you are bound to make a unique fashion statement. (It's a wonder the Iotians didn't laugh themselves sick at the sight of each other, but then, we survived the sixties in bell-bottomed hip huggers, white go-go boots, and paisley print shirts, and lived to talk about it.)

In this episode, not only do we get Kirk's rendition of an Edward G. Robinson-type gangster, but we also get an uneasy idea of just how efficient a Vulcan gangster could be if the concept could be made logical. It is also priceless irony that the man who can captain a ship the size and power of the *Enterprise* can't even drive a car around the block. I sincerely hope I never get myself involved in a high-stakes fizzbin game. I'm likely to lose my shirt—except on Tuesdays, when I would lose something else. I suppose contamination of a planet is serious business, but I wouldn't change a thing.

The Harry Mudd episodes ("I, Mudd" and "Mudd's Women") are pure enjoyment. Harry Mudd is slapstick all the way from his vaguely piratelike costume to his eternal run of bad luck. The fact that his antics can get on Kirk's nerves so badly only adds to the fun. Perhaps that's why we, the vengeful, get so much pleasure out of the idea that Harry is to be marooned on the android planet with thousands of replicas of Stella—Harry's wife and a typical intergalactic Hausfrau if I ever saw one—for what will certainly seem like forever. Mudd perhaps should have used some of the Venus drug on Stella. In "I, Mudd," Chekov calls poor Harry a Cossack after learning Harry programmed the pretty Alices to serve all of their lords' needs. I bet that was the only time Chekov meant that as a compliment.

Other episodes are not such broad comedy, but they are no less funny. "The Squire of Gothos" may be considered one long practical joke on the *Enterprise* crew, with the punchline being the fact that General Trelane is really a cosmic kid. He is hauled off by his overindulgent parents and, I guess, put to bed without his supper—whatever it was. But you see, the real trick here lies in the fact that although the concept is funny and Trelane is comical, we are made to feel rather sorry for him. A skillful mix of pathos and humor, perhaps? The same thing happens in "The Corbomite Maneuver." Not only does the powerful Balok turn out to be a small, childlike alien who is actually gentle, but we get a sense of his loneliness. (The joke here is really on Balok—there is no such thing as corbomite.)

Many times humor is injected for the fun of it, but never to the detriment of the story. In "Friday's Child," we are treated to the sight of an *Enterprise* officer becoming a father. (The only time we knew of, until recently.) McCoy tells the laboring Eleen, "Say to yourself, the child is mine." She promptly answers, "The child is yours." Thereafter she calls the baby McCoy's child to his inordinate discomfort and everyone's else's private amusement. McCoy has his revenge, though. He hands Spock the newborn and Spock reacts as if the baby carries something contagious. (Like emotions, maybe?) Even in an episode as sentimental as "The City on the Edge of Forever," we are treated to a priceless moment in which Spock enjoys himself at Kirk's expense. I hope in the years following this incident Kirk got plenty of ribbing for his lame idea about the "rice picker."

In "Shore Leave," the theme seems to be *"Star Trek* Meets *Alice in Wonderland"*—talk about science fiction! "Shore Leave" is in a class by itself.

As is another unusual episode. "Bread and Circuses" is unique because you can't call it a comedy, as everyone is in so much danger, but you can't call it a drama, either, as it is one of the funniest of the shows. "Bread and Circuses" is truly Spock and McCoy's episode. It starts out very lightly. After beam down, McCoy speculates on how much fun it would be to tell the locals, "Behold! I am the Archangel Gabriel!" Spock fails to see the humor in this, and McCoy assures him that it is only because no one could ever mistake him for an angel. The action quickly mounts and the humor right along with it. During the fight in the arena, Spock rather unnecessarily asks the struggling McCoy if he needs help. "Whatever gave you that idea?" McCoy responds sarcastically. Spock's opponent then calls him a "pointy-eared freak!" "You tell him, buster!" McCoy calls back. The incident is funny, but we believe in the danger of the moment anyway, even though I have trouble with the idea of a twentieth-century Roman Empire that televises its gladiatorial games. (If feeding Christians to the lions is regular TV fare, what do they do during the sweeps months?) Near the conclusion of the story, Kirk, fresh from the arms of a pretty slave girl, liberates the worried McCoy and Spock from their prison cell. Spock asks the captain solicitously, "What did they do to you, Captain?" Kirk answers, almost deadpan, "They threw me . . . a few curves, Spock." (Ah, the joy of gallivanting around the galaxy!)

I think we should be grateful not only to the writers of these and other episodes but also to the actors for their almost flawless handling of the rigors of precise timing and the monumental effort of keeping a straight face. (Although, according to rumor, they exercised their funny bones aplenty off camera, too.)

Another stroke of genius by someone was to "tag" many of the episodes, no matter how tense, with an amusing tidbit to leave us with a very human grin. "The Galileo Seven" is a great example of this. In spite of the constant contention during most of the story, we tune out laughing at the phrase "a very stubborn man." All the really comedic episodes end on a high note, but even shows like "The Devil in the Dark," "Wolf in the Fold," and "The Apple," leave us with a small smile. Unfortunately, most of these "tags" occur only in the first two seasons. In the third season they were disappointingly absent. In spite of a few shows some people consider laughable, the third season had the least amount of humor. For sanity's sake I must consider "Spock's Brain" to be a deliberate parody of fifties science fiction serials. Perhaps if they had kept (as did the Blish adaptation) Spock's joke, "It is a well-known fact that we Vulcans propagate our species by mail," in the script, the episode might have been saved ... maybe.

Evidently the powers that be don't realize how much they have spoiled us. We have come to expect this "Star Trek humor" and lately we haven't been getting any. The movies have been lacking in this department. True, McCoy makes a few successful forays in *Star Trek: The Motion Picture* ("To put it into simpler language, Captain, sir, they drafted me!")—not even Robert Wise could keep McCoy quiet. In *The Wrath of Khan,* we hear about Scotty's "wee bout" and get to see Kirk in the grip of paranoia as Spock asks Saavik to take the ship out of space dock. Asked how many times she has done so, she answers, "One hundred and ninety-three times ... in simulation. In real world circumstances—never." For an instant we see that Saavik is indeed capable of following in *all* the footsteps of her mentor. In *The Search for Spock,* it is significant that the universally accepted high point of the entire movie is comic-tragic. Poor McCoy thinks he can use the Vulcan nerve pinch on the security guard and he is astounded when it doesn't work.

Even with these few crumbs, we miss our "tag" and we do want to leave the theater with another of those human type grins. *ST:TMP* is the only picture where a funny tag would have been appropriate or desirable. With all due respect to the guys at the helm, I think it would have strengthened their movie. When Mr. Spock enters the story, he is closer than he has ever been to complete nonemotion. Through his contact with Vejur he discovers the validity of his human half. It would have shown that he'd come full circle if he'd been allowed to rediscover his sense of humor. We would have liked to have seen Kirk putting the ball into motion, then sitting back and enjoying (with the rest of us) one more battle in the Spock/McCoy war. It would have been nice to be reassured that some things never change.

Star Trek endures because it has so much to offer. In a tapestry woven of multilayered stories, complex and sometimes inconsistent characters, and an endless universe of never-ending possibilities, humor serves to add a little embroidery—and sometimes to patch up the holes.

HOW MANY SULUS?

By Mark Golding

Are there two Sulus in *Star Trek*? To be more precise, is the Sulu in "Where No Man Has Gone Before" a different man than the helmsman we see in the rest of the episodes?

Why ask such a question?

Star Trek's chronological framework makes it quite possible for two different Sulus to be involved. Most fans believe that "Where No Man Has Gone Before," which featured different compartments, hull, and personnel on the *Enterprise,* as well as different uniforms and insignia, happened before any other episodes. Also, fans logically feel that all second season episodes follow those from the first season, third season episodes follow the second, and so on. There is no mixing of episodes from different seasons.

In the second season episode, "The Deadly Years," Sulu said he had served under Kirk for two years, meaning either between 1.5 and 2.5, or between 2.001 and 2.999 years.

Chekov and Sarek are twenty-two and 102.437 years old in Season Two's "Who Mourns for Adonais?" and "Journey to Babel," and stated to be twenty-two and 102 at the time the information in *The Making of Star Trek* was current (pp. 250–1 and 227), which should be after Season Two ends. So *The Making of Star Trek* is at most 0.563 years after "Journey To Babel," and at most one year after "Who Mourns for Adonais?", making "The Deadly Years" at most a year before *The Making of Star Trek.*

The Making of Star Trek, pages 216 and 228, indicates Kirk was captain of the *Enterprise* for 4.001 to 4.999 years, and so for at least 3.001 to 3.999 years (the time of "The Deadly Years"), Sulu has served 1.5 to 2.999 under Kirk. "Where No Man Has Gone Before" could have taken place before the Sulu of "The Deadly Years" ever came aboard.

If *The Making of Star Trek* is not considered valid Star Trek lore, "Amok Time" and "Journey To Babel" indicate Kirk commanded the *Enterprise* for 2.001 to 4.999 years by Season Two.

In "Amok Time," Kirk says he has not known Spock to take leave during all the years he has known him. This should be at least 2.001 years. In "Journey to Babel," Amanda says Spock has not visited them (his parents) for more than four years, implying he did so 3.5 to 4.5 years, or 4.001 to 4.999 years ago, presumably taking leave to do so.

Together, these statements indicate that Spock became Kirk's first or second officer 2.001 to 4.999 years before the second season. "Where No Man Has Gone Before" could be before the Sulu of "The Deadly Years" began serving with Kirk.

The Making of Star Trek, pages 258–9, says "Errand of Mercy" was about two years (probably 1.5 to 2.5) earlier, and thus at least 0.5 to 1.5 years before "The Deadly Years." If Season One lasted .75 to 1.5 years, "Where No Man Has Gone Before" would be 0.75 to 3.0 years before "The Deadly Years," possibly before that episode's Sulu began serving with Kirk.

Even if *The Making of Star Trek* is not valid Star Trek lore, in Season Three's "Day of the Dove," Kang said, "For three years the Federation and the Klingon Empire have been at peace, a treaty we've kept to the letter." Kang could hardly claim the "Errand of Mercy" war kept to the letter any peace treaty then in effect. And if he meant the treaty the Organians imposed after "Errand of Mercy," "Day of the Dove" would seem to be 2.5 to 3.5, or 3.001 to 3.999, years later.

"Where No Man Has Gone Before" could still be less than 1.5 to 2.999 years before "The Deadly Years," if the intervening episodes were crowded as close together as possible. And even if "Where No Man Has Gone Before" is more than 2.999 years before "The Deadly Years," Sulu could still serve under Kirk in both episodes, his services being interrupted by periods of assignment elsewhere.

However, Sulu is a physicist (*The Making of Star Trek,* p. 136; *The Star Trek Compendium,* 1981 edition, p. 46, etc.) and head of the astro-science department in "Where No Man Has Gone Before." He hardly seems like the adventurous helmsman Mr. Sulu of the other episodes.

Could Sulu have changed his specialty in search of adventure? A helmsman might not go on exciting landing parties even as often as a head scientist. The Sulu of the episodes often changed hobbies and interests, but kept his helmsman's assignment for years. As an academy graduate, he should have a Bachelor of Science degree, but much more than that should be required to become head of the astro-science department.

After all, science is only one part of the Starfleet Academy curriculum. If midshipmen are not sorted into different career paths early on, they should all get generalized training, making them equally—but not highly—qualified as quartermasters, administrators, records officers (like Ben Finney), space lawyers, historians (like Marla McGivers), engineers, scientists, warriors, diplomats, and commanders. Specialized training for specific positions would largely come after graduation, in schools or on the job.

So Starfleet Academy would teach Federation and Starfleet loyalty, ethics, physical fitness, tactics, leadership, discipline, diplomacy, administration, laws, psychology, applied science, engineering, Starfleet technology, computer literacy, etc., in addition to pure science.

The average academy graduate might have only 1.25 or 1.5 or 2.0 times as much scientific knowledge as any of you readers (couched in twenty-third-century terms, of course), which would certainly not be enough to qualify as an astronomer, astrophysicist, astrobiologist, astrogeologist, astroarcheologists, or any other kind of astroscientist. In our era, a master's or doctoral degree is needed to obtain research positions equal to a starship's scientist, and by *Star Trek*'s era, increased knowledge and specialization should mandate much higher educational requirements for starship scientists.

Sulu would need to have obtained postgraduate physics courses to quality as a ship's physicist, and as head of the astro-science department, he should have at least the education and field experience of his subordinates. He might even be the *Enterprise*'s head scientist, director of all laboratories. The science officer may have that job, but his only duties shown in the episodes are to man the science station to inform and advise the captain. Since that is not a typical scientist's task, and Spock considers himself a scientist, he may do scientific research offscreen and/or head all the science labs. But it is possible that Sulu in "Where No Man Has Gone Before" directed all scientific research aboard the *Enterprise,* whether or not that task was later transferred to science officer Spock.

"Where No Man Has Gone Before"'s Sulu should not have gained such a position without a strongly scientific and/or ambitious personality. Why would a dedicated scientist become a helmsman? How could an ambitious officer abandon years of career advancement to start over at the bottom?

How could the familiar swashbuckling Sulu become a scientist in the first place, or think a console-bound helmsman faced more adventure than a desk-bound scientist? If he wanted adventure, why not become chief of security?

Physicist Sulu's change to helmsman Sulu of later episodes could have been the most traumatic change in Sulu's entire life, deserving a novel to explain. The change could be much easier if Starfleet does not require years of postgraduate education for its scientists. If Starfleet simply and routinely rotates officers into and out of science positions, Sulu did not abandon his life's goal and years of effort when he became a helmsman.

Of course, that requires Starfleet to put a very low priority on scientific research, perhaps just using it to disguise its military mission!

So the possibility that physicist Sulu in "Where No Man Has Gone Before" was a clone, twin, brother, cousin, or other relative resembling helmsman Sulu, being assigned elsewhere before the other episodes, avoids the problems involved with having only one Sulu in *Star Trek*.

What are the first names of the two Sulus? Are they Walter and Hikaru, or Walter Hikaru and Hikaru Walter?

Of course, it is possible that "Where No Man Has Gone Before" is in an alternate universe where Sulu became a scientist, and all episodes with helmsman Sulu are in alternate universes where he chose a different career.

If physicist Sulu did become helmsman Sulu, either Starfleet has the expected high requirements for its scientists, making it a very important change for Sulu, or else Starfleet has ridiculouly low standards for its scientists!

THE SPOCK/MCCOY WARS AGAIN: DYSFUNCTIONAL COMMUNICATION AS A DEFENSE AGAINST OVERPROTECTIVENESS

By Marie Greene

Last week I had the experience of teaching some principles of interpersonal communication styles in the college psychology classroom and coming home to see them in action in that night's *Star Trek* episode. What I saw was a bad example of what I had just discussed. Of course, the interchange I'm referring to was one of the verbal wars which exemplified the nature of the friendship between Spock and McCoy.

Paralleling this dysfunctional exchange were some really quality interactions between Spock and Kirk and between McCoy and Kirk. We have seen that both Spock and McCoy are able to carry on perfectly normal, healthy communication with other people, so we can make the assumption that there is something specifically blocking *their* interactions with *each other*. Since they are, otherwise, normal communicators, we can ask the question: What is the nature of the specific relationship they have which continually causes their dysfunctional interactions?

In the first place, authors and directors have a vested interest in maintaining characters with communication problems like this, for use as sounding boards for the exploration of ideas. Having two characters who will automatically argue about almost anything, no matter how much they are philosophically of accord, is a wonderful convenience to scriptwriting. Since the personalities of Spock and McCoy, in the television series, were designed very early to argue about almost anything, when the author needed to present two views, he or she could write a script to let the opposing sides be presenting by letting these two fight it out.

But many authors have used other characters to do this. McCoy and Kirk have argued, so have Spock and Kirk. New characters have been introduced to form opposing forces capable of counterpoint positions and views. So it is quite clear that our authors *do not have* to have Spock and McCoy continually at odds, yet these characters are continually in conflict. So there must be something intrinsic to these two personalities which has created the chronic defensive antagonism.

As oppositional as Spock and McCoy are in their interpersonal communication, the assumption could be that they are enemies, yet we know that they are friends. So what holds them together and what holds them apart? Like so many authors before me, I would like to investigate this question. And like so many others, I will be talking about *us* as I discuss the interaction of the two television friends whose behaviors we know as well, and sometimes even better, than our own. These two act as our alter egos as we make the same mistakes and make the same corrections. In addition, we see, through them, that a social communication error does not automatically destroy a friendship. Through examples of these errors made by Spock and McCoy, we learn of our errors, how to correct them (even when the example is a negative example), and how to forgive ourselves for them.

The chronic communication error which I perceive to be the problem is the overuse of interactions similar to what the psychologist Carl Rogers calls "supportive style." Since I am going to stretch this concept to the limit, I am going to adopt the term "protective interaction."

At first glance it may seem that to support and protect another person is a positive act. It would not seem a source of antagonism or harm to the other person. The truth is that an overuse of such behavior is an insult to that person. It may even weaken him, rather in the way a parent can harm a child by overprotection. The receiver of too much supportive or protective communication could come to doubt his or her own autonomy or power. At best, the person receiving such communication would feel that the sender did not believe in the strength of the person he was constantly protecting. That person would certainly come to resent such a subtle and chronic insult.

One measure of the quality of a friendship is the ability of friends to know when to support and protect and when to allow an individual to take his own risks and make his own mistakes. Spock and McCoy spend too much time and energy trying to protect each other and do not put enough effort into respecting the strengths of the other. So, despite the fact that they obviously care for each other, they are also constantly at odds with each other. I regard the constant arguing as a defensive pose on both of their parts to block the reception of insulting, weakening protective communications from the other.

McCoy wishes to protect Spock from the problems which could occur from pathological repression of emotions. This goal is both reasonable and legitimate from the perspective of McCoy's profession. He is not only a doctor, but considered to be an "expert" in the field of "space psychology." Although we can see the logic of this goal as it pertains to the professional *Doctor* McCoy, the friend *Leonard* McCoy would need to learn when to express this to Spock and when to leave his friend to make his own mistakes. Overintervention in an attempt to correct another person's problem is a sign of caring, but in this case, it is a sign of professional caring, not the tolerant behavior of a friend.

Spock is no paragon of virtue in this respect, either. Spock feels a responsibility to protect the ship's doctor from physical dangers. This is perfectly logical and rational as a professional goal on Spock's part. A doctor is not usually as well trained in combat as the rest of the officers. A responsibility for his defense falls to the officers around him. Spock is the natural choice for this role for two reasons. The captain has other obligations beyond the defense of an individual. His first officer is the next in line to assume this obligation. In addition, Spock has superior physical strength. So Spock the professional is obligated to fill this role. But if Spock wants to establish a more mature and quality friendship with McCoy, he had better learn to moderate this protective behavior, especially in verbal communications.

By illustration from both the television episodes and the movies, I want to argue four points: 1. How McCoy's overprotective behavior creates antagonism in Spock; 2. How Spock's overprotective behavior creates antagonism in McCoy; 3. How both McCoy and Spock are able to moderate their protective relations toward Kirk, thus establishing adult, satisfying friendships with him; and 4. How the relationship between Spock and McCoy has matured over the years, indicating mutual respect and tolerance.

From very early in the television series, Spock and Kirk respected their mutual differences, allowed for the other's uniqueness, and assumed that the other was reasonable in his decisions related to risk-taking and autonomous behavior.

Protectiveness and supportiveness was very limited in their interactions. Mutuality was much more common a theme. Like many friendships, a certain amount of supportiveness or protectiveness occurred early in the relationship, as if there was a need to show caring through such behavior. But the early episodes show such supportive/protective behavior happening without weakening the self-image of the receiver. For example, in "Balance of Terror," Kirk defends Spock against racial barbs by supporting a philosophy of equality, not by implying that Spock was unable to defend himself. The support was given in a limited and indirect way.

The same can be said of Spock's early support of Kirk in "Court-Martial." Spock continues to look for the weakness in the computer and eventually finds that Kirk has been made to look guilty by a change in the programming. Technical support is given without implying a weakness in the man in need of such support.

Through these and other early examples, we can see that the friendship is not yet complete so early in the relationship, nor is mutual trust fully and immediately established. But between Kirk and Spock, the development from protectiveness to mutual respect comes very early in the series.

In "The Menagerie," Spock protects Kirk from facing the death penalty alongside him by not allowing Kirk to know all the facts of the mission and by not allowing Kirk to make a commitment with him. Spock does not doubt that Kirk would have agreed to take the risk. Spock only wishes to protect Kirk from facing the same dangers he's chosen to face himself. Kirk is resentful of this. Spock's decision to exclude him implies that Spock does not believe that he, Kirk, is as strong as he is, and is, thereby, in need of this protection. It makes no difference that this message is not Spock's intention. This is the way we all feel when we are similarly protected.

We feel a similar negative response when a friend agrees with our words but not really with our ideas, indicated by a skeptical voice or phrasing of the agreement. Such is the case in "Arena." Kirk argues with Spock that the Gorns were vicious in their attack on the colony. He feels there was no other possible motive, or at least no legitimate motive; the attack was unprovoked. Somewhat condescendingly, Spock agrees. If that is what Kirk really believes, there can be no decision but to punish the offenders.

We feel, as we listen to this exchange, that Spock is giving verbal support without the belief that should accompany his agreement. If the friendship had been stronger at this point, Spock might not have given this purely supportive but incredulous response. A response based on such skepticism is actually an insult at some levels. It implies that the other person is not strong enough to receive the truth, or that the friendship is not yet strong enough for this truth to be risked by discussion.

Episode writer Steven Carabatsos gives us some interesting insights into the level of development of the three-way friendship in "Operation: Annihilate." The failure of the Spock/Kirk friendship to be fully developed is illustrated in the vacillation which Kirk shows between being protective/supportive of the injured friend Spock one moment and fully accepting of Spock's strength and integrity the next. It is an episode where mutual trust is repeatedly tested. The overall effect is to strengthen all relationships.

The initial response by Kirk, when Spock is attacked by the creature on Deneva, is disbelief that Spock could be so immediately and severely disabled. This leads, and appropriately so, to protective/supportive behavior by Kirk. When Spock indicates he is again in control and requests a return to acceptance of his strength, Kirk is not immediately ready to change from the supportive/protective mode. Since this reluctance is rational, based on the potential danger which Spock can be to the ship, no emotional repercussions result. Spock accepts the captain's logic and takes it on himself to accomplish the goal of capturing one of the creatures. When Spock plans to beam back down to Deneva to capture a specimen creature, Kirk ceases his protective behavior and returns to the assumption that Spock is strong enough and truthful enough to be allowed to name his own goals. In other words, Kirk grants both autonomy and strength as traits which Spock deserves and has. This assumption, versus unnecessary protectiveness, can act to cement any friendship.

McCoy responds to this exchange with professional protectiveness. He sees Spock the patient, not Spock the competent officer. Probably it is more than by chance that McCoy does not voice his concerns until after Spock has already beamed down. This restraint by McCoy probably reduces the instigation of further resentments by Spock, and we can assume that McCoy is astute enough to be aware of this.

Later, when McCoy surreptitiously checks Spock's condition with a medi-scanner, he makes a clear statement that Spock is still seriously ill, but in control of his pain. Despite the continued serious illness, McCoy does not make any recommendations to Spock that he should stop his research. In other words, McCoy the doctor feels the need for a few, well-aimed words of protective warning, but McCoy the person grants Spock his autonomy. To have said more would lead to defensive antagonism from Spock. As it was, Spock granted McCoy the professional need to express his concern, but warned by the tone of his voice that no more protective behavior would be tolerated.

The theme of autonomy versus protectiveness in this episode continues. When Spock announces that he may be losing control over the pain (and thereby implies that the creature could take control of his body and be a danger to the ship), Kirk responds with the assumption that Spock will be able to hold out longer. Kirk has not responded with protectiveness; he has assumed that Spock is capable of autonomous, responsible action. McCoy remains silent during this exchange, thus giving tacit agreement. This episode shows McCoy giving a very limited amount of protective responses, especially given the amount of chances he has to do so due to Spock's physical condition. Spock seems aware that McCoy is restraining himself from interfering with Spock's need for autonomy.

Caustic exchanges in this episode are brief and usually end with McCoy giving in to Spock's decisions, no matter how hazardous these actions are. When Spock suggests himself as the subject to test the power of light to kill the creature, McCoy protectively argues that the danger is too great. But McCoy shortly gives up his protective argument in the light of Spock's logic, although his concern continues to show on his face.

In that strained moment before Spock enters the experimental chamber, he takes a long look at both Kirk and McCoy. This moment could be read as a last questioning in the hope that some other alternative be found before he takes this risk. McCoy at this time has an opportunity to argue against, or even block, the procedure. He does not. In this episode McCoy has restrained his urges to be protective of Spock, and we see a closeness between the two which is rare.

In the end, ironically, it will be McCoy who will keep Kirk from being too overprotective of Spock. When the experiment is over, the creature has indeed been successfully killed and driven from Spock's body, but Spock is left blind. McCoy continues to perceive Spock as a functional being, even as the doctor feels the burden of guilt for allowing Spock to be blinded. Kirk, a man of action, is suddenly unable to perceive Spock as still competent: Spock locates a chair and starts to sit down; Kirk grabs him to guide him. If you think about it, once any of us locate a chair, we no longer need to look at it. It is behind us. We assume that it will stay there. Kirk's help is clearly redundant and dysfunctional. This hyperprotective response from Kirk comes from his own orientation toward life, one in which vision equals action. Kirk would be very handicapped were he suddenly to become blind. McCoy, less dependent on his vision, and thereby more aware of the degree of Spock's continued competence, is also aware of the damage Kirk could do to his friendship with Spock if he becomes overprotective. So McCoy pulls Kirk away.

I think that the next scenes, which show the depth of McCoy's guilt for his involvement in Spock's blindness, also tend to stand out as illustration of the degree of McCoy's caring. But these scenes *do not* illustrate friendship. They show that same professional protectiveness we have seen repeatedly from McCoy the doctor to Spock the patient. We have a mass of evidence available to us that McCoy cares professionally. What we seldom see is absolute evidence that McCoy's caring is based in friendship. The act of pulling Kirk away so as to grant Spock a feeling of autonomy despite his blindness is such an act.

The trouble is, too many of McCoy's acts of true friendship toward Spock are done in such a way that Spock will not learn of them. Spock cannot see this act any more than he could hear McCoy wish him luck as he took the shuttlecraft out into the giant amoeba. McCoy remains closed to Spock in defense against Spock's protective attitude toward the doctor. Only when Spock is able to cease being so protective will McCoy be able to openly express his friendship. So the two of them take turns being protective toward the other, then each responds by defensiveness because of the protection. In episode after episode, each maintains the distance created by their respective professional positions in relation to the other.

By the end of "Operation: Annihilate," Spock regains his vision. Ironically, if Spock had remained blind, he probably would have found his friendship shifting from Kirk to McCoy, for Kirk would have a difficult time continuing to treat a blind person as a functional, autonomous being. McCoy would not have that difficulty. As a blind person, Spock would no longer maintain an attitude of physical protectiveness toward McCoy, so some key issues of defensive antagonism would have been eliminated. The final results would have depended on how McCoy continued to try to protect Spock's psyche by trying to force him to express these feelings; Spock would have been the one to maintain a defensive wall against McCoy.

Although McCoy remains protective throughout "Operation: Annihilate," he remains restrained in order to keep this urge under control. In most episodes neither McCoy nor Spock refrain from expressing their respective protectiveness. The worst case of mutual protective/defensive abuse is the prison scene in "Bread and Circuses." McCoy has had to depend on Spock's superior physical prowess in the combat just completed. The doctor is both grateful and embarrassed by Spock's defense of him in the arena. McCoy is having difficulty expressing these mixed emotions. When he tries to express his ambivalent feelings, Spock does not allow the doctor to clear the air. McCoy, in defense against further put-down, attacks the Vulcan's emotional immaturity: his inability to experience certain emotions and to understand them in others. The scene ends with mutually hurt feelings and an increase in defensive walls between two people who are potential friends. Only their mutual friendship with Kirk keeps the interchange from becoming more volatile.

Any progress which was made between Spock and McCoy in "Operation: Annihilate" and not already destroyed by other confrontations is totally destroyed by the conflict over who would take the shuttlecraft out to investigate the giant "amoeba" in "The Immunity Syndrome." The mission is exceptionally dangerous, and as Kirk puts it, he wonders "which of his friends" he will "send to his death."

The project was devised by McCoy. If Spock had not also volunteered to go, Kirk would have been forced to send McCoy. The mission was so dangerous that Kirk could not send anyone except a volunteer, and originally, McCoy was the only one. Not only did

Spock volunteer himself, but he also gave several reasons why McCoy was not as competent as himself to succeed. So the decision of which will go is left to Kirk. Spock, with his greater physical strength and emotional control is, of course, chosen.

McCoy again sees himself as protected rather than treated as a whole and competent person. His anger is aimed at Spock, as it should be. Given the choice between McCoy and Spock, in a mission demanding physical endurance, Kirk's decision was predetermined. Only Spock could have allowed McCoy to go by not stepping in and volunteering in the first place. Spock volunteered for two reasons. The first was to increase the likelihood of success. Only secondly did he consider the life of McCoy. Still, McCoy interprets Spock's action as a personal affront; neither of Spock's reasons is complimentary to him.

McCoy's anger and humiliation is high but not total. However, it is high enough to cause him to refuse to wish Spock well until the Vulcan is clearly out of hearing. McCoy's anger and humiliation over his incident is enough to raise the doctor's defensive walls higher than ever. Spock's protective behavior and communication created a communication wall between the two which is never totally dropped by McCoy. Even in *Star Trek III: The Search for Spock,* we see the doctor telling Spock how much he cares only after Spock has been unable to acknowledge McCoy's queries.

So, through episode after episode, Spock continues to treat McCoy like the weak link in terms of physical abilities, and McCoy continues to treat Spock as a person incompetent in the healthy arrangement of his own emotions. The issue is not whether each is right or wrong in their perceptions, the issue is that both communicate a protectiveness to the other on the basis of these deductions. This respective professional protectiveness disallows either from forming the mutuality necessary for a fully mature friendship.

Only when McCoy is able to prove to himself that

he is able to face physical dangers as well as Kirk and
Spock is he willing to accept Spock's protectiveness.
In "The Empath," McCoy puts both Kirk and Spock
out of action with his hypo and goes to face almost
certain death in their place. "Not this time, Spock,"
McCoy says after Spock has shown his usual intention
to stand between McCoy and physical danger.

As McCoy lays close to death, having already defied
both Kirk and Spock, he is able to accept, even tease,
Spock for his continued protective, supportive manner. After that, the degree of open antagonism between Spock and McCoy seems to be reduced,
although on at least two more occasions it does flare
up. One such situation is in "The Tholian Web,"
where tensions between the two are only temporary
and mediated by some well-chosen "last words" from
the captain.

The final television episode (in terms of stardate),
"All Our Yesterdays," shows a continued pathological
exchange between Spock and McCoy based on their
traditional protective attitudes toward each other.
Spock saves McCoy's life by carrying him to shelter.
McCoy continuously analyzes and directs Spock's
emotions as the Vulcan begins to revert to his ancestors' ancient expression of the passions that nearly destroyed Vulcan before the reforms of Surak. Each sees
the weakness of the other as a critical, life-threatening
deficiency, and we are likely to agree with them. That
they are each correct does nothing to reduce the resentment of the protectiveness of the other, for such
protective attitudes are an insult and a demeaning of
the other's competence.

In the final scenes, Spock tells McCoy that the doctor can now cease his vigilant observations. Spock
finds that his emotional control has returned to his
norm: "I have returned to the present in every respect." Still, McCoy cannot let go of his concern for
the Vulcan. The doctor remains worried that Spock is
now repressing his true feelings of loss. "But it did

happen," McCoy insists. McCoy cannot cease his protective attitude over Spock's emotional processes any more than Spock could have left McCoy to die in the snow. But such protective behaviors and communications remain an obstacle to a fully developed and open friendship.

Another critical situation arises in *Star Trek: The Motion Picture*. In this case, Spock's social and emotional withdrawal has reached such a pathological level that any doctor would be remiss to ignore the symptoms. After two and a half years of absence, the first verbal exchange between these two "friends" is a caustic set of verbal defensive attacks. First McCoy identifies Spock's continued inability to express his emotions, then Spock hits back with an attack on the doctor's predilection for irrelevancies. McCoy has identified a weakness in Spock which, as a doctor, McCoy has an obligation to correct. However, the identification of this weakness is an attack on the Vulcan in an area which is a serious point of vulnerability at that moment. The only possible response is one of counterattack.

By the end of this movie, Spock has resolved the problem of emotional repression as well as we have ever seen. McCoy's goals have been achieved (although how much of the responsibility for this achievement can go to McCoy is questionable). The question remains: How much damage has been done between Spock and McCoy over the years? Can they now get beyond the antagonisms which have accumulated through tier defensive responses to their respective protective attitudes?

Although we see, and are intrigued by, exceptions to the McCoy/Spock wars, the general theme has been one of protectiveness leading to retaliatory attacks or defensive posturing between the two. Kirk, although he too has made exceptions to his usual behavior, has followed a theme of respecting the competence and individuality of his two friends, thus maintaining close, mature friendships with both Spock and McCoy.

As we look forward to more Star Trek films, we see that the basic reasons which have been keeping these two from a mature friendship have been resolved. McCoy has nothing more to prove, to himself or to Spock, regarding physical danger. He has faced a fatal blood disease, almost fatal torture at the hands of the Vians, risk of his sanity in the mind meld with Spock's *katra.* From here onward, any protectiveness offered by any of the crew members toward Dr. McCoy is likely to be at best a convenience and at worst a source of humor.

Spock has faced the issue of expression of his emotions in his encounter with Vejur. With his cadets and in conversation with Kirk in *Star Trek II: The Wrath of Khan,* we see a person who is easily accepting of his own feelings. Any continued pressure by McCoy toward Spock to accept or express emotion would probably be given due consideration without taking the recommendation as a threat.

Spock's continued contact with his father should also help to reduce Spock's neurotic fear of self-expression in two ways. Fear of paternal disapproval should be reduced by the expression of caring which Sarek has shown in his concern for what appeared to be Spock's death. In addition, Sarek is a rather openly emotional Vulcan. Spock, on the other hand, has exaggerated the Vulcan ideal of repressed emotion. Just being around his father's example should give Spock (a rational, autonomous adult capable of analytic observation) the opportunity to recognize the example Sarek sets, and this in turn should reduce Spock's fear of self-expression.

Thus, the reasons for Spock and McCoy's respective protective communications should now be gone. They neither have reason to protect the other, or reason to fear or resent the protectiveness of the other. They should be able to establish a mature, satisfying friendship. Ironically, it is Kirk who is now not secure in either of the areas—physical prowess and emotional expression—which McCoy and Spock have resolved.

Given the difficulty suffered by McCoy and Spock in learning the importance of respect for the autonomy and uniqueness of the other, I would not expect either of them to try being too overprotective of Kirk as he goes about achieving a new personal balance in these and other areas.

As I read some of the articles which bemoan the loss of the contrasts (and implied conflicts) between these three characters, I respond with some personal opinions.

In the first place, some of this contrast was lost as each of the characters matured and became more whole. Instead of needing all three characters to form a balanced triangle containing all parts of a complete person, each of these persons now forms a balanced being within themselves. This may be somewhat disappointing to new fans, but it is a pleasure for those of us whose careers paralleled the original crew. We have been able to watch them grow along with ourselves.

The *process* of growth was exciting to follow. Once the process of growth reached a certain level, some of the excitement was removed from an aspect of the program. The obvious answer is to include more new characters whose life as a *maturing* adult is just beginning, find a balanced group of them who form a whole as a unit, and watch them develop and mature to the point each of them forms a balanced individual. It will not make us love our already mature characters any less.

PAST, PRESENT AND FUTURE TENSE: A SPECULATIVE COMMENTARY ON CAPTAIN JEAN-LUC PICARD AND DR. BEVERLY CRUSHER—PART II

By E. A. Lowe

Part III—Tactical Maneuvers 1: The Captain's Strategy

Captain Jean-Luc Picard is a man with a problem. He finds himself strongly attracted to Dr. Beverly Crusher, his chief medical officer. The attraction is both physical and (here lurks the real danger) emotional. He is not at all attracted, however, to many of the personal and professional consequences of actual intimacy with her. He must, therefore, resist her ever-present temptation.

He can expect absolutely no support from Beverly Crusher in the regard because she, in turn, is strongly attracted to him.

So, he must be doubly resistant.

As *Star Trek: The Next Generation* reveals, Jean-Luc Picard resists temptation by avoiding it. Since he cannot avoid the woman (at least not entirely), he instead forestalls all familiarity in his dealings with her.

With Dr. Crusher, Captain Picard is polite; he is

formal; he is professional. Bluntly put, he is as stiff as a stick and about half as endearing. Only rarely does he remove the back brace that almost seems welded to his spine insofar as she is concerned.

The most notable tactic by which Picard keeps himself at a comfortable professional distance from Beverly is to use her title instead of her given name. This is common military usage designed to discourage unwanted familiarity between ranks. In "The Naked Now," Picard's preoccupation with the proper forms of address between them is nicely brought out and, in his intoxicated state at the time, it is a most befuddled preoccupation, indeed.

Picard almost never refers to or addresses Beverly in any other way than "Doctor" or "Doctor Crusher." The exceptions are significant: in "The Naked Now," when they are both intoxicated; not again until "The Arsenal of Freedom," after her immobilizing injuries, but even then only at a (presumably safe) remove from her; in "Symbiosis," at close quarters in the turbolift, but while she is engaged in a serious professional and philosophical disagreement with him (and not exactly in a receptive mood, romantically speaking); in "Conspiracy," when talking to Captain Walker Keel and, later, to Commander William Riker, but not in the presence of Beverly herself.

Picard's tactic is effective precisely because he and Beverly were formerly on a first-name basis, along with Walker Keel and Beverly's late husband, Jack Crusher.

The first time Beverly mentions Picard by name (to Riker in "Encounter at Farpoint"), she calls him Jean-Luc. Aboard the *Enterprise,* however, she is quick to pick up on the captain's formality. From their first meeting, he sets the tone by calling her Dr. Crusher. Afterward, she only occasionally addresses him as Jean-Luc and never again refers to him in front of others except by his rank.

In a related tactic, Picard also engages Beverly in

no casual socializing, no chatting over old times, or other personal matters. In this, too, Beverly mostly follows Picard's lead. Meetings and talks between them tend to be briskly professional (often, painfully so) and the topics for discussion are medically related, or, sometimes, concern Wesley.

After their conversation in sickbay in "Encounter at Farpoint," Picard never again even alludes to Jack Crusher with Beverly, except for an oblique reference in "Code of Honor" to Picard's also having seen his "share of death."

The closest Picard ever comes to a personal conversation with Beverly again is in "The Arsenal of Freedom," but even that stems from the medical situation of the moment. Picard is worried. Beverly is badly injured, in pain, and going into shock from blood loss. She must be kept talking in order to prevent her from losing consciousness. Picard speaks to her from a distance and starts off by asking her about the medicinal properties of some roots. A few details of her personal background follow from this, but it is hardly a cozy little tête-á-tête.

The discussions between Picard and Beverly in "Justice," although they concern Wesley's impending execution, are not personal. In the face of every parent's nightmare come to life, Beverly is naturally distraught. She is projecting more than enough emotion for the both of them, so Picard compensates by being very much the captain. Only later, when she has brought herself under somewhat better control, does he allow himself to share with her his own underlying sympathy and fear, but still as captain.

The threat to Wesley is ship's business. It is forcing Picard to struggle for a human interpretation of the Prime Directive that will permit him to save Wesley without also jeopardizing the entire complement of the *Enterprise*. Outwardly controlled, although deeply troubled, Picard is the professional anchor that steadies Beverly, by example, through her personal terror.

In his avoidance strategy with Beverly, Picard does not content himself with formality of speech alone. Another conspicuous defensive tactic he uses is to minimize physical contact with her, as if he cannot trust himself even to touch her (and he may well not).

Picard demonstrates the same restraint with Jenice Manheim in "We'll Always Have Paris," because of his still-powerful feelings for her, and even with holodeck construct Jessica Bradley, who vamps him outrageously in "The Big Goodbye." With women who have neither sparked his romantic interest nor shown such interest in him, Picard is not so inhibited.

Despite his general reserve (or perhaps because of it), and when circumstances warrant, Picard makes effective use of personal contact to convey any of several messages: to caution, warn or redirect; to signal approval or relief; or to lend strength, encouragement, support, or comfort.

He exhibits this talent, for example, with Lieutenant Natasha Yar in "Hide and Q"; with Counselor Deanna Troi in "Skin of Evil"; with Clare Raymond, one of the cyronic survivors in "The Neutral Zone"; with Kareen Brianon in "The Schizoid Man"; and with Dr. Katherine Pulaska in "Unnatural Selection."

Picard's behavior in these instances is not a sign of his immunity to the feminine charms of these or any other women. That Picard does recognize and appreciate a beautiful woman is borne out, for example, by his heartfelt admiration of Tasha Yar's loveliness, which he acknowledges to Lutan in "Code of Honor," and by his pleased reaction to Minuet, the stunning holodeck creation in "11001001." It is just that Picard's appreciation of a woman's physical beauty or other attributes (i.e., the natural response of male to female) is not necessarily transmuted into the mysterious emotional chemistry of romantic attraction. In the absence of such attraction, Picard is not afraid to allow his compassionate feelings open expression, even to the point of direct, physical display.

In "The Schizoid Man," the still-living personality of the late Dr. Ira Graves usurps the body and mind of Lieutenant Commander Data, then proceeds to make a fundamental error in assessing Picard's behavior with Kareen Brianon. Loving this young woman himself, Dr. Graves believe Picard to be manifesting desire for her. If Graves were better acquainted with the captain, he might realize he has no grounds for the intense jealousy Picard's attentions provoke in him. On the contrary, Graves would be entirely justified in feeling tremendous relief.

That Picard allows himself to touch Kareen Brianon at all, but especially so casually, offers the surest evidence he feels no desire for her, nor senses any for him on her part. At the first hint of such feelings, from either direction, Picard's emotional defense system would engage to shield him against the perceived threat.

As it does against Beverly Crusher.

In her capacity as chief medical officer, of course, Beverly must be able to touch Picard from time to time. This he allows, but only as needed. Aside from a perfunctory handshake in "Encounter at Farpoint," Picard himself touches Beverly in only two other first season episodes, "When the Bough Breaks" and "The Arsenal of Freedom."

In "Datalore," when she is relievedly hugging Wesley, Picard does reach out to Beverly, ordering her to sickbay to have her phaser injury treated. Again, in "Home Soil," he reaches out to urge Beverly to back away from the "microbrain" life-form generating the strange noise in the medical lab. In both instances, he falls short of actual contact.

In "When the Bough Breaks," Picard hesitates at first, but does rest his hand briefly on Beverly's shoulder during the conference with the parents of the kidnapped *Enterprise* children. His touching her in this fashion just then is very much a delibrate expression of his solidarity, not only with Beverly, but also, through her, with the other parents she will be representing in negotiations for their return.

As if to make up for the shortage elsewhere, "The Arsenal of Freedom" abounds in physical contact between Picard and Beverly: in their flight from the automated weapon; in their unsuccessful attempt to keep from falling into the underground chamber; and, especially, in the aftermath of that fall.

With a fine ironic twist, the medical tables are turned so that it is Captain Picard who must touch Dr. Crusher, and often, while he applies first aid to her injuries. Though gentle, he is also efficient and businesslike. He is just short of comically obvious in deflecting the doctor's sound medical advice to "keep her warm."

(Interestingly, it is Picard's very circumvention of this romantic cliché that proves ultimately decisive in effecting the Away Team's escape from the planet's weapons system. Had Picard lingered to serve as a living blanket for the shocky, shivering Beverly, he could not have discovered the master computer.)

Whether or not one is sympathetic to Picard's goal of avoiding emotional commitment to any woman, there is no denying the success of his strategy for achieving that goal.

In his treatment of Beverly throughout the first season, Picard repeatedly demonstrates his finely honed strategic sense and tactical skill, what Commander Riker describes in the second season's "Timed Squared" as the captain's ". . . ability to evaluate the dynamics of a situation and then take a definitive, preemptive step—take charge."

And "take charge" Picard does. His studied formality with Beverly, in both speech and manner, is the "definitive, preemptive step" from which he never allows her to recover. With it, he restricts her freedom of action. In fact, he decisively restricts her to *reaction* only, and reaction of an extremely limited variety, at that. An inspired stroke.

Picard is similarly inspired in the second season's "Manhunt" as he foils the obvious sexual intentions of Lwaxana Troi, Deanna Troi's widowed mother.

Constrained professionally by his regard for both Lwaxana Troi's "ambassadorial rank" and his own splendid working relationship with her daughter, Picard cannot reciprocate the Betazoid dignitary's romantic interest. And—it must be admitted—the haughty eccentric telepath engineers her approach, as she does everything else, with all the delicacy of a phaser blast; a trait guaranteed to put Picard right off from the start.

But he cannot reject the lady's persistent sexual advances directly, either, for fear of gravely insulting her. Picard's predicament is, indeed, as Katherine Pulaski teases Deanna, ". . . an excellent exercise for his reflexes and agility."

Cornered at the unexpectedly intimate dinner with Ambassador Troi, Picard finds two of his favorite stratagems unworkable. Formality proves entirely ineffective against this would-be lover, and diplomatic retreat is, for the moment, impossible.

Hard-pressed, the resourceful tactician resorts to an ingenious ploy: he calls in reinforcements. Lieutenant Commander Data obligingly (and, even better, quite unknowingly) renders his captain yeoman service as escort, shield, and diversion for the rest of the meal, much to Picard's relief and Lwaxana's frustration.

Next, Picard takes quick advantage of Deanna's entrance (at last!) to cover his own tactful escape. Later, after Counselor Troi has outlined the true extent of the threat her mother poses (i.e., a quadrupled Betazoid sex drive, plus marriage), the properly intimidated Picard goes to great lengths to stay out of sight, and out of range of Ambassador Troi, for the balance of the voyage.

Reminiscent of his fencing style in "We'll Always Have Paris," Picard's efforts to keep his dealings with Beverly Crusher (as well as Lwaxana Troi) on solid professional ground may sometimes display, to use Picard's own admission to his fencing partner, "the technique of a desperate man." But, as in the fencing match, what Picard's technique may sometimes lack in subtlety and grace of execution, it more than makes up in impact and efficacy of result. Picard actually wages an accomplished defense, worthy of the distinguished campaign veteran he is.

Picard's tactics with Beverly Crusher succeed on three fronts: they shore up his resolve to master his feelings for her; they erect a formidable psychological barrier between the two of them; and they deter Beverly from staging an assault on that barrier or his resolve.

In short: The captain's strategy works.

Tactical Maneuvers 2: The Big Exception

Regarding Captain Jean-Luc Picard's deliberate strategy of formal behavior with Dr. Beverly Crusher in *Star Trek: The Next Generation:* The big exceptions—the only true exceptions—cluster together in a single episode, "The Big Goodbye"; an exceptional episode in many respects.

In it, everyone gets to see a side of Jean-Luc Picard he seldom shows; a side that belies much of the stern, remote facade behind which he ordinarily camouflages himself; a side whose compassion, warmth, and humor are made all the more compelling precisely because he does allow himself to display them so rarely.

Here we see a Picard who embraces his recreational pursuits as avidly as he does his professional responsibilities. His boyish enthusiasm with the holodeck fantasy of Dixon Hill is almost contagious. When it bubbles over into his staff briefing, he delights his officers with unexpected exuberance. So caught up is he in regaling them with his account that he does not shy away from Beverly's touch. He not only permits her unmistakably intimate gesture of wiping lipstick from the corner of his mouth (in front of everybody!), he actually invites her to accompany him on his next excursion into Dixon Hill territory.

Pleased and surprised, Beverly accepts with alacrity.

Just when it looks to Beverly as if Picard is getting personal with her at last, he dashes her hopes by arranging for a chaperon, in the form of Mr. Whalen.

Actually, it is doubtful that Picard is thinking along the lines of needing a chaperon. He is so taken with the excitement and wonder of the Dixon Hill fantasy that he feels an almost childlike eagerness for kindred spirits to share his delight. Picard does not even seem to notice when Beverly's voice subsequently takes on a decided quality of pique.

For a few more fleeting moments, his staff is treated to Jean-Luc in full sail before he brings himself up short, suddenly realizing his enthusiasm is making him something of a spectacle. He then gets down to proper business.

(In previous episodes, we have been given only glimpses, mere hints, of Beverly's feelings. With this scene, we begin to appreciate fully what Beverly Crusher sees in this man, what she must know and sense and remember from those long-ago days of their first acquaintance—the sheer impact of the private Picard.)

By the time Picard and Beverly see each other again, on the holodeck, the cutting edge of his enthusiasm has been blunted. As Dixon Hill, he has just been released from a protracted and altogether too real session of police grilling.

The brief interchange that follows contains the one truly personal remark that Picard makes about Beverly during the entire first season: "I must say, you wear it well. I'm glad you could make it."

The statement may seem of little account, but Picard's delivery—revealing, as it does, in his quiet, understated way, the strength and depth of his feelings—imbues the words with a weight and significance all out of proportion to their objective meaning.

But this meaning is important on its own. Having dressed the part, and to perfection, Beverly supplies Picard with the missing ingredient. She completes the picture of the fantasy recreation of the private eye's seductive female companion. No off-limits Starfleet officer this.

The world of Dixon Hill assumes its own strange reality and Picard begins to view that world as something quite removed from the functions of the ship. The *Enterprise* seems far away, indeed; Picard's suggestion they "get back" to the ship brings this out nicely. It also highlights his contradictory feelings about Beverly; they need to "get back" to "normal."

Picard is obviously tempted to remain and play out the fantasy with her. Sensing the peril in this, he takes refuge in duty, but reluctantly. He is only too happy to fulfill Beverly's request to see Dixon Hill's office. In his willingness to accompany her from the safely crowded police station, Picard deliberately courts the dangerous privacy of that office.

As it turns out, neither of them is put to the test. Fortunately (or unfortunately, as the case may be) Lieutenant Commander Data and Mr. Whalen are on hand.

Ironically, neither of these *real* characters demonstrates even the tiniest fraction of the perspicacity shown earlier by the computer-generated Sergeant McNary. In fairness, we must remember that McNary reacted in light of Dixon Hill's well-known reputation with women. Mr. Whalen is not well acquainted with either Captain Picard or Dr. Crusher, and Data has some difficulty understanding the subtleties of interpersonal behavior.

From Picard and Beverly's point of view, the presence of these two unwitting—not to say, witless—chaperons is, without question, *un*fortunate.

Engrossed with each other, Picard and Beverly have for a few minutes happily forgotten their companions. When rude reality, in the persons of Data and Whalen, impinges on the beguiling fantasy world, one cannot help sympathize with Picard and Beverly's initial shock and vexaton. While Beverly's face is almost comically expressive, Picard, typically, assumes his unreadable captain's mask. Even so, one can almost hear his testy, "What cretin invited these two idiots along?" immediately followed by the self-professed cretin's suitably chagrined, *"Merde!"*

Making the best of the frustrating development, however, Picard is soon extolling the wonders of holodeck programming and regaining some of the expansiveness he lost during Dixon Hill's interrogation by police. He even displays a flair for the theatrical in the early dealings with holodeck construct Felix Leech, until events take an unexpected turn to the deadly.

From this point on, there are no personal moments between Picard and Beverly. Their respective professional priorities fully occupy their attention. Even when Beverly touches Picard, in a grimly twisted reprise of the lipstick incident, it is only to stanch the blood from his injured lip. Nor does the direct threat to Beverly's life provoke an overly personal response from Picard.

Emotionalism would be both inappropriate and counterproductive in this situation. Picard's tactical experience keeps him from giving his holodeck adversary, Cyrus Redlock, the great coercive advantage he already enjoys. Using self-control and reasoned psychology (plus the efforts of the holodeck repair crew), Picard is able to effect Redlock's destruction and save all of his people.

As impersonally as "The Big Goodbye" ends for Picard and Beverly, it showcases the only true exceptions to his "Beverly avoidance strategy."

In "The Naked Now," Picard's actions are the result

of the disinhibiting intoxicant, not a voluntarily chosen mode of behavior. As revealing (and later, embarrassing) as that behavior is, Picard manages to avoid a totally compromising incident. (Actually, the events of "The Naked Now" serve only to stiffen Picard's resolve. Hence, his "avoid temptation" remark at the conclusion.)

In other episodes, even under trying circumstances, Picard quite successfully maintains good working relations with Beverly while keeping his professional distance.

It is only in "The Big Goodbye" that Picard, by his own volition, runs the risk of letting their relationship venture beyond these safe boundaries. Before the trouble with Leech and Redlock erupts, Picard had begun to respond to Beverly in a distinctly man-to-woman manner.

There is no doubt that Picard's delight with the Dixon Hill fantasy overrides some of his self-imposed inhibitions, even in a staff meeting. He also assumes some of the characteristics of his alter ego. In a spillover effect, Picard's inhibitions concerning Beverly are likewise relaxed. Given what is known of Picard's actual history with women, ladies' man Dixon Hill is an intriguing choice of fantasy. Beverly reaps the benefits.

In "The Big Goodbye," Picard does not lose control, as he assuredly does in "The Naked Now." Rather, he allows himself a great deal more latitude with Beverly than he does at any other time. Much to her disappointment, Picard allows himself such latitude in no other episode during the series' entire first season. With the exception of this fantasy-based episode, the captain's strategy is fully online and operating.

A Second Opinion: Dr. Crusher's Dilemma

Evidence of Dr. Beverly Crusher's part in the tactical pas de deux with Captain Jean-Luc Picard, and her feelings about it, is widely scattered throughout first season episodes of *The Next Generation*.

Dr. Crusher's frankly sexual response to Captain Picard in "The Naked Now" surprises and dismays her but, while she is still intoxicated, does not shock her. The sobering effect of the antidote, however, brings acute embarrassment at her flagrantly provocative behavior. Until this point, at least consciously, Beverly has probably placed Jean-Luc in the category of "old friend of the family." One can imagine the rude jar to her psyche caused by the discovery that this particular old friend has become the focus for the kind of feelings she once reserved for her husband.

The tantalizing question remains: From where does her sudden, seemingly full-blown desire for Picard spring? She is already highly aroused by the time she arrives on the bridge, so these feelings must have erupted at the mere thought of Picard, while she was still working in sickbay, far from his physical presence. What is already there within Beverly's mind for the intoxicant to trigger and bring to the surface for public display?

Proponents of the theory that Wesley is really Jean-Luc's son (or, at the very least, that Picard and Beverly were once lovers) might see her conduct in "The Naked Now" as the linchpin of their argument. A long-ago affair between the two, even a one-night stand, would be ample fuel for the intoxicant's fire.

In fact, it would be more than ample. The intoxicant need not replay actual events. It requires no more than the concerns and yearnings of its victims, who may or may not be consciously aware of such yearnings in themselves. This seems to be Beverly's experience. Her very surprise at her reaction is eloquent testimony that her desire for Picard has never before found conscious expression.

Below the level of awareness, however, there has to be some attraction to Picard. It is doubtful that such attraction was newly born upon her arrival to the *Enterprise;* it likely dates back to their earliest acquaintance.

Through Walker Keel, Beverly met his friends, Jack Crusher and Jean-Luc Picard. In the early stages of friendship, Beverly probably found each attractive, in various ways and to various degrees. Here were three successful Starfleet officers; bright, ambitious, capable men, clearly heading to the top. They were close friends (according to Picard in "Conspiracy," "virtually inseparable") whose easy camaraderie would bring out the best in each. And although we get to see only two of them, and only then twenty years later, we know that all three were handsome and at ease in any company.

As her relationship with Jack developed, Beverly's feelings for him deepened, becoming quite different from the friendship she continued to feel for Walter and Picard. Courtship and marriage did not change this, of course; years later, in "Conspiracy," it is plain she still highly values Walker Keel's friendship. And by this time, her feelings for Jean-Luc Picard had progressed far beyond mere friendship.

But when did her feelings for Jean-Luc undergo this metamorphosis? Not during Jack Crusher's lifetime, I should think. Just about the time Jack began seriously courting Beverly, Jean-Luc would have begun implementing the first version of his avoidance strategy with her.

This unexplained cooling in Jean-Luc's behavior toward her would have left Beverly understandably puzzled. When she wondered about it, she might even have concluded, mistakenly, that his growing reserve was due to negative feelings about her, perhaps because of her intrusion into the three-way dynamics of the friendship he shared with Jack and Walker.

In any case, Jean-Luc's lengthier and more frequent absences, together with Beverly's increasing involvement with Jack, probably forestalled her dwelling overmuch on this distancing in the other relationship. After the first heady rush of romantic love had passed, the pressures of meeting the escalating demands of medicine, marriage, and motherhood would have supplied their own preoccupations and kept her too busy to wonder much about Jean-Luc Picard.

Then Jack Crusher was killed.

Beverly would have found some comfort in their son. Walker Keel, too, would undoubtedly have lent whatever support he could. From Jean-Luc Picard, though, she probably received little, if anything, in the way of either support or comfort.

Left almost as stricken as she, he was badly in need of support and comfort himself. Along with grief for the loss of his friend, Jean-Luc carried the added weight—the captain's burden—of responsibility for Jack's death. He apparently projected onto Beverly many of his own feelings about that death.

Angry with himself, blaming himself for his failure to prevent Jack's death, he assumed Jack's widow could do no less. How could Beverly not loathe the very sight of him?

Actually, Beverly seems to have been much less judgmental of Jean-Luc than he was of himself (although, being human, she was not entirely rational about him, either). At the time, even through her own shock and grief, Beverly would have sensed some of Jean-Luc's pain and understood at least part of his need to get away immediately after the funeral.

What would eventually have troubled her was his continued avoidance of her and Wesley through all the long years after the tragedy. Her relationship with Walker Keel did not suffer such estrangement. Friends of long standing, they refer to each other with unaffected familiarity in "Conspiracy." In contrast, Beverly had no contact with Jean-Luc Picard until she transferred to his ship, by her choice, in "Encounter at Farpoint."

Beverly's posting to the *Enterprise* is something of a coup in her already distinguished medical and Starfleet career. Her professional reasons for requesting the assignment are obvious. Less obvious are her personal reasons. Beverly herself may not have been fully aware of some of them until "The Naked Now."

In the years after Jack's death, Beverly devoted herself almost exclusively to the two passions remaining in her life—her son and her work—with notable success in both endeavors. Wesley's remarks to Will Riker in "Encounter at Farpoint" leave the impression that the boy's mother has made a habit of keeping men at a distance. In "The Naked Now," Beverly herself is disconcertingly forthcoming with Picard about her lack of sexual outlet since Jack's death, verifying that she had been without ". . . the comfort of a husband, a man."

Early in her widowhood, Beverly must have been wary of forming any new romantic attachments, fearful of risking another loss. A dozen or so years is a long time to maintain this attitude, however.

Beverly is a disciplined person, but her passionate temperament ill suits her to a celibate life. Over the years, as valiantly as she strove to sublimate them, the mounting physical and emotional tensions must have been terrific. So, why has she not remarried or taken a lover? Could it be that, subconsciously, she has been waiting all this time for just the right man, not to come along, but to come back into her life?

The clearest clue to the mystery comes in Beverly's bizarre statement, "You owe me something," directed to Picard in "The Naked Now." This refutes her earlier assurance in "Encounter at Farpoint": "My feelings about my husband's death will have no effect on the way I serve you, this vessel, or this mission." She was surely trying hard to convince the captain (and maybe herself?) that her feelings really had nothing to do with him at all.

At no time does Beverly appear to actually blame Picard for Jack's death (at least, not in the sense of considering him criminally guilty), but she does hold him accountable for it and her ensuing deprivation. But Jack Crusher's death, Picard's involvement in it, and the consequence for them both is the critical, unresolved issue between Picard and Beverly. It forever links them while simultaneously driving them apart.

The intoxicant in "The Naked Now" amplifies this truth, and lends it a quirky resonance, while dragging Beverly's sexual tension to the fore. Her besotted logic traces this tension to the loss of her husband, and that loss to Jean-Luc. By her inebriated reasoning, then, Jean-Luc Picard, the source of her sexual frustration, must become the agent for its alleviation.

Even though the intoxicant brings forth distorted and exaggerated reflections of feelings, it is important to remember that they are reflections, not inventions. The intoxicant does not fabricate emotion from nothing. It only expresses, however fancifully it may embellish, emotions that already exist.

With Beverly, it unleashes her long-suppressed sexual yearnings, her desire for male companionship to fill the void Jack's death has left in her life. It resurrects her heretofore subliminal attraction to Picard, an affection dating from the earliest days of their acquaintance. Not only does the intoxicant revive this attraction, it enhances it to the level of outright lust and thrusts it unmistakably into Beverly's conscious awareness.

From this point, even after the contaminant has been neutralized, Beverly cannot disavow the existence of these disturbing feelings for Picard. With sobriety restored, however, she can control her expression of them.

True, Beverly and Picard both appear to subscribe

to a tacit agreement not to speak of what happened to them in "The Naked Now." In later episodes, they perform a careful dance around each other, pretending (to use Tasha Yar's words) that "it never happened." If it had never happened, of course, most of this cautious choreography would be quite unnecessary.

With years of practice at the suppress-deny-avoid stratagem, Picard proves consistently better at this pretense than does Beverly.

During the first season, it becomes increasingly obvious that Beverly is much more willing to relax her guard around Picard than he is around her. This stems largely from a growing willingness, also on Beverly's part, to entertain the possibility of a more intimate connection between them.

And to want that connection.

Unlike Picard, Beverly has already had experience in combining a demanding career with marriage and family responsibilities. She knows what kinds of adjustments and accommodations are required, has weathered them before, and seems fairly confident she can do so again.

Also, having raised Wesley, Beverly has a lot more faith in him than does Picard, and credits their loving bond with the strength to withstand any stresses that a romance with Picard might occasion. Then, too, as Wesley will soon be a young adult with his own life to lead, and Beverly need no longer mold her life choices to fit the perceived requirements of a dependent child.

Although doctors have traditionally been wary of romantic involvement with their patients—Captain Picard is, after all, his chief medical officer's patient—Dr. Crusher seems prepared to leap this hurdle as well, without getting tangled up in the sort of professional knots with which Picard is so adept at hobbling his own emotional life.

This is not to say Beverly believes that developing their relationship would be easy, but she does not share most of Picard's personal and professional misgivings. Beverly has reached the point in her life where, beyond her desire for Picard, she is ready for the emotional risks and attendant complications of an intimate relationship with him.

What Beverly is not prepared for is a total lack of cooperation from Picard.

As the first season progresses, one senses beneath the brittle veneer of Beverly's self-control an increasing impatience to *do* something about her feelings for Picard. She is also growing impatient with his clear reluctance to do anything positive about his feelings for her.

Resorting to desperate tactics in the face of his obdurate formality, the very human Beverly is not even above exploiting Picard's weaknesses to further her own interests (i.e., her devotion to Wesley and, quite probably, her desire to forge through Wes a new link to Picard). She trades shamelessly not only on Picard's attraction to her but also on her status as Jack Crusher's widow, and on Wesley's status as Jack's son and heir, to advance the boy's career. She does gain extraordinary privileges for him from the captain, who would normally prefer children to be neither seen nor heard.

(As for the likewise very human Picard, it is difficult to determine what influences him most when granting these privileges to Wesley. Significantly, Picard does not go as far as to accord Wesley acting Starfleet rank until after the Traveler has pleaded Wesley's special case in "Where No One Has Gone Before.")

Now and then, as might be expected, Beverly's impatience with Picard gets the better of her. There is, for example, her annoyance in "The Big Goodbye" when Picard includes Mr. Whalen in his invitation to go to the holodeck. (A threesome is not what Beverly had in mind.) Then, moments later, Picard is groping for just the right word to describe being kissed by Jessica Bradley, Dixon Hill's holodeck-generated client. Misconstruing his feelings, Beverly pointedly suggests, "Exciting?" only to be countered by Picard's own exuberant, "Real!" (Granted, Picard was excited, but not so much by the client or the kiss as by the overwhelming sense of reality—"Sounds! Smells!"— of the whole Dixon Hill simulation, down to its finest details, kiss and client included.)

The events of "The Arsenal of Freedom" test Beverly's patience, too, while almost killing her. She finally gets Picard alone, only to suffer severe injuries and go into shock. Bluntly put: She is a battered, bleeding mess and not a whole lot of fun to be with. She even has trouble holding up her end of a less than scintillating conversation without repeated and frequent prodding from Picard just to keep her conscious.

What she wants from him just then (not to be confused with what she needs) is comfort and closeness. What he supplies is first aid and a steady stream of encouraging and medically necessary chitchat. And when the lady in distress throws hints in his direction about keeping her "warm," her hero neatly sidesteps them all in efforts to find an escape route out of their charming hellhole.

Small wonder, then, when Picard absently remarks from across the underground chamber, "... there must be a lot of things about you that I don't know," that Beverly's frustration seeps clearly into the tone of her weary reply, "Quite a few." True to Beverly's track record, it is a reply Picard fails to hear.

Impatience notwithstanding, Beverly is held more or less in check by Picard's formality, and by the embarrassing memory of her intoxicated advances toward him in "The Naked Now," where she was inarguably the initiator and aggressor. Both put her at a psychological and tactical disadvantage in all later dealings with him.

On the one hand, she wants to dispel any notions Picard may have that the desire she professed was solely the product of her intoxication and has no bearing on her now sober feelings. On the other hand, she also, understandably, prefers to avoid any suggestion of the aggressively wanton behavior she displayed on that occasion.

Beverly's quandary is how to unmistakably advertise to Picard her desire for him and encourage his own for her, without giving him the semblance of actual pursuit. For she knows, if she pursues him, she runs a high risk of being firmly and unambiguously rebuffed. Yet, if she does not pursue him, she guarantees losing by default her (admittedly slim) chance with him.

The choices she faces: probable humiliation if she acts, or certain failure if she does not.

Beverly is further hampered by having already made the first move. Standard courtship protocol specifies that she await some positive response from him, a response that Picard seems all too unwilling to make.

This situation must hold a certain galling irony for Beverly. Especially vexing must be her knowledge that Picard is actively resisting his attraction to her. After all, for years she has harbored a lingering resentment against him because of Jack's death; for years she has been keeping all men at a distance. Now that her own desires have been aroused—and by Jean-Luc Picard, of all people!—he steadfastly insists on keeping her at arm's length!

The irony is deftly highlighted in "Coming of Age," when Beverly tells Lieutenant Commander Remick, "My personal feelings about Captain Picard are . . . *none* of your business!"

The reality behind Beverly's statement is totally at variance with Mr. Remick's understanding (or, more accurately, misunderstanding) of the case. What Remick's intrusive investigation aboard the *Enterprise* utterly fails to unearth is that Beverly Crusher's "personal feelings" have moved as far beyond those of an aggrieved widow as they possibly could. Nobody on board—least of all Beverly—is about to enlighten the pest, however.

Picard's tactics and her own feelings twist together in a progressively exasperating tangle for Beverly. After "The Naked Now," Picard's physical proximity continues to fuel Beverly's desires. His psychological remoteness does nothing to extinguish them. Picard allows Beverly no outlet for the powerful feelings he arouses in her. Far from alleviating her emotional and sexual tensions, as she would like, Picard actually stretches them close to the breaking point.

Nowhere are Beverly's pent-up emotions made more evident than in "We'll Always Have Paris," during Deanna's abortive attempt to help the doctor come to terms with her feelings for the captain.

For Beverly, Picard's deliberately uncooperative tactics of avoidance and formality are both devilishly inconvenient and devastatingly effective. He has her stymied at every turn and unable to foresee any satisfactory resolution to the impasse.

So, her feelings for Picard persist, while the various deterrents to openly expressing them foster in Beverly an increasingly restive frustration. Trying to stifle this feeling, as well, only exacerbates her pressure-cooker predicament.

As the old saying goes, "Something's got to give!" From all indications—given what is known of Picard's personal history with women and of his determined strategy with Beverly—this "something" is shaping up to be Beverly.

"The Local Shrink": Counselor Troi's Prime Directive

Beverly Crusher's relationship with Jean-Luc Picard is a topic she is none too eager to broach with anyone, aside from Picard himself, perhaps. The captain, however, having carried his avoidance strategy to the level of a minor art form, skillfully deters Beverly from broaching it with him. Indeed, by virtue of his position and personality, Picard discourages discussion of his private life by anyone in his command.

Of all his officers (apart from Acting Ensign Wesley Crusher, whose excuse is the brash curiosity of youth), only Counselor Deanna Troi shows the audacity for such discussion. Of course, of all those aboard, only Troi is uniquely qualified, both personally and professionally, to dare so much with the captain (or any other *Enterprise* personnel, for that matter). Her empathic abilities endow her with the sensitivity required to delve into areas generally considered personal, private, and strictly forbidden. Her duty as ship's counselor may, on occasion, actually obligate her to do so.

Having to live and work cooperatively within the confines of an enclosed community like the *Enterprise,* and realizing how uncomfortable members of nonempathic species can be in the face of her talents, Troi makes special efforts to avoid unnecessarily reminding people that she is constantly aware of their emotional signals. Practicing her own form of the Prime Directive, Counselor Troi refrains from offering unsolicited advice or interfering in matters of purely personal import.

Therefore, for example, Troi largely opts against injecting her viewpoint into the already tangled emotions she senses between Captain Picard and Dr. Crusher. In only one episode, "We'll Always Have Paris," does Troi confront Beverly about her feelings for Picard. At no time does she confront Picard about his feelings for Beverly.

Where personal reactions may touch ship's business, though, "the local shrink" (as cryonic survivor Clare Raymond dubs Troi in "The Neutral Zone") is most ready with counsel, solicited or not.

In "We'll Always Have Paris," when Troi approaches the captain to discuss his response to the subject of Dr. Paul Manheim, Picard at first tries to brush her off. Troi refuses to be put off, pointing out that "unresolved, strong emotion can affect judgment." Discreetly, she refrains from specifying that emotion and offers him her "assistance" in her capacity as ship's counselor.

It is to Troi's credit that she stands her ground with Picard. He needs and deserves officers like this. It is to Picard's credit that he recognizes and accepts the legitimacy of Troi's concerns. So, putting his professional obligations ahead of his personal desire for privacy—and Picard is an intensely private man—he ends up not only asking for Troi's advice but acting on it, too. A less secure individual would have done neither.

At the same time, Picard's, "If I should need you further, I'll let you know," serves Troi courteous but clear notice that, having dared so much, she is to dare no more, at least not without an explicit request from him. Understanding her captain as she does, Troi is happy to comply. Later, Picard does enlist Troi's help in arranging his farewell meeting with Jenice Manheim on the holodeck.

Troi's stab at counseling Beverly in this episode meets with considerably less success, although it appears to get off to a promising start. There is even a touch of humor between the two when Troi jokes with Beverly, "I thought *I* was the empath." That Troi's mission with Beverly is more personal than professional, however, goes a long way toward explaining its failure.

Initially, Troi may have rationalized breaking her own noninterference rules by persuading herself that this mission was, in fact, professional; Dr. Crusher's feelings about Picard, and hence, about Jenice Manheim, might tend to color her emotional reaction to Paul Manheim, lying critically ill in sickbay.

Beverly, it turns out, does not need Troi's professional counsel. Paul Manheim poses several medical puzzles for the doctor, but no emotional uncertainties.

The consummate professional herself, Beverly has no difficulty separating medical judgment from personal feeling. Her treatment of Paul Manheim is in no way compromised by her private concerns about his wife, nor does it compromise her own emotional balance. What most upsets Beverly about Dr. Manheim is her admitted inability to prevent his death.

Sensing all this within moments of entering sickbay, Troi must realize, as quickly, that her continued presence there as ship's counselor is not justified. By her own rules, she ought to withdraw. Yet she remains. That she does so is Troi's compassionate response to the turmoil of emotions she reads in Beverly: the confusion of desires and fears, and the growing hopelessness about any future with the captain. Making an exception to her own policy, more in friendship than in any official capacity, Troi stays to offer personal counsel.

Beverly realizes Troi senses her feelings for Picard and her uneasiness about the possible effects of Jenice Manheim's sudden reappearance in his life. With Troi, Beverly does not even try to pretend she does not have these feelings. In fact, excluding her drunkenly aggressive honesty with Picard in "The Naked Now," Beverly is more candid about her feelings in this scene than she is with anybody else at any other time.

Of Picard and Jenice Manheim, Beverly frankly states, "I can't compete with a ghost from his past," adding later, "She may be in the here and now, but it's the ghost he sees."

Although Beverly does not bother to deny the obvious, she does derail Troi's well-intentioned efforts to discuss the issue, bluntly telling the counselor, "I don't think I want to talk about what I think you mean." By what she refuses to voice, as much as by what she actually says, Beverly lays bare her combined frustration and vulnerability about Picard.

Personal counsel on this problem is precisely what Beverly could use, but also, unfortunately, precisely what she is quite unprepared to accept. Troi's attempts to help Beverly open up about her feelings for Picard only put Beverly increasingly on the defensive.

Knowing when to persist, Troi also knows when to give up. So, when Beverly finally takes refuge in her work in order to escape the conversation, Troi chooses not to pursue the matter.

Troi's misstep here with Beverly confirms the merit of the noninterference policy Troi has set for herself. The Federation's Prime Directive imposes some difficult and uncomfortable decisions for Captain Picard, such as in "Code of Honor," "Justice," and especially "Symbiosis." Counselor Troi's own Prime Directive demands no less.

As greatly as her inaction must upset her, Troi forces herself to stand by as Captain Picard and Dr. Crusher, two people she likes and respects, continue their private struggles. Unlike any other person on the *Enterprise,* Troi actually feels, within herself, their warring emotions and their pain.

As long as Picard and Beverly do not seek Troi's assistance (and they do not), as long as their personal ordeal does not affect ship's business (and it does not), then the ship's counselor, empathic distress notwithstanding, mustn't try to make it her business.

Except for this one slip, she does not.

In "11001001," Captain Jean-Luc Picard tells Commander William Riker, "But you know, Number One, some relationships just can't work." The captain's observation could well serve as epitaph for his own awkward relations with his chief medical officer, Beverly Crusher.

By the conclusion of the first season of *The Next Generation,* the more off- than on-again personal relationship between Beverly and Picard has definitely stalled in the off-again mode. Throughout the series' first season episodes, apart from the embarrassing incidents of "The Naked Now" and the atypical interaction of "The Big Goodbye," Captain Picard has managed to maintain his professional distance from Dr. Crusher quite adroitly. Just barely, Dr. Crusher has also managed this distance, but with considerably less assurance and no satisfaction.

However mixed his emotions with respect to Beverly Crusher, Picard has charted a course of his own in dealing with her. He holds to that course with great (if not altogether unswerving) determination. To Beverly, though, has fallen the unenviable chore of matching another's course, a flight plan that carries her precisely one hundred and eighty degrees off the mark of her own desires. She can feel neither enthusiasm for the itinerary nor anticipation at the prospect of journey's end.

There is also the matter of Beverly's personal pride—or vanity, if you prefer—which takes quite a beating during the first season. Unrequited love is, frankly, demoralizing. Beverly lacks the necessary streak of masochism to suffer this kind of ordeal gladly or for very long. Therefore, although disappointing, it is really not so surprising that the second season opens to find Beverly already transferred off the *Enterprise.*

Personal considerations aside, if her *Enterprise* posting was a career coup, this appointment as head of Starfleet Medical was even more so. Beverly was probably elevated to a rank somewhere in the captain to admiral range. The promotion greatly widened her scope of responsibilities and sphere of influence, and enhanced her power to get things done.

And personally, Beverly may well have felt a move that put a few parsecs between herself and one Jean-Luc Picard was for the better. After all, when she first signed on to the *Enterprise,* she had not bargained on the particular set of emotional complications that ensued.

So she left. But Wesley stayed.

This was a bracing challenge for Picard. Determined to care for and guide Jack Crusher's son, Picard must try to fill the shoes of an absent mother. Wesley Crusher is the living embodiment of both his parents and, as long as he stayed on the *Enterprise,* served as a continuing link between them and Picard.

Perhaps Beverly recognized the potential for Wesley's personal growth and development, and how it would be enhanced by he and Picard getting to know each other on their own terms, without the complicating presence of a woman for whom, each in his own way, they both care. It is a tribute to Beverly that she grants this opportunity to the two people in her life for whom she cares most deeply: a fine example of her "... fierce devotion ... no matter what the personal cost," so admired by the late Tasha Yar.

REQUIEM

By Miriam Ruff

Gene Roddenberry died tonight. The Great Bird of the Galaxy is gone. How can we begin to express the loss, both for ourselves and for the phenomenon of Star Trek that he created? The loss will undoubtedly touch each one of us in unique and personal ways, but I feel compelled to write about its effect on me in the hope that not only will I be able to come to terms with it myself, but that others will find something of value and of consolation in my experience as well.

I think it is fair to say that Mr. Roddenberry revolutionized an entire era with his visionary show, not only in this country, but around the world. The evidence is all around us: Phrases like, "Beam me up, Scotty," "Space, the final frontier," "Live long and prosper," and the terms "Trekkie" and "Trekker," have fallen into common usage. NASA named its first shuttle test orbiter *Enterprise,* after the future starship. Mr. Spock is—excepting, perhaps, Mickey Mouse—the most recognizable fictional character in the world. Representatives of the U.S. Navy, impressed by the layout of the starship *Enterprise*'s bridge, toured the set to determine how they duplicate certain features on current military vessels. Many devices first seen on *Star Trek,* such as diagnostic beds and retinal scans, are becoming part of our reality.

There is another side to this revolution, responsible

for creating an environment where all of these manifestations are able to flourish. This side speaks to us on a more personal level, with a kind of insistence, and will, in fact, be the true legacy left behind by its creator.

Each *Star Trek* fan has a story of how and why they got involved with the show. In this way I am not much different than many others. I had watched and liked the original series as a child, but for some reason I cannot even begin to fathom, my parents forbade me to watch it. I read, watched, and enjoyed other science fiction, but there was something missing that I couldn't define, a hole in my life that needed to be filled.

During my first semester of college, I was reintroduced to *Star Trek* by a friend, and needless to say, I was very quickly, and completely, hooked. My appetite for *Star Trek* was insatiable, and fortunately there was much to satisfy it. There was episode after episode of new and exciting adventures that I either didn't remember or hadn't seen. I came to know and cherish the characters. The expanded version of *Star Trek: The Motion Picture* was making its debut on television, and a brand new, exciting movie, *The Wrath of Khan,* was out in theaters.

This was Star Trek at its best, a bold adventure full of hope and loss and promise, with a great script and characters who were real; both as people and as the heroes with whom I had come to identify.

The movie was hard on me, for unfamiliar with the storyline and circumstances of the situation (I had not yet seen or heard of "Space Seed"), I was not prepared for the death of Spock. Here was a character whom, essentially, I had just met, and who I regarded (much as did Saavik) as a mentor. To have him killed off so abruptly was devastating, and the sense of loss was almost overpowering. With every new line I hoped that someone was going to tell me that it was, like Spock's coded message to Kirk about the *Enterprise*'s condition, an exaggeration. That was not to be.

I returned again and again to see this movie, trying to come to terms with Spock's death, or maybe more simply, with mortality in general. And in those viewings, I came to recognize the magnificence of that death scene, both in terms of the character's development—what more of interest can you do with a character who had found peace within himself?—and cinematically. Quite simply, it has to be one of the most beautiful death scenes ever filmed. With that recognition, I vowed that this would not be the end for me. I wanted, even needed, more of this universe, and suddenly it was there.

It was a Trekker's dream come true: Gene Roddenberry himself was actually coming to speak at my university. I couldn't wait—but I had to. Catastrophe struck: Mr. Roddenberry had to postpone his engagement due to an illness in his family. For months I waited, pestering the poor guy at the ticket counter to distraction with my demands for information. Finally, new posters announcing the date and time were placed around campus, and much to the ticket seller's relief, I made a beeline to his counter, purchased my tickets, and just as quickly got out of his life.

After all the delays and anticipation, I wasn't disappointed. There was, of course, a showing of the first *Star Trek* pilot episode, "The Cage," and Mr. Roddenberry's personal blooper reels. (Both in black-and-white and horribly scratched, but food for a starving Trekker.) Mr. Roddenberry spoke about not only the series and its creation, but about his philosophy of life and humanity, his hopes for the future, and the advances in "real" space travel which we could help make reality. This was stuff you couldn't get anywhere else, and leaving the auditorium, I was so exhilarated I was sure that someone had turned on an anti-grav unit.

My friends and I talked about it for days, going over every scrap of information we could remember. We spoke about the series and characters, our own hopes and aspirations, and anything else we could think of. This may seem pretty routine for most fans, but you have to understand that I knew nothing about organized fandom, so I clung to every moment of these discussions as if each would be the last.

It was this lecture that served to reinforce the message I saw in the episodes and movies, and it was this message that served to change my life. It was a message of hope, of potential, of possibility. It showed me a goal to strive for, a future to build, a universe to explore. Through the series it gave me tangible characters to hold onto and learn from, and abstract philosophies to contemplate. In short, it not only showed me a future that was worth working toward, and a way of life that was worth living, but it helped provide the means for me to achieve them.

The *Star Trek* characters were firmly grounded in Gene Roddenberry's philosophy of life, and each embodied different characteristics that were essential to creating any single, unified whole. Their guidance and example have been invaluable in helping me to define and foster those qualities within myself. For that, I am forever in their debt.

Mr. Spock taught me the most, for in many ways he is the most complex. His actions continually demonstrate the importance of rational thought and the consideration of all possibilities before arriving at a conclusion. More importantly, he imparts a sense of dignity and honor, despite the struggle constantly going on inside him. The lone Vulcan among a crew of humans, he managed to regain his sense of self and his principles without feeling the need to capitulate to their emotional desires. I am not easily swayed by peer pressure, but Spock's behavior has served as an important example for me.

I am a strict vegetarian. Though I always leaned that way, I must admit that it was Spock and his rational arguments for such a lifestyle that helped me follow through with my convictions. Over the years I have endured a lot of ribbing and pressure, especially in business situations. I believe very strongly in what I do, but sometimes I have to question it in terms of the difficulties it creates. Spock presents a powerful example of commitment and resolve, and fueled by that, I have consistently refused to compromise my position, and I have never regretted it.

Spock also speaks to all of us who have ever felt trapped between worlds. A prisoner, in his mind, of the conflicting demands of his highly disparate heritages, he admits to Kirk and McCoy in "The Enemy Within" that "I have an alien half as well as a human half, constantly at war with each other." His mother, Amanda, also tells Kirk in "Journey to Babel" that he is "neither Vulcan nor human, at home nowhere except Starfleet." We know from references in the series that he spent his entire life trying to reconcile his two halves; we also know that he chose the Vulcan path after the *khas wan* test when he was seven years old. After years of denial, he recognized the importance of his human, emotional heritage only after his encounter with the cold, emotionless Vejur in *Star Trek: The Motion Picture,* but he didn't know how to incorporate it into his life. It was not until *The Wrath of Khan* that he found the balance between his two halves, only then possessing the accumulated knowledge and wisdom to appreciate what he had achieved.

We can appreciate Spock's struggle, for each of us battles our own internal conflicts every day. It is not important if ours arise because of differing heritages, or peer pressure, or as with Spock, the struggle between emotion and logic. What *is* important is that we fight the battle and search for inner peace. Not to do so leaves us essentially in a state of anarchy, each side free to reign unchecked and able to wreak havoc in our lives. We learn from the struggle and the balances we strike in ourselves and the universe in which we live. Though he spent a lifetime in the pursuit of his goal, Spock shows us that both the time spent and the

REQUIEM **121**

goal itself are worthy of our effort, and that each of us not only can, but should, undertake the quest.

McCoy, the brilliant but cynical doctor, demonstrates that emotion does play a part in our lives. Realizing that most sapient life forms (read: humans) are ruled by feeling rather than logic, he serves as a vital counterpart to Spock. He constantly challenges Spock's assumptions in any discussion, and thereby forced the recognition that both sides of a question, the rational *and* the emotional, must be considered in order to understand it fully. He, much like Commander Troi from *The Next Generation,* forces each person to look within themselves and analyze their reactions on both levels, forcing them to become self-aware. It is something that each of us can't afford not to do if we are to function at the best of our abilities.

Kirk, the bold captain, embodies strength and bravery and a strong sense of self. Though often rash and impulsive, he, like Spock, has strong convictions and demonstrates time and again that we must be willing to stand and fight for them, even if the cost is our lives. His most important quality, at least for me, is his ability to see not only both sides of an argument, but to strike a balance between them and act on that decision. It is that ability which allows a person to be able to control their own destiny, to make for themselves the future that they want and not be deterred by others. It is a quality that has enabled me to go after much of what I seek in life.

Data, the android second officer in *The Next Generation,* is unique among both of the crews. Kirk commented to Marlena Moreau in "Mirror, Mirror" that, "You can be anything to want to be if you put your mind to it." It was a theme that was prominent throughout classic *Star Trek* and served to develop many of the characters. We certainly see it in Spock, and in Data.

What Data wants most of all is to be human. Very much aware he will never achieve this, no matter how much he tries, he recognizes there is something to be learned, and gained, in the attempt. It is in his pursuit of the unattainable that he will finally learn what it means to be human. I respect him for his willingness to persist in the face of adversity, and I have come to share his eagerness for the experience of awareness.

The *Enterprise*, in all her manifestations, is perhaps the most important character of all, for she is the expression of our collective dreams. Designed to "seek out new life and new civilizations," she embodies centuries of reaching for the stars, the hope of taking humanity beyond the confines of our planet and out through the universe. Her very presence gives us the means to become more than we are and touches a basic need in all of us. She is, in essence, the embodiment of Mr. Roddenberry's ideal.

I have thought long and hard about this ideal and his assertion that each of us could make a difference in our world and help usher in the future. It was with these ideas in mind that I took my interest in zoology and began to work toward a career in space biology, learning how Earth-based organisms could adapt to the cold, dark, weightless environment of space. It was a small step to take, but one that I know is essential to help this planet's population move out among the stars. Though I subsequently left the field to pursue a career in film production, my motivation and goals have not changed. I realized that no matter what area we choose to work in, each of us has the power to help pioneer the future. It's a heady thought, but one that is true. It's only up to us to make it work.

To that end, I joined and later became executive director of a local space group. Its goals were primarily educational, and we spent much time distributing literature, holding seminars and conferences, and trying to reach the community through television, radio, and interesting events. We were even asked to introduce a Star Trek film festival at a local cable station, and we used the time to talk about and promote colonization of space. It was, unfortunately, always an up-hill battle, due mostly to finances and apathy of the general public toward anything that didn't make immediate, easy money. I kept thinking back to all the battles and victories and hard-won lessons I had shared with *Star Trek,* so I dug in and braved the storm. Though I and the group certainly didn't change the world in any immediate, earth-shattering way, I know that we did reach a number of people with our efforts. It is the knowledge that you have accomplished something positive, and perhaps quite meaningful, that makes it all worthwhile.

The show's message and influence have been particularly important to me during this past years, which have been personally very turbulent. There were many occasions during that time when I thought that I simply couldn't go on anymore, that there was nowhere to turn. Through the desperation, however, Star Trek, in one of its myriad forms, invariably would appear like a beacon and give me the strength to continue. This future it spoke of, one of hope and beauty, was where I belonged, and I knew again that I had to be a part of its creation. Without wanting to sound melodramatic, I think that the show literally saved my life. It is just as Edith Keeler said in "The City On the Edge of Forever": "Someday . . . we'll be able to give each man hope and a common future, and those are the days worth living for."

Many people have been speculating on how Mr. Roddenberry's death will affect the production of the new series, and Star Trek as a whole. Can it go on without its creator and navigator at the helm, and if so, how? Star Trek is an ideal, one that transcends any one specific character or starship or even—dare I say it?—creator. No, it can never be exactly the same, and we certainly should not try to keep it so. As Star Trek demonstrated again and again, attempting to maintain the status quo can only lead to stagnation.

If that is what we wanted, we wouldn't—and *couldn't*—be fans of Star Trek in the first place.

Like any good teacher, Mr. Roddenberry has given us—the viewers, the writers, the producers—a seed, his idea of the way things are and the positive way they should be, in the hope that we would learn and benefit from it. He helped us to plant and nurture that seed for twenty-five years, and now it is up to us to see that it continues to flourish. The future of Star Trek depends on us. What it will or will not become is a direct result of how we choose, as individuals and a collective whole, to deal with this gift we were given. If we choose to write, to discuss, to hold and attend conventions, or simply to continue watching, we help to carry its message onward. Because Star Trek has affected us so positively, we cannot help but take it to new and greater heights. To paraphrase Surak from "The Savage Curtain," in our efforts together we can become greater than merely the sum of our parts.

As long as a single person continues to look out into space and dream, as long as a single person believes that it is possible for us to work together to build a better future, Mr. Roddenberry's legacy will continue. It is up to us. With our help, the Great Bird of the Galaxy will fly again.

For myself, I have lost a great mentor and friend. Though I never spoke personally with Gene Roddenberry, he succeeded in changing my life more than any other individual. He gave me purpose, and hope, and I grieve his loss. I am reminded of Dr. McCoy's statement at the end of *The Wrath of Khan*. Said, of course, about Spock, it applies equally as well to Mr. Roddenberry: "He's not really dead, as long as we remember him." As long as there is Star Trek, we cannot help but remember Gene Roddenberry.

TREK ROUNDTABLE: LETTERS FROM OUR READERS

Terry Jones
Huddersfield, West Yorkshire,
England

I recently discovered your *Best of Trek* books and was fascinated to find an article on the age of the *Enterprise*. Fascinating to me, because two years ago I worked out the age of the vessel myself. The original writer's guide, television series, and the *Federation Reference* series form the basis of my analysis, so read and enjoy.

In 2225, the Starfleet shipbuilding division submitted a design for a heavy cruiser which could be constructed cheaply and whose major components could be reconfigured to produce other starships. With the approval of the Federation Council in 2226, work began on the first of these heavy cruisers, USS *Constitution*, NCC 1700. Three years later, the *Constitution* was commissioned and so pleased the council with test results that work began on thirteen other starships.

Three years later, in 2232, the USS *Enterprise,* NCC 1701 was commissioned under the command of Captain Robert April. Over the next eighteen years (one year shakedown, three five-year missions, with a break of one year between each mission), April and the other starship commanders expanded the sphere of

Federation influence, creating new starbases and making contact with new civilizations. During this period General Orders One to Six were created, and the Federation had the first contact with the Klingons. Robert April's wife, Dr. Sarah April, spent her eighteen years in space working on the subjects of xenobiology, alien psychology, and the treatment of space diseases. All of her work became standard medical texts at the academy.

April returned in 2250, and the *Enterprise* was decommissioned for repairs to the PB 31 warp drive units and the fitting of the Daystrom Duotronic M4 computer and support systems. The vessel was recommissioned in 2252 under the command of Captain Christopher Pike. Under Pike's eighteen-year command (one year of trials and testing of the new Daystrom systems, three five-year missions with a break of one year between each mission), significant advances were made in the field of exploration, the discovery of new materials, and the creation of General Order Seven after the Talos IV incident in 2259. On Pike and his new science officer Spock's findings, and because of the potentially dangerous nature of the telepathic powers possessed by the Talosians, Starfleet Commander Robert Connell recommended that penalty for breaking General Order Seven be death.

The *Enterprise* returned in 2270 and Christopher Pike was promoted to Fleet Captain. The vessel was decommissioned for standard repairs to the onboard systems and warp engines. It was recommissioned in November 2271, under the command of Captain James Tiberius Kirk. Having his command transferred from a Saladin-class destroyer to a Constitution-class cruiser, Kirk used the two-month patrol to acquaint himself with the vessel's operations. In early January 2272, the *Enterprise* returned to Earth, where the vessel was uprated to BonneHomme Richard specifications, and in late February 2272, command was officially handed to Kirk by Fleet Captain Pike.

The *Enterprise* returned in February 2277, whereupon Kirk was promoted to Chief of Starfleet Operations. In late January 2278, the ship entered the San Francisco Orbital Navy Yard for the start of an eighteen-month refit. In the space of one year, between the vessel's return and the start of the refit, all computer system memories were downloaded into the Master Control at Fleet Headquarters and all onboard systems were shut down ready for the refit.

The *Enterprise* was twenty hours away from launch in August 2279, when an intruder into Federation space brought Starfleet to full alert. Admiral Kirk assumed command of the *Enterprise,* replacing Willard Decker as captain. Upon interception, the intruder turned out to be a returning *Voyager* probe launched three centuries earlier. Decker disappeared on this mission, so Kirk was rewarded command. The *Enterprise* was recommissioned in October 2279, and embarked on a second five-year mission. The ship returned in October 2284, when Kirk had the ship placed on training status, with Spock as captain. Pavel Chekov was assigned to the USS *Reliant* as first officer, and the other command officers from the *Enterprise* teachers at the academy.

In January 2287, the *Enterprise* was stolen from the spacedock by Admiral Kirk. Although mission details are still secret, actions by the admiral resulted in the destruction of the *Enterprise,* ending fifty-five years of faithful service from the vessel.

Here is more food for thought about Kirk's pre-*Enterprise* career. The following is based on information from the writer's guide and the episodes "Court Martial," "Where No Man Has Gone Before," "Obsession," and "Dagger of the Mind."

Jim Kirk was born in 2239 (the writer's guide states he was about thirty-four; it wasn't until "The Deadly Years" [2273] that he stated his age as thirty-four). At the age of seventeen, he joined the academy in the three-year command program as a midshipman. He was assigned aboard the USS *Republic* as part of his training and met Ben Finney. In 2259 he graduated and was assigned to the USS *Farragut* under Captain Garrovick. Despite the death of Garrovick and half the crew when the ship was attacked by a cloudlike entity in 2262, Kirk completed his first tour of duty, proving to be a fine young officer, rising quickly in rank. On his return in 2264, he earned the distinction of being the youngest captain in Starfleet. His first command was a Saladin–class destroyer. In 2266, while the vessel was on rotation to the academy as a training ship, Kirk became friends with Gary Mitchell, who was completing his first year in the command program. Mitchell graduated in 2268 and was posted to the USS *Enterprise* as navigator while Kirk carried on his destroyer command. In November 2271, Kirk received his transfer of command order and took the post of captain of the *Enterprise*. His first assignment was a routine, two-month patrol mission. In mid-December 2271, the vessel encountered an energy barrier which damaged the warp engines and caused the deaths of Gary Mitchell (23) and Dr. Elizabeth Dehner (21).

Repairs were done and the *Enterprise* limped home. On the way back, uniform designs were transmitted by subspace radio to reprogram the clothing fabricators. The new communicators, phasers, and tricorders would be issued on the vessel's return to Earth in January 2272. She underwent an uprating: new armaments were installed, the bridge was modified, and the old PB 31 engines were replaced by PB 32 models, increasing maximum sped to warp factor eight.

Thomas Noonan
Manchester, CT

First, let me say how very much I enjoy all of your *Best of Trek* books. I find them informative and entertaining, and a welcome change from the not-too-realistic fiction stories published by your competitors. (By the

way, isn't it time we readers demanded that Pocket
Books give us better stories? Perhaps a wider selection
of authors would help. I know I, and many of my
friends, get tired of seeing many of the same names.)

Sorry, got a little off the track, there. What I really
wanted to discuss was the almost universally adverse
reaction among fans to *Star Trek V: The Final Frontier*. I simply don't understand why this movie, which
contains so much of value and information about all
three of our Star Trek heroes, is so maligned by fans.
Sure, William Shatner's direction wasn't the greatest,
but neither was Leonard Nimoy's the first time out.
Direction and acting are important to a movie, sure,
and I'm not willing to concede the point that either
one was bad in this movie, but what is really important
here is the story. This storyline is one of the best ever
to appear in Star Trek, movies or TV. It is a story
which discussed human relations, the need for us to
forgive ourselves for our errors and to forgive others
for their faults, and our need as living beings for
friends and comrades to share in our triumphs and
failures.

Forget all the stuff about finding God; that was just
trappings, and pretty standard Star Trek trappings, at
that. ("Finding God" was one of Gene Roddenberry's
favorite jumping-off points to tell a story; we really
can't blame Bill Shatner for wanting to follow in the
footsteps of the master, now can we?) What this story
is really about, and what Star Trek is really about
when we get down to it, is relationships. How we deal
with other people. How we deal with the decisions we
make. How we deal with the blows life gives us. How
we survive from day to day, and more, carry on and
eventually succeed.

Sybok, who "released" others from their guilt and
pain, had no one to do the same for him ... except
God. So he sought for years to find a way to reach
the one embodiment of God which legend said could
be found: ShiKar, the center of the galaxy. There,

Sybok felt, he would find a power so great that it could answer all his questions and ease his pain and guilt. His suffering would end with acceptance into the infinite, and he would be one with the universe.

Everything he thought was in error, of course. It was wrong to remove the guilt and pain of others; as Kirk said, it removed a vital part of their essence as living beings, of what they are, and deprived them of what they could become. There are no shortcuts, Kirk was telling Sybok. Only by accepting and overcoming one's own fears and doubts could one truly grow and mature into a superior being. And in the process, help the race mature, as well.

Spock pointed out another error that Sybok made. Sybok, indeed *everyone,* was *already* in harmony with, and one with, the universe. Seeking that which was already within oneself was illogical; using others to do so was immoral.

Many fans have both praised and condemned this film as being overtly Christian in outlook and message. I disagree. The film does reinforce the values held by Christians (as well as by countless other religions, of course), but that's about as far as it goes. Indeed, looking at the message discussed above, the film can be seen as the antithesis of Christianity: It could be construed as saying that the true God is found only within ourselves, not without, and certainly not by following a charismatic leader or organized worship. This is hardly a message designed to warm the hearts of down-home fundamentalists. (Though it would probably delight the logical Spock and the ever-breaking-down-of-restrictive-societies Kirk.)

Those who went into the theaters thinking, "Oh, this is just a little movie with a plot we've seen before, and the only reason they made it is because William Shatner threw a hissy fit and they had to let him direct one," were probably not disappointed. There is much in the movie that is downright silly and pretty illogical. But with repeated viewings, those things can be ignored, and the important message and the excellent acting and production values during the scenes conveying that message can be all the more appreciated.

Everyone, Shatner included—heck, Shatner especially!—does an excellent job during the scenes of confrontation with Sybok. Although Spock and McCoy seem at first to succumb, we know their will and intelligence will help them to overcome Sybok's power. This is especially true when Kirk refuses to allow Sybok to "remove his pain." Kirk's reasons, as we stated above, are completely logical and correct, but we get the feeling that, even if he allowed Sybok to try, the effort would end in failure. Why? Because Kirk is not the kind of man to allow the past to affect his present. And this is the point that many fans miss; they say, this is where Bill Shatner failed, where Shatner made Kirk the superman, the only one who could resist, the hero of the piece—typical Shatner, typical, typical. This time, they are wrong.

You see, William Shatner understands Jim Kirk better than anyone. Much, very much, of Kirk is Shatner. It was Gene Roddenberry and Gene Coon and Bob Justman who created Kirk, but it was William Shatner who made him live. It was Shatner who gave Kirk many of his own qualities, good and bad; he exaggerated some, underplayed others, but with the skill of a fine doctor, he honed and refined them into a lasting, living character. Shatner knows how Kirk will react; he knows what Kirk thinks; he knows Kirk's desires, fears, wants, needs, lusts, ambitions, regrets, angers, and moments of despair. What Shatner knew about Kirk that most of us did not know—and, yes, *we should have known*—is that Kirk does not want anyone to take anything from him. He wants all of his experiences to remain with him, within him. Shatner knew that Kirk was nothing more, and nothing less, than the sum of his past experiences. Kirk doesn't need a god to lift his pain, Shatner was telling us. Kirk needs a god to tell him to keep striving, to never give up, to keep working and struggling and fighting until the last moment, when Kirk would finally find the answers and, time enough at last now, be with God.

William Shatner was smarter than almost all of us Trek fans and—wouldn't you know?—we hate him for it.

Please go back and once again watch *The Final Frontier*. This time, forget the hoopla, forget the occasionally bad line or slightly embarrassing acting, forget to sneer when you see Shatner's name on the credits as "Director." Just sit back and enjoy the film, and see if you can't tap into the message which is so subtly stated throughout.

Don't follow, it tells us. Lead. Love. *Live*.

Shannen Forslund
Minneapolis, MN

I really enjoyed *The Best of Trek #16*. Please allow me a few minutes of your time to comment on several of the articles.

My favorite article was "*Star Trek*'s Third Season: A Worthwhile Mixture of Success and Failure." I, too, have always been one of those people who feel that the third season of *Star Trek* was every bit as well-made and entertaining as the previous two. Just consider the number of episodes most fans consider "excellent" that appeared in the third season: "The Paradise Syndrome," "The Enterprise Incident," "Is There In Truth No Beauty?", "The Empath," "The Tholian Web," "Plato's Stepchildren," "The Lights of Zetar," "Requiem for Methuselah," "The Savage Curtain," and "All Our Yesterdays." A pretty good line-up, wouldn't you say? I'll bet many readers wouldn't recognize this line-up as being comprised of all third season shows; there are many "fan favorites" here. Looking back from a twenty-year perspective, I don't think we can any longer blame Mr. Fred Freiberger for *Star Trek*'s demise. Yes, there were some clinkers produced under his banner, but there were some real stinkers in the first two seasons, too. A more rational explanation of why *Star Trek* never made it to a fourth season is that it was never that popular in the first place and had simply run its course, and the network, NBC, no longer felt it necessary to support the show.

Whew! Seems as if my planned few comments turned into a sermon. I'll try to keep it from happening again, but no promises!

One article I take great exception with is the "Critique of Spock's World." Mr. Lou Mason seems to have something of a grudge against Diane Duane, doesn't he? It seems as if, in his opinion, she can't do anything right, and if she does, then, why, it must be someone else's doing, or something she was forced into doing by the show's history, or some kind of lucky accident. I found Ms. Duane's novel to be exciting and educational; it told me things about Vulcan and Vulcans I had never known and provided an excellent background to all the adventures featuring Spock, Sarek, and other Vulcans. So what if there are a few inconsistencies? The original series was rife with them; so is *The Next Generation*, which seems to contradict itself every couple of weeks, unthinkable in this age of continuity and fan scrutiny, but there it is. I've never been a big fan of nit-picking (sorry, Leslie Thompson, but your mystery-solving sometimes bores me), and I would rather have a good story than a consistent one. *Spock's World*, in my view, meets that simple criteria, and that's good enough for me.

I thoroughly enjoyed Joyce Tullock's "Star Trek and the Miracle Myth." Ms. Tullock's articles are always enjoyable and thought-provoking, and I found this one to be no different. Although I do not always agree with some of her opinions, I find myself marshaling arguments against them even while I'm reading, and to me, that's a sign that I'm both interested and having fun. Thanks again, Joyce, for a half-hour's brain exercise.

I also enjoyed Walter Irwin's review of *The Next Generation* premiere. Although it's been quite a while since I've seen the show (like many other fans, I haven't yet begun repeated viewings of the *Next Gen.* episodes), I seem to recall having reactions very much like those reported by Mr. Irwin. I shouldn't be surprised; after all, his opinions are usually perfectly in synchronization with Star Trek fandom in general. Paramount ought to consider hiring Mr. Irwin as a sort of "story tester"; if he doesn't like it, chances are most Star Trek fans won't, either. One little carp: Mr. Irwin says in his review that he was intentionally giving Deanna Troi "short shrift," as he wanted to wait and see what would become of her character over the course of the series. Now, that's an article I would love to see! Mr. Irwin's views of the fairer sex in Star Trek are always interesting (and generally sympathetic, if occasionally misogynic), and it is apparent that he has a great affection for females and likes seeing them on the show. As Deanna has proven over the past seasons to have an extremely multifaceted character, I'd truly enjoy having Mr. Irwin delve into the psychic depths of our favorite half-Betazoid.

Of all the articles in *BOT #16,* I found myself most enjoying one of the simplest: "Uniforms," by Lieutenant David Crockett. (Is Crockett truly an officer in one of the services, or just using one of those bogus "Starfleet" rankings?) [*Editors' Note: David Crockett is a lieutenant in the United States Army.*] Crockett's skillful description allowed me to enjoy the article without referring to reference books or photographs, and it also made sense within the framework of the series "history." His opinions as to why certain changes were made in the uniforms or why certain elements were present were also logical and consistent. A good, meaty job on what I would have originally dismissed as a minor sidebar to Star Trek lore.

The remaining articles were informative and entertaining, but none of them have aroused enough ire or admiration in me to inspire further comment. Let me just say that they were all up to your usual excellent standards, and that I enjoyed each and every one of them.

In closing, may I make a suggestion for future volumes? Please go back to your previous practice of providing introductions to each of the articles. I enjoyed the glimpses into the lives of the writers, as well as your occasional comments on your relations with them. As an aspiring writer, I am always looking for tips on how to get along with editors. (A good one would probably be to not write letters with negative comments about articles in the publication you wish to write for. Hmmmm.)

Also, could you provide a tag line indicating when the article was originally written? There have been so many *Best of Treks* now, and so much Star Trek over so long a time, that it can occasionally get confusing to the reader. I get a better feeling for the author's meaning and intent if I know when the piece was actually written. For instance, I know that my feelings are different immediately after my first viewing of a Star Trek movie than they are after my third or fourth viewing. Consequently, a review I'd write the day after my first look would be quite different from one I'd write after a later screening. Just a suggestion.

Thanks again and keep up the good work.

Lou Scroggy
Stockton, CA

Just a brief note to tell you how much I enjoyed Volume 14. I especially liked Tom Lalli's article, "The Empath." This is one of my favorite episodes, and Tom did a great job delving into the intricacies and philosophies of it. One thing I think he missed, though, is even though Gem was a representative of her entire race, she was still acting and reacting as an individual. The purpose of the Vians' experiment was not to have her learn self-sacrifice, which would then be passed on to the rest of her species, but to see if one individual could rise above fear and self-preservation and, yes, even prejudice.

We must remember that Kirk and the others, although humanoid and apparently identical to her in appearance, were, to Gem, aliens. Aliens who made strange sounds with their mouths and strange gestures with their hands. She was rightfully frightened and perhaps even repelled by them, and overcoming this fear and offering to help them was equally as important as her later willingness to sacrifice herself. If she were able to do this, as an average representative of her race, no one special or specially prepared, the Vians knew that any one of them would do the same under similar circumstances. It was nothing they had to "learn," nor was it something Gem could pass on to them. The capacity was already within them, as demonstrated by her, needing only the proper circumstances to bring it out.

It is interesting to note that Gene Roddenberry, for all his faith in science and progress, so often depicted advanced alien races as lacking in what we feel are the "finer virtues," such as compassion, self-sacrifice, sharing, and individuality. Perhaps it is not so strange, though, for he constantly warned us of the need to maintain our individuality and sufficiency from science and technology. The message was: "Use the tools you have, but never let them use you." Some of the politicians and military men of today would be wise to heed those words, I think.

I was completely thrilled by Sally Jerome's tale of "Walking the Decks of the Real *Enterprise*." Hurrah for her and her prize; one which we would all dearly love to have. Now that those production sets have been broken down (and perhaps destroyed, if rumor is to be believed), it may well be that such tours are ended forever. Just let me say that although I never had the privilege of walking the decks, I was able to get a good idea of what it must be like thanks to Sally's beautiful article!

Claudia Groiss
Vienna, Austria

Greetings from the other side of the Atlantic Ocean. Excuse me if I won't compliment Messr. Irwin and Love on the *Best of Trek* series—carrying coals to Newcastle by definition represents an action lacking sense. (Briefly: *Best of Trek* is great.)

As you might already have surmised by looking at my address, the articles touching me nearest were those dealing with the mutilation and hence meager reception of Star Trek in the German-speaking countries. I take gross exception to Ms. Davis' comment, "The German voices are relatively well selected" (*Best of Trek #7,* "Star Trek Lives in Germany").

Come on, lady, the synchronization speaker for W. Shatner made Kirk sound like a cheap hooker. Personally I've never been overly fond of Kirk's character, because his smile struck me as syrupy. But in the American original he at least was portrayed as a brilliant commanding officer.

In case you're interested whether the sync studios have acquired enough brains and taste within the last one and a half decades to provide their audience with a translation faithful to the original—well, they haven't. Not even approximately. When I discovered the pilot to *Star Trek: The Next Generation* in my video store, I yelled with delight. When I had finished watching both the American and German version, I boiled with rage over the latter. No omissions, no cuts—but a defective, imprecise, and sometimes simply wrong translation. Some prize examples?

Take the dialogue between Picard and Riker in the lounge. The charm of the scene results from the fact that Picard downplays Riker's performance during re-connection, thus eliciting an ironic remark from the first officer. Not so in the German version:

Picard: Manual reconnection is not easy. That was good work.

Riker: Thank you. I'm glad if you're content, sir.

Picard: I nevertheless have some questions for you.

Riker: Yes, sir. That was clear to me.

The remaining conversation is not contradictory to the original, albeit faulty, until towards its end, when the probably worst offense occurs:

Picard: ... You know, in the eyes of children the captain has the aura of ingenuity [!!!]—and this illusion I want to preserve for them.

Damnit, Picard doesn't want the kids to adore him like a god, but not to scare them! Or take the little scene, again between Picard and Riker, just before Q's celestial appearance:

Picard: Have you signaled the *Hood*, Commander Riker?

Riker (in a level and matter-of-fact tone): Your exact message: Bon voyage, mon ami.

Since I saw the German version first, I had no inkling why Picard was laughing—later I found out that actually Riker was mimicking him.

Or take the moment after the two aliens have floated away, when Picard turns to Q, asking, "Why do you use other life forms for recreation?" Believe it or not, "recreation" was replaced by "rebirth"—and the captain's legitimate question sounded like an excerpt from a piece of the Theatre Asburde.

In the German version, Picard's words "its mate" were entirely ignored, being dubbed by "we'll free it." No horrible distortion, I admit. The nice touch, however, that only the Frenchman perceived the intimate relationship between the creatures was lost.

Needless to stress that Picard's and Riker's rather high-pitched German voices are a handpicked maltreatment to my ears—the captain's mellow inflection in particular is as far from Patrick Stewart's authoritarian tone as one can get.

Now please mix up all mentioned alterations and see whether you can still deduct any sense in the mess. I can't.

The quality of the recent Star Trek novels borders on the deplorable. I'm tired of reading the umpteenth rehash of the story of how some superbly talented female officer aids Kirk and company to save the galaxy. I'm aware of the intriguing opportunity this sort of plot offers, which is to study the regular cast of the *Enterprise* from a number of different angles, and it worked quite well when employed once or twice. Unfortunately, from #25 or so on, it had become redundant. The introduction of fresh thoughts won't hurt the series. (My biggest personal problem: I've got ideas for ten novels and vocabulary for a bare tenth!) Still, I'll continue to buy the novels—each one sports at least some minor scenes making their acquisition worthwhile.

The best of them? *The Final Reflection,* because it deepens our understanding of Klingon culture. The worst? *The Vulcan Academy Murders* and *The IDIC Epidemic.* Jean Lorrah's Vulcans invariable behave like good American middle-class families. Sorry, that's not my idea of an alien society. But you who liked them, be glad. Tastes, despite all religious and ideological efforts to the contrary, still differ.

Melissa Steidman
Brantford, ONT, Canada

With regard to Hazel Ann Williams' commentary on *The Voyage Home* in *Best of Trek #13,* and Les Leist's commentary on it, I must say that one thing about both reviews considerably irked me—no, irritated me—to no end.

And that is that both reviewers were dismayed at the absence of rookie actress Robin Curtis, and by extension her character, Saavik. Mr. Leist says that we can accept Saavik's absence in the fourth Star Trek opus by virtue of the fact that she had such impressive moments to shine in both *The Wrath of Khan* and *The Search for Spock*.

And Miss Williams says that one particular scene in *The Voyage Home* should have been cut out in favor of an explanation why Saavik was left on Vulcan.

Well, I for one, am glad—glad as hell—that Miss Curtis was left behind on Vulcan. As for Leist's comments, the only similarity (in my opinion) between the Saavik of *Wrath of Khan* and the one in *The Search for Spock* is her name.

Everything about Robin Curtis was wrong. Her rank insignia (she wears a junior lieutenant's rank during *The Search for Spock* and wears a full-fledged officer's white collar) to her hairstyle. (Vulcans wearing California afros? Come on. That's like saying T'Pau wears cornrows.)

In addition, Curtis is so bland, waspish, and suburban-looking that she can't possibly play a Vulcan successfully. Leist mentions that Saavik has her moments to shine in *The Search for Spock*.

Get real! Like where? All she does is walk through the movie like a zombie, with her thick yellowish application of facial tone and corpselike mannerisms. Considering she is supposed to be a science officer, she asks David everything ("How could they have evolved so quickly?" with regard to the microbes on the tube's surface), and so on.

And will someone please tell me how her eyes changed from jade green to dark brown? That's another thing that bothers me about Curtis—the fact that she has brown eyes precludes any possibility of Romulans and human blood. Romulans—and only Romulans—would have green eyes. That's how you could certainly tell in *The Wrath of Khan* that Saavik was a Vulcan/Romulan hybrid (in addition to her arched eyebrows).

As Walter Irwin and G. B. Love pointed out in *The Best of Trek #8,* all the Romulan influence is gone—the flash, the fire behind the cool exterior, her temper, and difficult (almost impossible) control of her emotions. In short, how does she go from running the gamut of emotions to not showing any emotion?

I feel that Curtis was too easily excused (and has gotten away to some extent) for the fact that she didn't show any emotion. More than that, almost every second person seems to find a new reason—or excuse—to justify an emotionless and wretched performance. Why don't we all put our hair down for once and admit that she is an ugly and talentless actress that was deliberately hired by Bennett and Nimoy to destroy a consummate and interesting character?

Walter Irwin and G. B. Love called her "a fine actress" (despite their criticism of her) and on this count, I don't feel people have been hard enough. She is not a fine actress—every possible thing was wrong with her. As for the moments in which she shines, consider this: "Sir, David is dead."

Real emotion! Somebody is killed in front of her and she reacts like she just saw someone finish a meal—completely no reaction! A trivial reaction to a highly emotional and dangerous situation!

What about the fact that the Klingon could have easily opted for killing Spock rather than David or herself? She would have done nothing—matter of fact, the Klingon was going to kill her and she just stood there!

It is a shame that the Saavik character in *The Wrath of Khan* is so interesting that she overshadowed Spock, whereas the Saavik character in *The Search for Spock* was so boring we were clamoring for the return of Spock (which was Leonard Nimoy's intention).

On this count, I believe that Bennett and Nimoy have gotten away with too much—mucking up an interesting character and making her into a bore, while making a sequel (to an excellent and entertaining movie, *The Wrath of Khan*) into the worst movie ever made—*The Search for Spock* (right up there with *Return of the Jedi*).

In closing, I hope never to see that ugly, talentless rookie again, and I hope you never publish any more articles by "Robin Curtis lovers."

Hannah Thomaston
Paterson, NJ

This is the first fan letter I have ever written to anything that is Star Trek or just science fiction/fantasy. I am a fourteen-year-old girl. I go to a private, Christian school. I am a quite normal teenager, except for one thing: my private obsession, Star Trek.

My obsession began quite unexpectedly. One day I was at the library looking through the young adult section. I was very frustrated because I had read almost everything there. The science fiction books just happened to be next to the young adult section, and in desperation for something I had not read before, I started to glance through them. One book caught my eye: *Star Trek IV: The Voyage Home.* I remembered seeing previews of the movie and wanting to see it, so I grabbed the book and checked it out.

I began reading it that night. Some of it was a bit boring to me, but you have to remember this was the first time I had ever really had anything to do with Star Trek. Strangely enough, when I was much, much younger it make me have bad dreams, even the animated episodes. I remember only one episode from my young childhood: "For the World is Hollow and I Have Touched the Sky." (Gosh! You never realize how long that title is until you write it out.) I remember that episode probably because it never gave me bad dreams. (I can't imagine why the others did; they most definitely don't now.)

Anyway, the one character I absolutely loved was unfortunately left on Vulcan. That little bit of disappointment scarred my enjoyment for the rest of the book. (I'm sorry to all the Star Trek fans since the series began, and also to all Saavik haters, but there is a younger generation out here.)

I didn't immediately fall in love with Star Trek, and I didn't rush out and rent the movie, but I did want to find more about Saavik, so the next time I went to the library I got *Star Trek II: The Wrath of Khan.* When I finished reading it, all I wanted to do was rush to the bookstore and buy everything I could find that was Star Trek. I rented all four movies within a month and combed the bookstores and libraries from top to bottom.

I don't know how I survived all these years not watching and reading and just experiencing the wonderful joy Star Trek has brought me. I promise that my future children will experience it from the time they are old enough to understand it, and I sincerely hope they will love and enjoy it as much as I have and always will.

Daniel Bahuaud and Henri Pintkowsky
Winnipeg, Manitoba, Canada

We have been avid Star Trek fans for a good decade now, and it must be said that we've been content with the way "the human adventure" has continued over the years. Star Trek, with its humor, intelligence, and insight, remains the yardstick by which the quality of televised and cinematic science fiction is measured.

With all that Star Trek could be, it is disheartening to see *Star Trek: The Next Generation* go the route of playing it safe. The complacency marking the latest season does little to advance the Star Trek saga to new heights. Where is the drama, the excitement and the variety that has make Star Trek successful in the past? It is sadly lacking, and what we've been given, with a few notable exceptions, seems dull by comparison. We realized that such general, sweeping statements are useless without specifics. As to that, we'd probably be killed by a mob of angry "Treksperts" if we didn't elaborate. Bear with us, then, as we embark on a tour of our *Next Generation* pet peeves. . . .

1. *Trivia.* Trivia is nice. Trivia is fun. One can talk Star Trek until the wee hours of the morning (trust us). However, trivia does not a good Star Trek experience make. In the past, we've enjoyed learning about Vulcan history and mores, about Kirk and his family ties, and a plethora of other interesting facets of the Star Trek universe. Somehow, most of this trivia was presented in a way that *served* the dramatics of the story. It wasn't trivia for its own sake. For instance, in "Amok Time," we weren't simply told about the nature of Vulcan marriages, it was dramatically demonstrated. Last season, we learned about the Klingon death ritual and it was used in "Heart of Glory" 's most poignant scene. This year, we've been given all sorts of Klingon trivia that had no bearing on the stories. Frankly, we don't care about tea ceremonies unless someone's life depends on them.

2. *The "Love Boat" Syndrome.* Let's get away from beaming guest stars aboard the ship every week. There's no variety in that. We realize that planets are hard to come by. Still, we'd rather see a studio set, whose horizon seems to extend for a few meters, than stay aboard the *Enterprise*. Besides, did a cheap set distract us from enjoying "Amok Time"? It's high time some writer got back to meeting Star Trek's basic mandate: to boldly go where no one has gone before. Sorry, *Next Generation* corridors don't quite cut it. Nor does the holodeck, for that matter.

3. *Character conflict.* Yes, a family feeling is a necessary ingredient. But does the crew *have* to get along so well? In the show's format, Gene Roddenberry has purposefully set up potential conflict between Riker and Picard, Picard and the chief surgeon, and even between our "stodgy captain" and Wesley. So far, conflict has only been hinted at. What's wrong with

Riker objecting *strongly* to an Away Team decision? Why can't he put his foot down for once? Why doesn't Picard completely lose patience with Wes? And why doesn't the doctor stop threatening Picard with her authority and simply act? It is our humble opinion that the family feeling can survive such incidents. Realistically speaking, they're bound to occur once in a while. Perhaps then the show could come across as more believable. After all, this is not *The Cosby Show*.

4. *Jeopardy.* Conflict must also exist between the *Next Generation* and whatever is "out there." It is the basis of any drama. So how about more straightforward drama? (Notable exception: "Q Who?") By the way, we're not talking about the kind of story that takes fifty minutes to get to what little excitement there is left. "Risk is our business," Kirk once said. Obviously, it's just not the case in the twenty-fourth century.

5. *Issues.* Last season, Roddenberry promised us a look at current affairs. They delivered. Not only was drug addiction ("Symbiosis"), the environment ("When the Bough Breaks"), and the arms race ("The Arsenal of Freedom") touched upon, we were also treated with insight on the Iran/Contra affair ("Too Short a Season") and the philosophical problem of evil ("Skin of Evil"). Star Trek should challenge the status quo, not simply maintain it. So why not challenge us with these biggies? Freedom of expression. Religious fundamentalism, pros and cons. Détente. Apartheid. Political repression. And, hey! How about some political dissent in the Federation; what, up to now, has always been portrayed as a utopia? Judging from Dr. Crusher's reaction in "Symbiosis," it's clear that not everyone jumps for joy at the words "Prime Directive." Perhaps we are expecting too much. It is sadly obvious that the powers that be have sacrificed the issues. In their pursuit for the Almighty Dollar, they have given us safe stories that won't keep us up

at night. Forget "A Private Little War," just give 'em a *Family Ties*-style flashback episode.

6. *The Bizarre.* Let's see more far out and bizarre ideas (i.e., "Where No One Has Gone Before" and "Encounter at Farpoint"). True, a one-hour episode pales in comparison to the cerebral quirks of a Frank Herbert or a Robert Heinlein, but one *can* try. Speaking of "Where No One . . .", how about the return of Diane Duane? Now there's someone who uses trivia correctly (Picard's mother, Tasha's planet, etc.). She can write, too, which is more than can be said of others who attempt Star Trek novels.

7. *Fans.* This theory might not sit well with some. One of the reasons that this season has been so complacent and self-satisfied is that the production staff seems to be catering too much to the fans. Dedicated fans are one thing. They are intelligent and passionate. But the fans we have had contact with can scarcely be placed in such a category. These people are highly conservative, wishing to preserve their precious Star Trek "universe" as it is, and damned be the person to suggest otherwise. They read their comic books and brag about their uniforms while discussing the possibility of Lieutenant Saavik bearing Spock's child and other mental pabulum. Such blatant and constant disregard for drama, which is what makes Star Trek tick, reduces all the wonderful content of the show to one vast adolescent role-playing game. We are aware that Star Trek isn't a paragon of science fiction. We know that pulpy elements mingle with its headier aspects. But we would rather have *The Next Generation* be accused of portentousness than silliness.

In conclusion, let it be said that we care about *The Next Generation,* which is, in spite of our criticism, a highly enjoyable experience. Let's face it; Star Trek is still one of the best shows in the "vast wasteland" of television. The exceptional language level of the program alone can attest to this fact. It is, however, a show with untapped potential, content for the moment to rest on its laurels. Good drama and controversy must not be ignored. Gene Roddenberry's long-awaited opportunity for "doing it right" should set the standard and not merely follow it.

Rita Bemish
Pelham, NH

I love your *Best of Trek* books. I have all of them and am looking forward to the next one. I have just finished reading your article "Wrathfully Searching for Home: The Star Trek Trilogy" in #14. I've had many feelings and thoughts on many previous articles in the *Best of Trek* series, but this one prompted me to actually sit down and write to you.

I do not agree with your opinion that each of the two sequels in the trilogy trivialized the events of the one preceding it. People learn from their mistakes and people make sacrifices every day of their lives. Also, what happens today will inevitable affect what will happen tomorrow. Such is the theory of cause and effect. To me, making the ongoing storyline consistent throughout the three movies added to the realism of Star Trek. We saw the growth of the characters through the trilogy, but then Kirk again becomes the obsessive person he was before the end of *Wrath of Khan*—this is also growth. This is not a case of "backsliding" from his positive acceptance and peace. As you say later in the article, Jim Kirk has merely realized that "obsessive behavior" is what has made him an excellent starship captain, and a legend.

As to the fact that David admitted he used proto-matter in the Genesis matrix, this does not mean that Genesis can now only be used as a weapon. We are not given a lot of technical background on Genesis, but the results of the first detonation on a planetwide scale might not be the results they would've been had the test been done on the proper planet in the proper environment, and under the proper conditions by the proper people. In other words, protomatter in the matrix may not be the only reason Genesis' first use was a failure.

Also, we are never told that only David knew of the use of this unstable substance. When we learn of it, the only other person who could substantiate or denounce the fact is David's mother. All of the other scientists involved in the Genesis project have been killed. David might not have been the one who came up with the idea in the first place and may just have been trying to keep the names of the other scientists, including his mother, clean.

Science fiction is just that: fiction. We cannot possibly expect everything to have a scientific explanation. However, when things do happen that do not seem feasible, we must remember that we are talking about 300 years from now. If you told someone only a hundred years ago that by the 1970s a man would walk on the moon, or that there would be machines you could type on and rearrange words without paper, the response would be the same as the one some of us are giving when we see Spock's body regenerated from infancy to adulthood: "Poppycock!"

I remember when my boyfriend and I went to see *The Voyage Home* for the first time. We arrive at the theater a half hour early and were told that the first show was sold out. We then bought tickets for the next show and waited. The next show was sold out an hour before it started, because, like us, people who had gone to see the first show had already bought tickets and there weren't many left. We finally got into the theater after what seemed like a lifetime and found a seat. The people behind us were dressed in tuxedos, and after listening to their conversation, we found that it was a groom and his wedding party. They had left the reception, and his new wife, to come see *The Voyage Home*. I couldn't believe it. Everyone could be heard discussing what they thought was going to happen, but when the movie started, there was dead silence.

The most memorable part of that experience was when we got the first glimpse of the new *Enterprise,* the entire audience, unashamedly, clapped and cheered, laughed and cried. It really was an experience I won't forget.

The fourth movie brought in more money than the previous three. If that is any indication of how much the fans were disappointed by the trilogy, I wish I could disappoint people as much.

Star Trek has played an important role in my life. Not only does it give me something to collect and be involved with, it gives me a sense of pride and hope that the world will eventually return to the morals and beliefs that people should be living by now. Many people do not see these messages in Star Trek. All they see is that the ships aren't as neat looking as the ones in *Star Wars,* or that the sets look phony. Try to explain things to these people and all you get are rolling eyes and comments about being "weird."

I actually put Star Trek as my hobby on my resume, and it was the only thing that prompted a comment from everyone I handed that resume to. My now current boss said during my interview that he knew people who would leave a golf or a gin game early to go see a rerun of *Star Trek.* He asked if I knew people like that, but I didn't say anything. I knew I would be one of those people if I played golf or gin.

The *Best of Trek* books have let me see that there are millions of other fans out there feeling the way I do, and I thank you for that. Even sitting down and watching the show with my boyfriend, who isn't a Trekkie, gets me strange looks. While I'm cracking up at McCoy's comment about not knowing if the aging is caused by a virus, bacteria, or evil spirits, my boyfriend is looking in *TV Guide* to see what is on when this is over.

Being a Star Trek fan in a small town can be lonely,

but just knowing there are plenty of others somewhere is comforting enough so that I do not admit myself into the nearest mental home. Being the only real Trekkie in my high school was an experience, and because of Star Trek, I have had the opportunity to experience more things I would not have experienced without it.

I am referring to the two most exciting things that have happened so far in my life (besides meeting my boyfriend). The first is my attendance at my first Star Trek convention in the summer of 1987. Taking place right after the release of *The Voyage Home*, the convention had many people there selling posters and whatnot from that movie. The real reason for our attendance was the fact that Leonard Nimoy was one of the guests. My boyfriend's father agreed to drive us down to Boston. We spent the day looking around the hall and then eagerly awaited Mr. Nimoy's apppearance.

Of course, me and my camera edged our way up to the very front of the stage, ready to start snapping shots as soon as he walked out. My boyfriend saved us some seats as close as he could.

Then it happened. They introduced him and out he came onto the stage. Everyone was clapping and cheering, but I just kept that camera working. It was the most exciting feeling to actually see Leonard Nimoy six feet in front of me. I finally tore myself away from the stage about fifteen minutes into his talk and went and sat with my boyfriend. His father was supposed to pick us up at 3:00, but since Nimoy was still talking, I made him stay. At 4:00 my boyfriend literally pulled me out of the room so we could go meet his father. Needless to say he wasn't happy, but it was worth it. I had seen Leonard Nimoy in person! Life couldn't get any better!

Then I heard on the radio that William Shatner was going to be in Boston at the World of Wheels. Could it be true? Seeing my most favorite actors within months of each other? My boyfriend's father refused to take us down this time, so I had to find a ride. The day came and I was heartbroken because neither one of us wanted to drive into Boston. Then a miracle happened. My brother's friend called looking for him. I asked why, and he said he was inviting him to go to the World of Wheels in Boston. I persuaded him to take my boyfriend and me instead. After getting lost three times on the way there, we finally arrived.

The lines to meet William Shatner were almost completely around the building! Since the rest of my crew refused to wait in that line, I stood there by myself for over an hour. Just listening to people talk and ask each other trivia questions was fun. Then it was my turn. With my camera ready, I walked up the stairs, snapped a picture, and shook hands with William Shatner. He said, "Hi," then turned around, still holding my hand. He was talking with the men behind him for almost a minute. I thought I'd died and went to heaven. They were asking him if he wanted to take a break, but he said no. When he turned around and smiled, I knew I had died. It was the most exciting experience in my life.

Jason Barney
Swanton, VT

A couple of years ago I stumbled onto the fifteenth *Best of Trek* that you had put out. I had read most of it inside of a week and I must say that I was pleasantly surprised. The viewpoints that some of your writers have are interesting and most of them are informed about the series.

About twenty minutes before I was to see *Star Trek: Generations* I bought your newest volume and I enjoyed it quite a bit, as well. Here are some general points I'd like to make about some of the things that appeared in these two books.

About the time that I picked up *BOT #15*, I was

debating if I should read all the Star Trek novels. When I read Kari Skouson's review of all the earlier novels, I decided to go ahead and read them all. I agree with most of what she says, except I think that she could have gone into a little more depth in regard to some of the really early novels.

Tom Lalli's article about sexism, on the other hand, was the down point of your combined works. I respect Mr. Lalli's views, but he should remember that the main characters in the Start Trek universe (especially in the original series and *The Next Generation*) were mostly men. Whenever I watched anything from either of those great shows, I would say that I watched it for the quality of writing and the story. I really don't pick things apart in the Star Trek universe to see how sexist they are. I would, however, like to see Mr. Lalli's views on the Kira and Dax characters from *Deep Space Nine* and any of the female characters from *Voyager*.

I would say the articles I enjoyed the most were the two by Kenneth Reeler. In #15, Mr. Reeler did a very detailed overview of when the Star Trek universe does or doesn't take place. By now, Mr. Reeler has probably seen *The Star Trek Encyclopedia* and the *Star Trek Chronology,* and in a future volume, I'd like to see what his views are on these books.

In your latest edition of *Best of Trek,* Mr. Reeler wrote a very specific identification of where Vulcan should be located in the stars, and put forth some interesting ideas about some of the specifics that a planet such as Vulcan would have. I would like to add one thing to his research, something that he has probably thought about as well. If Vulcan truly were within forty light years of Earth, then the Romulan Empire (the Vulcans' distant cousins) would have been really close to Earth. Probably too close for the establishment of any realistic space exploration by man.

And finally, I'd like to comment on Michelle Kusik's article on the fate of the female Romulan commander throughout the novels. Continuity is something that I look for in all the novels, so I must say that I enjoyed her article. There are going to be mistakes in the Star Trek universe; our imaginations are what can make those mistakes tolerable. I must point out that the two Bantam novels need not be put into any part of the time line. The Pocket Books novels are the ones that the Star Trek universe is currently being explored in, and most of the Bantam novels, if put into any form of time line, would most likely screw up continuity one way or another. Dan Day's article following the one I just mentioned also offered an interesting viewpoint.

Thanks for putting together these neat little collections of Star Trek information, and until the next volume appears, live long and prosper.

Pauline J. Alama
Rochester, NY

I read with interest Ruth Barker's article "Spock and Uhura" in *Best of Trek #17*. It seems you've had some debate on the question of the ideal lover for Spock; while I'm hampered by having missed the article on Chapel to which Ms. Barker responds, I'd like to take the question in a new direction.

Barker makes a pretty good case for Uhura as a compatible mate for Spock. But what intrigues me the most about both sides of the argument—Barker's article on Uhura, and what she reports on Chapel—is how they need to make so much of so little. A glance, a silent gesture, an idle joke—when it comes to the women of classic *Star Trek*, there's not much to work with. I'm a devout fan of the original *Star Trek,* but not uncritical. I love its sixties optimism, but not its sixties sexism. While I'd like to have seen a romance between Uhura and Spock developed in the show or movies—if only because it would have given more screen time to Uhura—I just don't see it. Her teasing Spock can be seen as a sign of affection, as playful flirting with a "safe" man, or simply as a ploy of the writers to throw Spock's alien, unemotional demeanor into sharp relief by contrast with Uhura's "feminine" emotionalism. The character of Uhura is unfortunately never developed enough in the show for us to know what she really feels.

But with all respect to Uhura and Chapel (and to the wish that they'd gotten bigger, juicier parts), I think that both articles ignored the obvious candidate for the position of "love of Spock's life." I refer, of course, to James T. Kirk.

Now, don't get me wrong: I'm not a writer of K/S erotica. I don't necessarily mean that Spock and Kirk were physically intimate, though I don't rule out the possibility. (Spock and McCoy were *spiritually* intimate in *The Search for Spock,* and so McCoy would be my second choice for "love of Spock's life" ... but I digress.) Let's take into account all that "love" means—which is a lot more than what happens under soft lights with violins playing and a suggestive fade-out.

Kirk, Spock, and McCoy have repeatedly shown their willingness to die for each other. (In "The Empath," for example, they all fight over who gets to die for the others.) If that's not love ... then how about companionship? On that score, again, Kirk wins. How about the sheer inability to leave someone alone, because you love them too much to let them out of your life, even for a greater good, or for your own good? When Spock tries to abandon all emotion through *Kolinahr,* it's Kirk whom he must say good-bye to. And it's Kirk whom he *can't* say good-bye to. Spock dies for Kirk and McCoy, and they can't let him stay dead. *That's love.* That's love the way we'd all like it to be: stronger than death. Whatever may be implied by Chapel's brooding or Uhura's teasing, it can't compare to the intense relationships we've seen between the male heroes. The one Spock loves best is Kirk—and if not Kirk, then McCoy.

That doesn't mean they're hot under the covers, pals. The love of comrades-at-arms is a traditional theme of heroic literature (and Star Trek, especially classic *Star Trek,* is heroic literature). For example, the heroes of *The Song of Roland* are famed for their mutual love, though unlike the comrades/lovers in the *Iliad,* Roland and his comrade Oliver are explicitly heterosexual. The *Morte D'Arthur* speaks of "love" between the flagrantly heterosexual knights Lancelot and Gawain. It's only the twentieth century that has a hard time using the word "love" for friends.

But what if Kirk and Spock *are* more than friends? It's not unlikely. In "Amok Time," Spock seems to lose his entire mating drive once he has fought Kirk, as though his sexual impulses have been transferred from his bride to his friend. Thinking Kirk dead, he says he will neither live long nor prosper; he seems to be contemplating suicide. What if Spock's feelings for Kirk *are* sexual? What would that mean for the Vulcan?

I don't know if Star Trek novelists or fan writers have developed a tradition on Vulcan attitudes toward homosexuality, but I'd imagine the picture would be pretty bleak. Their philosophy devalues and denies emotion. I'd imagine that sex outside the seven-year cycle of *pon farr* would be seen as a deplorable surrender to passion (and you thought the Rhythm Method was tough!). Sex in *pon farr* presumably serves two purposes: reproduction, and cementing alliances between families through arranged marriage. But even within the sanctioned union, Spock seemed pretty ashamed to admit he even *had* sexual feelings: Vulcan sexual taboos must be intense. Sex outside *pon farr,* having no purpose but emotional fulfillment, would be "illogical." Homosexuality? Probably damn near unthinkable for a Vulcan. No reason for it, unless you consider passion a reason, which would be terribly "human"! Please note that these are not *my* views on homosexuality; I'm not Vulcan and emotional reasons are good enough for me. But if Spock has erotic feelings for Kirk, then, well, poor Spock! Could he admit his feelings, even to himself? It almost seems to be a love that could *only* express itself in sacrifice.

Kirk and Spock's intense, die-for-each-other love is the kind you don't see much in *The Next Generation*. That's why I like classic *Star Trek* better. I guess I just can't resist a good love story.

Tim Wilson
Milan, IL

A thousand thank you's! *Trek* has quenched the thirst of three years! Three years of no *Best of Trek* collections, three years of wondering, "What would Walter and G. B. think of this movie or episode?" I was in the wasteland of Star Trek fandom, but your *Best of Trek #17* (December 1994) has led me back to paradise!

On December 1, 1994, I was perusing the stock of a local secondhand bookstore. They had the usual castoffs, seconds, rejects, and whatnots. Then, under a stack of Star Trek novels, I saw a *Best of Trek* collection. I figured it might have been a reprint of one of the other seventeen *Best of Trek* volumes (not counting, of course, the two *Best of the Best of Trek* collections). I am proud to say I have all seventeen volumes printed since 1976. This particular book shocked me, though, because it was in mint condition, and the copyright was current. So new was the volume that the very day matched the December copyright date! I snapped the book up immediately and read it in a day and a half.

The only thing which surprised me was that this *Best of Trek* collection, the first in three years, had no overview of the Star Trek phenomenon to date. I felt that it should have been proper for an essay from Mr.

Irwin, Mr. Love, Leslie Thompson, anybody willing to tackle the tidal wave of information on Star Trek. The articles in this collection were first-rate, but after eighteen volumes, they were still original-series heavy, with any *Next Generation* articles dealing only with its first two seasons. It made me wonder, "What would Walter and G. B. think about *Deep Space Nine* and *Voyager?*"

Here is my answer to that question:

Star Trek, the original series, spanned three seasons of seventy-nine episodes in the late 1960s. *Star Trek,* the animated series, lasted two seasons of twenty-two episodes during the mid-1970s. *Star Trek II,* the proposed second television series, was canceled three months before its scheduled debut in the fall of 1977. *Star Trek: The Motion Picture* was a hit in 1979, giving us the movie series: *Star Trek II: The Wrath of Khan* (1982); *Star Trek III: The Search for Spock* (1984); *Star Trek IV: The Voyage Home* (1986); *Star Trek V: The Final Frontier* (1989); and *Star Trek VI: The Undiscovered Country* (1991). In 1987, the phenomenon returned to television with *Star Trek: The Next Generation,* launching an unprecedented seven seasons and one hundred and seventy-eight episodes. Then *Star Trek: Generations* marked *Next Generation*'s move to the cinema in 1994. The sequel series *Star Trek: Deep Space Nine* succeeded *Next Generation*'s spot as number one in syndicated television. It is in its third season, with more than seventy episodes aired so far. And this past January, *Star Trek: Voyager* made its long-heralded debut, winning its Monday, January 16 time slot against all four competing major networks (including a two-hour episode of *Melrose Place*). Not bad for the Continuing Human Adventure!

But classic *Star Trek* started it all. It gave us the frame of reference: everything started here. It endures because Star Trek was, and is still, about people. The original series is the first "Human Adventure." We love the *Enterprise* because our friends were there on her; she lived because they lived. The newest generation of fans complain about "cheesy special effects, heavy-handed morality plays, poor acting," and more. These fans do not grasp the scope of original *Star Trek*. It cannot be dated, because almost all of these adventures take place *in the future.* The so-called cheesy special effects were state-of-the-art for their time. Scripts portraying "heavy-handed morals" of the 1960s are no worse than the "politically correct" tripe hitting the airwaves today. The acting, like in any TV show, was both good and bad. A little perspective goes a long way: if classic *Star Trek* was *so* bad, *nothing* would have followed it. Star Trek is because *Star Trek was.* Thanks to the original series, we fans have the rich smorgasbord of today.

The animated series is very important to me. Although Paramount Pictures and Star Trek's current producers do not consider the animated *Star Trek* as "official" or "true Star Trek," consider: Gene Roddenberry created the animated version and produced it. All of the original cast took part in the show. The program was nominated for Hugo and Nebula awards, and won a Peabody and an Emmy for Best Children's Series in 1974. All things considered, I think it is "official" enough for me.

In fact, it was an episode of animated *Star Trek* that hooked me as a fan in 1973. I was eight years old and was watching "Beyond the Farthest Star," about an energy creature that tried to destroy Captain Kirk and the *Enterprise.* It was creepy and full of drama, and scared the bejeezus out of that eight-year-old. It was within a year that I began watching reruns of the original series. I have loved both versions ever since.

The film series came about as an extension of this love, shared by millions of other fans like me. We hit the theaters in 1979 to see *ST:TMP.* Though critics (and some fans) derided the film as "Boring ... A three-day sightseeing tour ... Visually pretty, but familiar ... Should be called the 'Motion Sickness' ..."

the movie did what no single adventure of Star Trek has: change the status quo. It moved the entire Star Trek universe forward, moving the Human Adventure along.

For me, the next three movies were a single story, combined to tell one good tale of how to have it, lose it, get it back, and enjoy it afterward. *The Final Frontier* served as a flawed affirmation of the Big Three's friendship, and *The Undiscovered Country* was a fitting end to the best crew in Starfleet.

The Next Generation showed us that different is good, and in some ways better. *Generations* was a bridge, a well-made connection between old and new. The great debate, "Who's the better captain, Kirk or Picard?" was answered: they *both* are. It did what the first movie did—it moved the entire Star Trek universe forward.

Deep Space Nine has disappointed some, thrilled others, and has bothered just about everyone. The three seasons broadcast so far have contained three kinds of episodes: good action adventure, good SF soap opera, and a few real duds. The remedy of the new starship USS *Defiant* will cure the ills of the stuck-at-home crew of DS9.

I had a long and difficult wait to watch the premiere of *Star Trek: Voyager* because I do not have a local television station which broadcasts the program. Though I am trying to talk my Fox affiliate into picking up *Voyager* (they have *Next Generation* and *Deep Space Nine*), friends and family are sending me and my local fan club, Starfleet Sectors, copies of the show on tape. This has proved fortunate, because *Star Trek: Voyager* is good, *darn good* Star Trek.

Of the five pilot episodes of the *Star Trek* series, "The Caretaker" is the best at defining and launching a new part of Star Trek. The plotline is simple, straightforward, lean, dramatic, and well-acted.

In the last three decades, there have been hundreds of hours filmed and broadcast by the producers of Star

Trek. Through all these episodes there has been an overriding sense of hope, of humanity being able to measure up and overcome against diversity. Whether it is Captain Christopher Pike rebelling against a paradise like prison on Talos IV, or Captain Kathryn Janeway destroying her only means to get home in order to save a civilization, each story affirms the best in our natures. We fans of Star Trek are there because we enjoy a good story. It is said that the best literature and the best entertainment is a simple story well told. Thanks to Gene Roddenberry and others who really care about Star Trek, we will be enjoying the best in entertainment for decades to come.

TECHS, SPECS, AND *PON FARR*

By Bill Wirth

I must say that *The Best of Trek #13* was very interesting. It reminded me of soap opera: everyone was mad at someone because no one understood anyone!

People were bent out of shape because the Klingons all looked different, or they didn't think such-'n-such was possible, and so on. This is highly annoying to anyone who owns the *Starfleet Technical Manual* and/or *Mr. Scott's Guide to the* Enterprise. Why? Simple. The answers to many of those technical questions can be found in those two books.

Seeing as how some of you obviously don't have either of these two books, or an understanding of some sciences, I'll tell you the truth. (At least the truth as I see it.)

The first question I came across was, "How does a photon torpedo, after being fired, hit a target in warp space?" Now anyone who has taken physical science knows this. If you are on a train traveling 200 mph, then you also are going 200 mph. If you run to the front of the train, then you are going your running speed plus the train's 200 mph. So if the *Enterprise* is traveling at warp six, then the torpedo, which is on board the ship, is also going warp six. Now if the torpedo is fired at 50 mph, then it would not be going warp six plus 50 mph. If it is going warp speed, then it is in warp space and can thus "contact" another object, or target, in warp space, right? Right.

The problem is not "How do you hit a target in warp space?", but "How do you (going warp six) hit a target going away from you, at, say, warp six point one?" You can't; you must be going the same speed as the other craft and you must be in the same warp field. But some of you say that each craft has its own warp field generated by the warp nacelles. This must be incorrect and probably is.

When going warp speed, you enter a new "dimension" which we call warp space. Warp space is a duplicate of normal space, except you can travel faster than light. (Because it is a duplicate, there are objects to plot courses around.) Because we do not belong in warp space, we create stress barriers, or fields, which have different stress parameters depending on speed. To physically "contact" another ship, you must have identical stress barriers. If the stress items inside the barriers contact each other and are not identical, then the items inside the barriers will, probably, deflect each other (like the same poles of a magnet). Sometimes objects may get trapped in the barrier's parameters and create the wormhole effect seen in *Star Trek: The Motion Picture*.

The navigation and weapons officers work together to figure out how fast the ship must be going so that the photon torpedo, when fired, will penetrate the "target's" barrier and "destroy" it.

"How come the *Enterprise* destroyed the asteroid but just damaged *Reliant*?" Okay. The photon torpedoes easily defeated the "fragile" asteroid, but it didn't destroy it. Think about it: the asteroid was not blasted to space dust. The photon torpedo blew the asteroid into smaller sections that were diverted out of the barrier, off course, and their speed changed; thus the *Enterprise* passed by without harm.

The *Reliant*, however, is basically hollow and built to take a pounding. This prevented her from being blasted to space dust. Her hull structure carries objects that help hold her hull together, such as atmosphere and framework, respectively. Remember, space is a vacuum; thus, the entire ship and its contents want to fill that vacuum. Because of this need to expand, the hull is forced to maintain its inflated position. The asteroid, however, had none of this.

In *The Wrath of Khan, Reliant*'s port warp nacelle was "knocked off," but there was no matter/antimatter explosion. Why? We must assume that *Reliant* and vessels of her class have a safety feature which seals off the intermix chamber if it is ruptured, thus keeping the ship from exploding.

Even if it had exploded, Spock would have had to die. Being that close to a matter/antimatter explosion means you'd be engulfed and vaporized.

Some people asked about the *Enterprise,* "Where does the vertical intermix chamber go? It should go right through the center of the photon launch system." No, but it almost does. The vertical intermix chamber is located approximately ten feet in front of the area we saw Spock buried. We know that there are two torpedo tubes, but we saw only one. What we saw was the photon loading zone; it is about fifteen to twenty feet wide, in the center of M. Deck. Because of the antimatter involved, only one torpedo can be loaded at a time. (The antimatter has some use that I cannot recall and assume it is the explosive.) Thus only one loading zone. The loading belt enters a forward chamber and forks into two belts. These two belts load the torpedo tubes we see from the outside. The vertical intermix chamber is between these two launch tubes.

Also asked was, "Where is the turbolift for the photon torpedo launch system [M Deck]?" According to *Mr. Scott's Guide to the Enterprise,* the turbolift is located behind the loading zone; therefore, we cannot see it. However, there are no turbolifts connecting the secondary hull to the dorsal and primary hull that I could see. The only way to get from N to M Deck is by stairs and one-man lifts.

Before I carry on, let's discuss the blurring effect

seen in the second and third Star Trek movies. How did this happen? We know that when something goes by us faster than we can perceive it, it will blur. We saw *Enterprise* speed up for warp space and blur, but instead of our viewpoint "stopping" when it entered, we "followed" it in. As stated before, in warp space it is possible to go faster than the speed of light. As the speed is constant, the light that allows us to see the ship blur originates from the ship itself—engines, running lights, etc.

Someone also asked, "Why do we see stars when watching the *Enterprise* in warp space?" Remember, warp space is a duplicate of real space. As the stress barrier is transparent from outside the ship, that viewpoint allows us to see the stars. In *The Next Generation,* the viewscreens and viewports are calibrated to see "through" the stress barrier, and display the starfield.

"The damage seen on the *Enterprise* in *The Search for Spock* was more severe than what happened in *Wrath of Khan,*" someone stated. Now wait a minute. Usually the same sets and props are used for movie sequels; it wouldn't be thrifty to build new ones when you've got the ones you need. I think that you have been a victim of either a memory lapse or an optical illusion. However, if you haven't been, then the extra damage was probably caused by Genesis' debris and the stress from the journey to Earth. Besides, the damage had to be bad in *Wrath of Khan;* the shields were damaged before they even got raised, and Scotty's engines gave out. What are the odds on that? And didn't Scotty say something about a refit? She'd just had one!

"How could the *Enterprise* back out of starbase at one-quarter impulse power?" That is answered in the technical manuals twice! In the *Starfleet Technical Manual* it says, right next to the impulse engines diagram, "Power is reversible by proper control of external vent shields," and *Mr. Scott's Guide to the* Enterprise says that, ". . . to aid mobility a particle thrust reaction-control system was installed at strategic points on the *Enterprise*'s hull." If you look at photos of the refitted *Enterprise,* you can see them easily.

In *Wrath of Khan,* we saw Spock and Kirk use a combination code to override *Reliant*'s command console However, when Kirk stole the *Enterprise,* Starfleet didn't use it. Why? Well, maybe Starfleet tried. Spock did say, in *Wrath of Khan,* that changing the code was possible; maybe Kirk changed the code. If not, that leaves us with only two illogical choices. One, Starfleet forgot about the codes, or two, they really didn't want to stop Kirk. The first is unlikely because the codes would have been mentioned in Kirk's report as the determining factor in the confrontation between the *Enterprise* and *Reliant.* (Remembering these kind of details is what makes good command material.) The latter is most unlikely because they sent *Excelsior,* thinking her operational, after *Enterprise.*

But if they did want *Enterprise* back, why wasn't a tractor beam used? Well, maybe starbases don't have tractor beams. When *Enterprise* came home, starbase was given helm control; they didn't use a tractor beam. But why didn't *Excelsior* use one? Scotty took out not just the transwarp controls from the engineering computer, he took all the little brains out of it. Kirk and Scotty knew of tractor beams; they're not stupid enough to leave something working that could inhibit them. They had to get Spock!

Someone asked a couple of questions about Genesis. The first was, "Why didn't the scientists notice the protomatter David used in the device?" We must assume that they didn't because David covered it up. He was intelligent enough to "play" with the formula and programs. Besides, didn't the book say that the scientists designed their own sectors on Genesis? If it did, David could have concealed the protomatter in his sector.

The second question was, "How come the Genesis wave expanded and contracted, breaking the laws of motion?" That may not be totally correct. The Genesis wave expanded and spread out. By spreading out, it used more energy, thus causing it to slow down due to lack of energy. (Genesis will keep expanding and slowing until it uses all its energy, which is what the wave is. This point in time is probably billions of years in the future.) Genesis at the time of detonation and for probably five minutes afterward used the majority of its energy to pull and break down matter caught in the wave. After that first five minutes, Genesis became too weak to continue; thus it became just light and heat, still expanding. In the movie the outgoing wave was a bright white-blue color; the incoming wave was a dull blue-white. Obviously it was utilizing its energy resources to pull in that matter, which is what we saw returning. But how did it pull in without contracting? If *Enterprise* has artificial gravity to hold its crew "down," then why not create Genesis to utilize artificial gravity to gather matter?

"How did Spock soft land? Why didn't he asphyxiate in the torpedo?" I think because the Genesis wave was in flux it not only acted as a buffer, but also as a flight path. It could have glided him in and soft-landed him. Those of you who know about space flight also know that soft landing doesn't mean that you land like a feather. You land hard and jarring, but not so hard that it could kill. (Hard landing leaves the possibility of death, if I remember correctly.)

Besides, Spock was dead until he arrived on Genesis and was then rejuvenated. The life form, remember, appeared at the same place as Spock's "coffin" when Saavik and David located it, not some distance away. If the life form had rejuvenated earlier and left when it landed or soon afterward, then two life forms and an older Spock would have been found (remember the microbes). If it was rejuvenated before landing, Spock would have died from the reentry heat, unless that damage rejuvenated at the same time. He still would have been older if that's when rejuvenation began. He couldn't have started rejuvenating before he landed because Genesis was just beginning to evolve when he landed. Remember that Spock was in sync with the planet, aging years in a matter of minutes. Spock was reborn (rejuvenated to a ripe, young age) at Genesis' creation and looked as he had at his death when Genesis self-destructed.

But even if he began rejuvenating after he landed, Spock should have been asphyxiated, right? Not necessarily. We know that Vulcans can control their breathing and heart rate. Maybe Spock slowed down his breathing until he was able to open the torpedo tube. This is all assuming that the tube was airtight. Photon torpedoes need magnetic fields to hold in antimatter, not an airtight tube.

Spock was dead; a dead man doesn't need air, thus no need for an airtight tube. If it wasn't airtight, Spock would have received air from Genesis' atmosphere. Spock could have forced the tube open even though he was a child; recall that Vulcans are strong even when young.

How did Spock gain weight on Genesis as he got older? If Genesis could take the weight away, why could it not give it to him? It was an amazing device. It made those microbes pretty big and strong, so why couldn't it do the same for Spock? Genesis was a miracle device that was as inexplicable as God. Let it work its miracles; besides, "One man's Star Trek is another man's science and yet another's religion."

So someone believes that Klingons have invented a size-changing device, eh? The Klingon ship, supposedly, was huge alongside the merchant vessel, but dwarfed by the *Enterprise*. I don't think it changed size at all; definitely not twice in one movie. The merchant ship, for one, was only about one deck high; we saw cargo stored on the bridge! The Klingon cruiser was about two decks high, and it was cramped, too.

Every time we saw out the cruiser's viewscreen, we saw things far away and unmagnified. Every time we saw out of a Federation vessel's viewscreen, the view was magnified. The view from the merchant vessel was reduced because the cruiser was so close. Thus the seeming changes in the cruiser's size. To me, the merchant vessel and Klingon cruiser's fuselage seemed about the same size. However, the cruiser's wingspan made it look bigger than it actually was. The *Enterprise* was twenty-one stories high (A-U Decks) and the cruiser was only one or two stories high. The view we saw of the cruiser from *Enterprise* was magnified to fill the viewscreen. The view from the cruiser was not magnified; this was the actual view. It was only through magnification and reduction in the viewscreens that the cruiser seemed to enlarge and reduce.

The chronology in *Best of Trek #13* cannot be correct. *Enterprise* was launched, supposedly, in 2190. The *Enterprise* lived to a ripe old, mechanical age of more than twenty-five years. She was destroyed in the year 2215, but the chronology says she was destroyed in 2241. That means she was fifty-one years old. "Out of date" is right! I think we have many dates that no one can agree on. Does this one satisfy anyone?

2164—Spock is born seven years before the first Klingon delegation to Terra.

2171—Leonard H. McCoy is born. First Klingon delegation.

2173—James T. Kirk is born.

2181—Hikaru Sulu is born.

2189—SS *Columbia* crashes on Talos IV.

2190—*Enterprise* launched.

2191—Kirk enters Starfleet Academy.

2194—Robert T. April receives *Enterprise* after major refit and overhaul due to problems discovered after four-year deep-space shakedown cruise; *Enterprise* seems to be brand-new. Beginning of first five-year mission.

2199—End of *Enterprise*'s first five-year mission. Lieutenant Kirk injured in *Farragut* disaster. Christopher Pike receives *Enterprise*. Robert April becomes

Federation ambassador-at-large. *Enterprise* visits Talos IV. Sulu enters Starfleet Academy.

2200—Kirk receives *Lydia Sutherland.*

2202—Kirk receives Palm Leaf for Azanar Peace Mission.

2203—Kirk receives command of *Enterprise.*

2206—Individual ship uniforms employed.

2208—Beginning of second five-year mission.

2212—Gray uniforms. *Enterprise* command emblem used as Starfleet emblem.

2213—End of second five-year mission.

2215—After two and one-half years as head of operations, Kirk retakes *Enterprise.* Vejur invades solar system.

2217—Launch of Enterprise-class vessels.

2219—New red uniforms.

2222—Events of *Wrath of Khan, The Search for Spock,* and *The Voyage Home. Enterprise* destroyed; Kirk court-martialed; Kirk receives NCC 1701-A.

Note: The destruction of *Enterprise* in 2222 makes her thirty-two years old. Harry Morrow said, "She's over twenty-five years old, Jim . . ."

Note: I do not remember anyone saying Kirk's age in *Wrath of Khan,* just that it was his birthday. If my chronology is correct, he would be forty-nine or fifty years old. In a time when the average life expectancy is over a hundred, turning fifty would be treated the same as turning forty is now—terrible.

"Where did the new *Enterprise,* NCC 1701-A come from?" Get a copy of *Mr. Scott's Guide to the* Enterprise. It states that Enterprise-class vessels were designed and built to become the pride of the fleet, as the Constitution-class vessels once were. Further, these vessels have state-of-the-art technology, such as Leeding Engines' FTWG-1 Transwarp nacelles, an Daystrom Data Concepts M-6 logic system.

Ti-Ho was the first Enterprise-class vessel to receive the transwarp nacelles. She was on her way back to Earth from her deep-space shakedown when the

Probe crisis began. When she returned, *Ti Ho* was immediately rechristened *Enterprise* and placed under the command of Captain Kirk.

And the voyage continues.

What is *pon farr*? Is it psychological, physiological, or psycho-physical? Let's first state what we know of *pon farr*.

Pon farr—the burning of the Vulcan blood—comes once every seven years of a male Vulcan's adult life. (Knowing the Vulcan propensity to state all the facts, and seeing that no Vulcan ever said female Vulcans experience *pon farr,* we can assume female Vulcans do not.) It is a period when a Vulcan cannot control his emotions. If the Vulcan denies *pon farr*—the time of mating—too long, he will eventually die from the stress. The female soothes her mate through touch telepathy and physical exertion, possibly sexual intercourse. We also know that this is not the only time Vulcans have sex.

What do we know about Vulcans? We know that some Vulcans, by tradition only, are bonded telepathically during childhood. Bonding creates a telepathic bridge between the two mates. We consider it marriage, and the bond can only be broken by death or mutual consent. Vulcans devote themselves to *arie'mnu,* emotional control, not emotional suppression (see *The Wounded Sky*). Vulcans can control their entire body, and by doing this they have lengthened their lifetimes. For this to seem credible, it means they must have slowed down all of their hormone releases because they all affect aging.

We know that Amanda would not allow Sarek to completely bond Spock. She still wanted Spock to choose his own wife as Sarek had. This must mean that bonding comes in stages; the first stage could possibly be what humans call engagement. The second stage is most likely marriage. Spock is, in my opinion, only on the first stage. Why? Because the first stage lets him choose a wife and allots him a mate if *pon farr* comes before he finds one.

If this is true, we know that Spock went through *pon farr* unbonded (at first stage bonding) and survived. This must mean that a Vulcan can die not from putting off each day of *pon farr,* as some people seem to think, but by putting off each cycle, or coming, of *pon farr.*

After Spock "killed" Kirk in *koon-ut-kal-if-fee,* it didn't stop. The emotions changed to sadness and depression at a level Spock could barely control. This shows that physical and emotional exertion can help "defeat" *pon farr,* just as they reduce stress in humans. Stress is psycho-physical, meaning it comes from, and can be cured by, physical and psychological actions. Because stress and *pon farr* can be defeated in the same way, I think that it is safe to assume that *pon farr* is psycho-physical.

Could it be that holding back the growth hormones, a process which by now has probably become natural for Vulcans, causes *pon farr?* Yes, by refusing to release hormones, which a body continuously creates, the body is caused physical stress. And by holding in their emotions, specifically pain and anger, Vulcans double that stress by adding psychological stress.

Because *arie'mnu* has been happening for two thousand years, since the Reformation, it has probably altered the Vulcans' genes that control hormone release and thus created *pon farr.* More evidence that *pon farr* started after the Reformation is that we have never heard of a Romulan experiencing *pon farr.* (The Reformation is when the Vulcans learned *arie'mnu* and body control. The Romulans, as we know, are the ancestors of those who refused to follow Surak and his Reformation. They left Vulcan because they could not live among all those who chose the Reformation; they devoted themselves not to life and logic, but to honor and dignity.) *Pon farr* is probably an explosion within the body, which releases an overload of hormones, most likely testosterone, causing changes such as physical maturation at an alarmingly painful rate. A rate that causes so much pain that a Vulcan cannot defeat his emotions.

The touch telepathy with the female is probably used to help the Vulcan male slow down the hormone release to a less painful rate. It is likely that physical activity is used to give the male an opportunity to "eat up" the excess hormones.

There is evidence to support this in *The Search for Spock*. Saavik was able to soothe Spock by creating a telepathic bridge. We don't know what she said or did with that bridge; perhaps she bonded. However, we do know that a Vulcan automatically creates a bridge when touched, and Spock was relieved by this touch from Saavik. We know physical exertion relieves some stress, because we saw the young Spock somewhat relieved and a little more able to control himself by striking the Klingon on Genesis.

Why don't females experience *pon farr*? If *pon farr* is caused by a hormonal explosion, and females don't have *pon farr*, then we must assume that the hormone that causes the "madness" is found only in males.

In *Best of Trek #13*, it was put forward that females cause *pon farr* in the male through the psychic bridge between bonded couples. This emotional projection would cause similar feelings and responses in both; in other words, the female would feel the pain the male feels. The calm actions of T'Pring refute this: her body language didn't betray distress of discomfort, or even that she was making Spock feel distress or discomfort.

The same person who said females caused *pon farr* tried to say that Saavik "diagnosed" the young Spock incorrectly; that Spock wasn't even in *pon farr* on Genesis. She may be only half-Vulcan, but then so is Spock. She knows everything Spock knew, and he knew very well what was happening when *pon farr* came upon him. We must presume she knew what was happening and what to do. Besides, it was a necessary element of suspense to the movie; wouldn't everyone have been confused if Spock didn't experienced *pon farr* as he "aged" every "seven years"?

STAR TREK: THREE FACES, SAME MIRROR

By A. H. Wokanovicz

The twenty-fifth anniversary of the original *Star Trek* series premiere has come and gone. We have seen a favorite television show that made us think, grow, and evolve to take its rightful place among the cultural icons of our time.

Star Trek's characters and themes are now nearly universally familiar. The starship *Enterprise* is instantly recognized by millions all over the world, nearly always with a fond smile. Expressions like "Beam me up," and "Warp speed" pop up in the speech patterns of pundits, professors, critics, children, and presidential candidates. The many incarnations of Gene Roddenberry's hopeful universe have achieved enduring mainstream popularity under the careful stewardship of Paramount Pictures.

Science fiction at its best is more than mere entertainment; it is a medium in which we can ponder the progress of humankind through an infinity of alternate futures. We can explore the issues that frighten, compel, and intrigue us by setting them in an allergorical "otherwhere," allowing us to illuminate them from a safe intellectual distance.

Some have said that Star Trek is not "true" science fiction, but rather an amalgam of science fiction and fantasy best described as "space opera." Unlike "hard" SF, Star Trek has never been primarily about futuristic hardware and wildly abstract concepts; its territory is more the exploration of the "human adventure." And in this it succeeds admirably. It has become a mirror in which to see ourselves as we wish we were and as we really are, warts and all.

Art is supposed to reflect life, not the reverse, though even that casual relationship is suspect where Star Trek is concerned. And if this form of art is then a clear reflection of those who made it, what does it have to say about us?

In 1966, America was a nation which had taken some heavy blows to its shining self-image. Everything had been turned upside down—it was hard to know what was "right" and "wrong" anymore. Awful things were happening all around us, seemingly at random, and the traditional places people went for answers suddenly didn't have any that worked. A generation had grown up in the shadow of the Bomb, believing annihilation probable within their lifetimes. Assassinations. Race riots. The Red Menace. The war in Vietnam.

At the same time, an explosion of new ideas was taking place. Civil rights. Gender equality. The youth movement. Computers. And, of course, the reality of space travel. The time was ripe for science fiction, previously relegated to a fringe following, to become mainstream entertainment. People hungered for new ideas to replace some of the old ones that no longer fit the new visions and challenges.

The ways in which Gene Roddenberry's television creation of an optimistic future touched the collective consciousness of a generation are too well known to need repetition here. The fact is that a great many seekers of hope found a future they wanted to believe in and make happen through Star Trek. And that phenomenon has echoed down the years to Star Trek's most recent incarnations.

We watch "the old show" through different eyes

these days. The perspective of twenty-five years has shown us that some of our most cherished sacred cows were questionable attitudes, at best. Whom among us has not lately squirmed in our seat watching a young, brash Captain Kirk summarily disregard the Prime Directive to give some alien culture an attitude adjustment? We now can see a subtext of simplistic self-righteousness behind our assumption that "The Federation is always right." The Federation of 1966 seems a thinly-veiled "American Way," enforced through Starfleet under a doctrine of "Peace through superior firepower."

While the humanistic and science-fictional aspects of such shows as "Balance of Terror" and "City on the Edge of Forever" ring eternal, many Trekkers now find entries like "The Omega Glory" and "Turnabout Intruder" so dated they are almost disturbing. Were we really like that? Were those attitudes actually *progressive* not such a very long time ago? Perhaps we have, as Gene Roddenberry had hoped, made progress toward "growing up" after all.

We step through the Guardian of Forever and it is now the 1980s. The generation which marched on Washington and took on the Establishment is now making a deeper mark on America. We have marched forth into the Real World with our ideal and have begun bending it to who and what we are.

Some of us are now raising families of our own and pondering the world we will leave them. Some are fulfilling our wildest dream in ways that would have been impossible a generation ago. Women astronauts. Black governors. Precocious twenty-six-year-olds turning garage workshops into corporate dynasties. "Money for nothin'" in the form of junk bonds to leverage any buyout spawning an ethic of instant gratification through buy-now, pay-later economics. Glorifications of high living, casual sex, and substance abuse. Smugness as we beat our parents at their own materialistic games, with style.

Onto this scene in late 1987 exploded *Star Trek: The Next Generation*, and lightning was caught twice in the same bottle. Like the original, the new Star Trek is a perfect mirror for our perceptions of ourselves. And though the show is still in first-run as this is written, enough time and changes have elapsed to give us a perspective.

The Federation of *The Next Generation* had plainly matured. Our ship was now a magnificently refined work of space-going sculpture. Space itself had been tamed enough to bring our families aboard for the voyage. Many of the problems that had plagued Kirk and Scotty could now be cured with the touch of a keypad. The mighty Klingons had capitulated; the Romulans called it a standoff. We had conquered disease, poverty, hunger, and want. We were free at last to explore the outer limits of human knowledge and possibility.

In fact, the twenty-fourth century of Gene Roddenberry and Rick Berman has been accused of solving *too many* of humanity's problems, and too easily for either credibility or dramatic tension. *The Next Generation* employs much subtler forms of conflict that Captain Kirk's old tunic-rippers.

Like its predecessor, our new *Enterprise*'s adventures reflect our perceptions of ourselves at a given place in time. The "strange new worlds" we explore are more likely to be within the human mind and heart than on some planet of styrene rocks, and even Trekkers don't always agree on what we find there.

Some have argued that *The Next Generation* takes fewer chances than the original show. But how does one define the progress of thought? Are not stories which explore the nature of sentience or the motivations for homophobia shaking our applecart just as surely as the first interracial kiss or the morality of war did a generation ago?

There are those who say that the original *Star Trek* was better entertainment, because it had more fisticuffs, sex, and shooting. But how many of us today truly consider violence to be a desirable way to solve the problems of nations or individuals? How many think wars are inevitable? How many consider Kirk's "alien-babe-of-the-week" antics admirable?

We had grown up, and not grown, by 1987. Work hard, play to win, live it up. Anything is possible.

And so we went forth in our padded cocktail lounge in the sky, with our supremely self-confident Captain Jean-Luc Picard, who always had the right answers. Humanity had won, and we were reaping the rewards. We could afford to be inclusive and compassionate to all we encountered, and had learned to allow them free rein to make their own mistakes along the way, as we had done. A Klingon, former enemy, was now our protector. A blind man piloted the ship. And even an android could aspire to the joy and challenge of being human.

About the time the Borg arrived in sector 001, things began to get much more complicated in America, too—and a whole lot darker. True, the Iron Curtain had fallen, and with it the seeming inevitability of Mutually Assured Destruction, but the real chance for a future of hope and promise was quickly obscured by the complexity of the problems that replaced it. With our economy in decline and our people looking for scapegoats, it was time to clean up the mess.

There is a certain ironic symbolism now in Picard's capture and alteration by the Borg to be used as the Federation's ultimate weapon against itself. By 1991 we had met the Borg, and they are us. We have become something we didn't even recognize.

We step through the time portal again, and it is January of 1993. In some ways the changes that have taken place since 1987 rival the ones we saw in the twenty intervening years between classic *Star Trek* and *The Next Generation*. The world today is literally changing faster than we can update the maps. Thanks to instant satellite feeds, the global village of the media is a done deal. The tragedy and misery of an entire planet is beamed to us as it happens, produced by CNN. Everything from food to love contains a hidden threat; there is no longer even a pretense of innocence.

We stand today on the cusp of history. On one hand is a real change to come together as the Family of Planet Earth, infinite diversity in infinite combinations, side by side in peace. The other is the far likelier possibility that we will let our differences continue to divide and conquer us, turning what could be our greatest strength into a fatal weakness.

The human race is compartmentalizing and fragmenting at a rate not seen since before the First World War. We are dividing along racial, ethnic, religious, even sexual lines. Could it be an instinctive, momentarily confused reaction to the realization of how far we have come? That there's no "them" anymore, but only "us"? None can know the future.

And so the latest incarnation—*Star Trek: Deep Space Nine.* We aren't along for the ride on a shining flagship of enlightenment anymore, folks. We've been dumped off at the edge of the unknown, charged with rolling up our sleeves to salvage and retrofit what's left from the ruins of the former empire. All the aliens aren't cooperating, and we're not even cooperating too well among ourselves. We have real interpersonal conflict these days, and in our frustration we don't always take care to respect the opinions of others. We question authority, sometimes loudly and spitefully. We grimly bite our lip and power up the phasers without apology when necessary. Even the motivations of the Federation itself are open to constant question and debate.

But even through the "darker, grittier" lens of *Deep Space Nine,* we can see ourselves as we'd like to be and find some real role models to sustain us for the job ahead. Commander Sisko, who vows to do the best he can in spite of his own self-doubts. Major Kira, pointing to the difficulty of adjusting cultural attitudes we once thought absolutes. Odo and Dax, holding up a mirror in which to see our paradoxes. And Dr. Bashir, who, with the light of the original *Star Trek* vision in his eyes, can still make us believe that "this is the place where heroes are made!"

I wish all of them, and us, warp speed.

WHY DO I LOVE THE KLINGONS?

By Sue Frank

My little green Jedi conscience is muttering, "Love or love not! There is no 'why'!" "But," I protest, "there is! What in space can I mean when I say 'I love the Klingons'? What kind of idiotic assertion is that, anyway? I love the most dangerous, explosive killers who ever terrorized a television series the way I love my folks? My native land? Gooseberry pie? Surely not!"

You Kor-susceptibles can help me out. Just stop a minute and reflect on your reactions when you watched your favorite Klingon military governor stride into the council chambers or Organia for the first time. And the tenth time. I'm talking about what happened on the surface of your skin, inside your liver. Come on and describe the sure signs of falling into Klingon love.

If it has happened to you, you know that you can't do a blessed thing about it except drop under the spell. You don't have to be female to be caught this way. I have heard some formidable males declare their love of Klingons. We would need a Teiresias,[1] who

---

[1] Teiresias is a mortal male from Greek mythology who, by a set of curious circumstances, got to live in a woman's body for a time. So the Olympian gods turned to him when they wanted to settle the question, "Who has more fun in love—men or women?" The answer from two-way Teiresias: the women, easily. I won't be such a female chauvinist as to transfer that ancient conclusion to this special problem. We need more data.

could try out both the men's and women's versions of this experience, to make a proper evaluation of the differences and report who has more fun. But let's not worry about that now. I'll stick to what I know best—my own experience.

My credentials as a lover of the bad guys are as good as you'll find. When I was ten and living for the next TV installment of the Flash Gordon serials, I found Flash admirable and Dale lovely, but they couldn't fill the place in my psyche reserved for Ming. He is the one whose picture I drew. He is the one I would have married, given a choice of any of the players. (Why is it that when we were ten, my friends and I expressed our approval of fictional characters by offering to marry them? I don't think we were obsessed with sex. It seemed a way of saying, "I wouldn't get bored teamed up with this guy over the long haul, and I'd sure enjoy watching him operate!")

I was busy deciding that I wanted to be Jewish and not Episcopalian when I was twelve, but that didn't interfere with falling in love with Yul Brenner's Pharaoh in *The Ten Commandments* and passing over Charlton Heston's Moses. Like Ming, Pharaoh is exotic and wrong. He is also totally dedicated to his resistance of the approved line of conduct, ready to die (which he does!) for the privilege of exerting his *perverse* will. I mean, how many times, in how many different ways, does the Lord have to tell you to let a bunch of scruffy Hebrews *go,* already? I love a guy who can just say "no" to God.

So, my pattern was set. My adolescent heart beat for the dark and the doomed. Who cared about the fair-haired winner? What could taste more like dust in the mouth than a moral victory? I wouldn't want one! Give me the life (and death) of Ben Hur's unscrupulous opponent Messala or—Great Galaxies! could this be my first Klingon?—that wretched liar, Kras[2] This might be only a remnant of teenage rebel-

---

[2] Kras is the Klingon agent who dies negotiating for minerals on the planet Capella in "Friday's Child."

liousness expressing itself in a preference for those who would turn the world upside down to get what they want. But hey! I haven't outgrown it yet! I gather a fair percentage of you are hanging tough with me, too.

Star Trek came and went while I was in college. Then I went off to grad school. I didn't watch TV or see many movies for almost ten years. There just didn't seem to be any time if I were going to get properly serious about all the ancient, dead languages I wanted to learn. So, in 1980, when I went to *The Empire Strikes Back,* my shields were down. When a certain tall, dark, scary guy exploded into the rebel ice fortress on Hoth, he breached all my defenses. Lord Darth Vader seemed to say, "You may be thirty, but age confers no protection."

Remember the seduction invitation Vader makes to Luke: "Join me and together we will rule the galaxy"? He wouldn't have had to ask me twice! Turn down the Dark path? No problem! Wait for me!

In Vader's wake came other excellent science-fantasy villains. My mother gave me a way of describing and assessing the physical contact these characters can make with their audience. One of her schoolmates, intimidated past endurance by an examination give by a teacher she adored, wrote at the end of her torched paper a sort of apology: "When I hear your foot upon the stair, all my organs turn around in their cavities!" Well, I can instantly tell that I have met a worthy "bad guy" because my guts are right there with the report. Max Von Sydow's Ming, Ricardo Montalban's Khan, Sarah Douglas's Evil Queen in *Red Sonja,* and the super bully in *Superman II* all made my innards shift.

This is not an indiscriminate preference for the villain. No, let my be perfectly clear. I do not love that blob of thlup, Jabba the Hut. I am not moved by the drooling chestbusters of *Alien.* James Earl Jones's Thulsa Doom in *Conan* doesn't work for me, much as

I want to like him. I get no thrill from the Cylons. Even *Dr. Who*'s Master, although his look is close to "right," doesn't make the grade for me. And the Ferengi—my lights will never jump for money-lust.

There are even some of *Star Trek*'s Klingons who disappoint. Although most all the Klingons of the TV and movie series have been gloriously fulfilling, it must be admitted that old What's-His-Name the Unforgettable[3] was wasted in the episode "The Savage Curtain." But this is a negligible lapse compared to the Klingon trashing that goes on in the "pro" novels. Except for John M. Ford, most of the writers of these pulp wonders pull out stock Klingon types who are stupid, conceited, mad for sex and torture, and bound to end up ingloriously dead or humiliated. The creepy sadists of *Dwellers in the Crucible,* drugged Kalrind of *Time Trap,* the mutually abusive, thrown-away crew in *Covenant of the Crown:* I am not amused. What are the editors of the series thinking when they allow such characters to be published? Can't you just hear Mara? "Feh! We have seen how we are portrayed in your pulp fiction!" How in space are people like this supposed to run an empire?

Some Trek fan writers have taken this tack with their Klingon characters, making of them lifeless stereotypes. This probably happens for the same reason Uhura get slighted and we rarely hear from Mr. Scott: people are busy writing about the Big Three and the characters around them get reduced to dull conventionalizations. Along with everyone else, especially aliens, the Klingons lose dimensionality and shrink to plot devices used to hurt people and get hurt back. For someone like me who fell in love with the Klingons as bad guys but got hooked on them as beings in their own right, that's a major let-down.

I'm not saying I could write a good Klingon. Just that after all these years, I trust my instincts and I

---

[3] Linda Slusher's pet name for Kahless.

know a convincing Klingon when I meet her or him, on the screen, in the books, in the zines. Here I'd like to offer a preliminary report from the field: a survey of the Klingons I have encountered and will always love—a little description, some analysis. Who knows? Maybe some of the "why" of it will float to the top.

But I need to preface this excursion with a disclaimer. I haven't by any stretch met all the Klingons who are out there to know, especially the fannish ones. Zines go out of print or just never cross your path. So I make no claims of exclusiveness. My project here is to acknowledge some happily met personalities who make me want to keep mingling in this strange Klingon society—half a universe full of worthy opponents and coconspirators.

Video Klingons, Old and New

In the beginning are the Klingons of television and film. They are a choice crew. No wonder the Klingons have such a devoted fan following!

"I am Kor, Military Governor of Organia. Most of my soldiers are taller than I am and look like they could run circles around me, but I've got an insinuating voice, a wolf's grin, and a sneaky wit that will put me in front every time. Look at me from any angle you choose. I used to being studied, admired. And why not? I am the sexiest! And I'll do a strategist's job of appraising you. Count on it. I know how I can use you."

Security Chief Murashaka's Summary Report of Commander Kang: "Aptitude for leadership and loyalty are superbly integrated in Kang. Rely on him to maintain Klingon dignity at all costs. He works well with his wife and science officer, Mara. Their mutual devotion is an inspiration to us all, but clearly does not interfere with their first, best aim: service to the empire. Kang is a magnificent figure of a male, unconscious of his beauty, but objective about his abilities, which are totally dedicated to imperial victory."

Kras, you slimy animal. How do you put out all that wattage with no disruptor on your hip, so little hair on your head? Why can't you resist any opportunity to irritate those Earthers? Why are you doomed to take bad step after false step until there's only one path open for you—a field promotion to the Black Fleet?

My *dear* Captain Koloth! Yes, we have met before. Organian negotiation, wasn't it? Whatever. You may bring your *men* onto this station for shore leave, but I'll have one of my people here for every one of yours. Don't give me that crooked grin, you effete excuse for a Klingon. No, I'm sure you'll manage to keep your nose clean, but your friend Korax, here . . . More the Klingon ideal, wouldn't you say? Still, I must confess to a certain fondness for you both. Could I interest you in a charming little tribble? Maybe 1,876,431 of them?

Is it any wonder that even in those old *Star Trek* episodes (remember "A Private Little War" and "Elaan of Troius"?) in which Klingon characters appear for only a few seconds, they are highlighted in the previews?

While some of us miss the superior sophistication and intelligence of the old series' officers, the movies and *Star Trek: The Next Generation* have brought us challenging "knothead" characters. Someone important must have been seeing to the survival and success of the Klingon species, even after *Star Trek* got canceled. The opening sequence of *Star Trek: The Motion Picture* shows a battle group of Klingon warriors (led by Mark Lenard! Thank you, IDIC!) demonstrating the only sensible way to say "Hi" to Vejur.

Khan holds the Klingons' place in *Star Trek II: The Wrath of Khan* in high style. He even casts a Klingon proverb into Kirk's perfect teeth[4]

Then comes *Star Trek III: The Search for Spock,* in which the wifty Klingon of my dreams, Kruge, buys the Big One in a sea of Genesis lava. But not before he laughs defiance at the prospect of destruction: "Exhilarating, isn't it?" and has a chance to display utter incorrigibility, trying to drag Kirk down with him instead of accepting his rescuing hand.[5] And not before he disturbs every peaceful organ between my brain and my knees.

Scotty and McCoy can make those unkind remarks about the hardy little Bird of Prey that carries them home to the 1980s and back in *Star Trek IV: The Voyage Home,* but we know that is just a clever Klingon way of maintaining a presence. Any form of publicity, you know . . . And here is *Star Trek V: The Final Frontier*—whoopee!—bringing us a rousing musical theme for the Klingons with its peacock screech orchestration and almost a full hand of new and memorable knotheads. I ask you, how do *you* feel when Captain Klaa slaps his chest and cries, "Qapla!"? And *Star Trek VI: The Undiscovered Country,* the supposedly valedictory film in the series is a Klingon story pure and simple. It fills in the historical evolution in Federation—Klingon relations which take place between "classic" and "Next Generation" eras, as well as giving us a feast of splendid new Klingon characters to contemplate.

[4] Where do you suppose Khan picked up a Klingon proverb? Makes me believe R. Jan's tale of the encounter between a group of Klingons and Khan's company on Ceti Alpha V, "Joachim," in *Katra VI,* Lana Brown, ed., New Zealand, 1987.

[5] Some of us already know that Kruge, like Maltz, is still alive. See Linda Slusher's "Behind Every Great Man," in *Katra IX,* Lana Brown, ed., New Zealand, 1988.

I must say, *The Next Generation*'s Worf has been a test of my Klingon love. Worf is simple. Will all the Klingons in this show have to be simple? Will they always have to endure the condescension of Earthers and others? I worry about Worf being exploited as Starfleet's token growler and strong-arm. Is pain the only thing he enjoys? I can't help preferring untamed types—the ridiculously single-minded, feisty Captain Kargon, worthy friend Klag, and those reckless outlaws Korus and Kanmil. And how nice to meet *you*, Vekma and Kehylerh!

Klingons in Story and Art and Song

A few crucial professional writers have made contributions to Klingon lore which have extended the horizons of Klingon fanciers. Games designers, a linguist, and an extraordinary novelist have all brought us closer to these particular alien love-objects.

There are impressive Klingon characters to meet and impersonate in the scenario literature created for gaming systems based on Star Trek material. In the FASA universe, players are helped to imagine themselves in the characters of Star Academy cadets, planetary governors, espionage agents—you name it—all from the Klingon point of view.

Operating in a separate sphere, the combat simulation games of Starfleet Battles support their world with exciting fictional offerings. These have introduced several classic Klingon warriors. I found the exploits of Commander Korath against a Juggernaut invader inspirational,[6] but my favorite is a female commander, Kaita Kor,[7] who gets to preach a sane gospel, "Survive to fight another day!"

[6] Christopher Allen, "Objective: Juggernaut" in *Captain's Log* #1, published by Task Force Games, 1982.
[7] Mary Beth O'Halloran, "What Price Victory?" in *Captain's Log* #7, Task Force Games, 1989.

A Klingon emulator can improve his grasp of Klingon cultural concepts and even learn how to ask for a good restaurant in Klingonaase if he studies Marc Okrand's *Klingon Dictionary* (New York: Pocket Books, 1985). The book is, of course, much more than a word list. It is a richly conceived approach to the language as a whole. I had looked forward to the day when someone would get Garrison Keillor to tear his throat out recording sample dialogues for "Klingon Language Systems for Earthers Who Don't Want to Feel Like Strangers When Visiting the Homeworld." Well, it's here now: Michael Dorn (Worf) and Marc Okrand have produced just such a tape to accompany the *Klingon Dictionary* (Simon and Schuster, 1992).

Matt Leger's description of favorite Star Trek novels in *Best of Trek #14* led to me John Ford's *The Final Reflection* (New York: Pocket Books, 1984). I have read Ford's action epic a number of times. It keeps giving back more than adventure. I have been disappointed to find that friends to whom I loan the book recoil from the characters. They are, apparently, too bizarre. We who ordinarily identify with the Federation cannot imagine a world in which races other than our own are frankly reduced to object-servant status, where electronic torture opens the minds of enemies to our inspection, where the state sponsors assassination of our loved ones to suit its own inscrutable ends. An odd failure of the imagination, considering the world we live in.

But *The Final Reflection* also gives us Klingons in all their irreducible otherness. These beings can't be contained in a human's account. The characteristic ellipses of Ford's style conveys this fact perfectly. You try to read between the lines and realize that you can feel the consistency, the rightness, but you can't ease out all the logic. Mystery and wonder—fear, too—lodge in these places.

Aside from Ford, I look to my fellow fans for further Klingon entertainments in the literary zone. By the way, I don't mean to slight Majliss Larson's novel, *Pawns and Symbols*. Any story in which a captured Earther female finds herself confined to the Klingon captain's cabin to serve him dinner and warm him up is exhibiting a classic, enjoyable fannish pattern. So I look at *Pawns and Symbols* as an excellent fan work which by some happy fluke got published by a big commercial house.

Most of the rest of us won't get that kind of circulation (not to mention the financial renumeration!), but at least we know where we can turn for reliable Klingon fixes: the zines. Here I have found handsome continuation of "canonical" Klingons by writers who have transcended old "set 'em up to knock 'em down" scenarios. Dennis Bahm's story of Kor and Kirk, trapped together in a wine cellar, made me feel like I'd again met old friends.[8] The hero of the aptly titled "Koloth Hatches His Revenge" is just right, too, and the Klingon "wins" in this one.[9] Mary Aldridge's "A Place in the Stars," a sequel to "Day of the Dove," brings us an effective depiction of Kang and his sister.[10]

The *Katra* zine crew did an extraordinary service, bringing us Klingons old and new, lavishly drawn, convincingly characterized, on a regular basis. Here we find Lana Brown's Krantz (wait till he gets that Terran chick Sean into *his* cabin!), Robert Jan's Atrpoos, Sue Isle's Keth, Leon Gammel's tough guys, not to mention good old Kor, Kang, and Maltz. All are alive and well here—and loved. (Katra is the best antidote to that James Blish nonsense about banning Klingons from space.[11] Don't hem us in, dammit!

Part of what's wonderful about Klingons (like Tig-

---

[8] Dennis Bahm, "... And Thou Beside Me", *Baseline 2*, Official Publication of Starbase Kansas City, Publisher: Kay Johnson, Editor: Cathy Strand, March 1982.
[9] Gina Martin, Carol Yocum and Linda McLaren in *Enter-Comm 5*, Canadian Contingent Press, Darien Duck *et al*, eds., January 1982.
[10] Mary Aldridge, *Ibid*.
[11] See James Blish, *Spock Must Die*. New York: Bantam, 1970.

gers[12]) is that they are fun and funny. Shona Jackson, Linda Slusher, Robert Jan (again!), and Melody Rondeau draw and write them with a light touch. They turn up all over the place in zines, startling unsuspecting Spock or Data fans with Cupid-quick zings of Klingon hilarity.

Gennie Summers, Bonnie Reity, Richard Pollet, Bobbie Hawkins, and Sat Nam Kaur are artists with the *klin* in them to take us well past video. Roberta Rogow's muse inspires her with Klingon songs. And I think it's time to drag out the old concertina and see how the music printed in *Alkarin Warlord*[13] sounds. By the way, if anyone out there knows dance notation, we need to start collecting the native dances of the homeworld, too.

Sometimes you need a sustained universe, a source for continuing Klingon divertissement—something that approaches the Darkover series in comprehensives. Devra Langsam and friends have for years been building a world which centers around students of a Klingon martial art. The Kersuh fighters, Klingon, Terran and others, are mischievous, infuriating and lovable by turns. Off in another direction, Carol Walske and Fern Marder have generated a fantasy world for Klingons in their Nu Ormenel series. *Alkarin Warlord*, mentioned above, is one of theirs. Kor and a lovely blond Earther? Here is a courtship and a wedding to die for. Another large-scale Klingon project is Ann Schwader's epic of a Starfleet xenosociologist who becomes involved in a Klingon revolution. Get hooked on *Beyond Diplomacy* and find other segments of the cycle in issues of *More Missions, More Myths*.[14] Robert Endres' series about the extra-hyper-ultra-bloodthirsty Khmer Klingons isn't for the squea-

---

[12] See Mac's "A Silly Klingon Filksong" in *Rerun #7*, Lorraine Bartlett, ed. Rochester, NY, 1989.

[13] Fern Marder and Carol Walske, *Alkarin Warlord*, Winston A. Howlett, ed., Mpingo Press Special Issue, 1978.

[14] See issues #9, 11, 12 and 13. Wendy Rathbone, ed.

mish, but it has a large concept and vast cast that will pull you in. Pick up Sue Isle's novels, *The Far Side of War* or *Elba*, and you'll be scrambling for the issues of *Katra* and *SPOCK* that contain further stories of Keth, Kalek, and Treven.[15]

Let me finish my bows to the fannish enhances of Klingon glory with a kowtow to Kalin den Teke Lorad Sharma. Faithful spouse, father, reluctant warrior, possessor of an inordinately large pair of feet—this Klingon has as much trouble with bureaucratic red tape as he does with Kzinti cannibals. I mean, his socks get dirty, he draws a paycheck, and he has trouble with his kids. (Yes! That's one of the things I'd been missing in Klingon stories—Klinglings and other noncombatants!) You can find his adventures recorded in *Maisform-D, The Clipper Trade Ship, This Side of Paradise* #7, and various other out-of-print zines. Linda Slusher has her own distinctive, utterly consistent take on Klingon society, and she can keep you regally entertained on the Klingon channel for hundreds of pages. No lover of the Klingons should miss this answer to Jane Austen/Groucho Marx.

There are favorite themes in the fannish work. Fan writers are enchanted with the Klingons' strangeness and "outliness" (nice word; I learned it from *Katra*). They often bring Klingons and Earthers together (usually a Klingon male and an Earther female) and let their readers watch the two work on their relationship. The Klingons are usually beautiful, powerful, and bound by social codes of decorum that make Earthers seem like undisciplined children (barbarians, even) by comparison. They are also dangerous. They will do serious damage to your Earther physique if you push them too far, which generally involves being hopelessly rude or trying to "un-Klingon" them. Most fan writers protect the alien integrity of the Klingon char-

[15] In print and available from various zines agented by Bill Hupe, Lansing, MI.

acters. Like so many Star Trek fans, they are glad to meet the "other" and take a stab at getting to know it on its own terms. Much of their rewarding fiction documents this effort.

The Evolving Relationship Between Klingons and the Federation: Fannish and Pro Visions

The Klingons of television and film have made a fascinating sort of progress which sometimes parallels the concerns of us Klingon fans.

In the original *Star Trek* shows, the Klingons' main occupation is pestering the Starfleet heroes. They can be old-timey villains, enormously entertaining in their determined resistance to the Federation. As Kang points out, they need no reason to hate Earthers.

But, hard as they try, they rarely get to really hurt anybody. Only tribbles die from the grain poisoned by the Klingon agent in "The Trouble With Tribbles." The two hundred Organian hostages "disrupted" at Kor's command ("Errand of Mercy") are not physical beings, so no one actually dies. And Kor's scary mind-scanner doesn't give Spock, with his Vulcan "mental disciplines," so much as a headache. The Starfleet security man stabbed in the guts by one of Kang's swordsmen ("Day of the Dove") heals right up due to the controlling energy being's powers. The *Enterprise* crew suffers no permanent casualties in this trying incident, although the cruel enemy alien destroys four hundred Klingons on Kang's ship to set up its hate lab. Kras of "Friday's Child" does actually get to phaser a Capellan or two out of existence (there's that much less Day-Glo fake fur in the galaxy!), but Kirk and Spock do as much damage to their hosts with their bows and arrows. Of course, Kras pays with his life for this delinquency. The *Enterprise* boys get away with the laurels and the topaline mining contract!

So, in the original series, all these Klingon characters "lose"—in the sense that their aims and means come to naught against the Federation. At least the scriptwriters had the grace to build complexity into their personalities, and terrific actors gave them depth of character creative fans could build upon. They get to rattle human complacency, but with little long-term impact. Things have changed, however, with time's passing. Stakes and risks have risen in the Klingon-Federation game.

The Klingons of *ST:TMP* perish, but they surely die well! As for Kruge, he is the first Klingon who gets to really hurt Kirk and make it stick: he kills the captain's son. Kruge pays many times over for his "success" with the loss of Valkris, his crew, his "prize ship" (the *Enterprise*), his ship, and finally, his own life. It's expensive being this kind of Klingon, but he commands our attention, and—hey!—a little of our respect. I think we Earther's (especially soft, liberal types) are fascinated by beings so dedicated to their goals that they live genuinely prepared to die. Is there a place for us to meet these people and commune a bit before the shooting starts? There have always been fans who thought so.

And there may yet be hope for *The Next Generation,* if only this series can follow up on the promise of Worf's one great script, "Heart of Glory." Here Worf shows that a Klingon can join the Federation without having his incisors drawn. He is totally satisfactory as he lines up the civilized virtues of internal control against the berserker glory-seeking of the Klingon renegades who seek to win him over. Korus may have been unable to hold on to the thought, but he sure is right when he says to Worf, "They ask you to change the one thing you cannot, and you do. That, too, is the mark of a warrior." Here Worf, along with the little-mentioned Konom of the Star Trek comic book series, models one of the possible trajectories of Klingon-Earther relations.

Linda Slusher provides an alternative view of Klingon-Federation encounter. Her Klingons usually come out ahead of the Feds they happen to meet. They display more charm, wit, strength, and, bless 'em, goofiness. Kalin outmaneuvers the legendary Kirk in a struggle to win a planet's valuable minerals.[16] He has the good grace to rescue Federation colonists threatened by cannibals without getting all cozy with Starfleet.[17]

I must say, I prefer the way of Kalin, Krenn, Krantz, and Co.—those who would maintain the utter independence of the Klingon Empire while defusing some of the more war-happy elements. We need those guys out there saying, "You can take your Federation and (bleep) it. How dare you condescend to us, lecture us with your feeble morality? We, like you, are determined to succeed and survive. So push us. We'll push back. We might even come out and push you first, so stay sharp."

The designers of the FASA Star Trek game see fit to remind players that, "The authors find Klingon society to be a fascinating alien culture. We do *not,* by any means admire Klingon ideals and practices! As Mister Spock would say, 'Finding a culture fascinating does not imply approval ...' (We don't suggest that you be a Klingon, only that you try playing a Klingon!)"

Good words, but who is listening? Some of us do admire "Klingon ideals and practices." We have even found rewarding company in which to try them on and explore them: fan-designed, fan-run clubs. I am grateful to *Starlog Magazine,* which first cued me in to the existence of Klingon organizations late in 1988.

[16] Linda Slusher, "The Life of a Warrior is Short" in *The Clipper Trade Ship* #63, Melody and Jim Reondeau, eds., San Jose, CA, 1989.
[17] Linda Slusher, "Neither Man Nor Spirit" in *The Other Side of Paradise* #7, Amy Falkowitz, ed., San Jose, CA, 1987.

I met the Klingon Strike Force, a Seattle-based Klingon military organization, and watched the Klingon Assault Group come to birth out of that lion's head. Both these groups have an international sweep and sponsor newsletters and encourage correspondence. Smaller groups operate independently, reminding us that Klingons thrive on diversity and carve out local spheres of influence. Whenever you are, you need not die alone. No need to hide your *klin* behind an Earther's smile. Come forward and embrace your comrades-in-arms.

I can appreciate the FASA folks' little reminder not to go overboard in identifying with the tricky folks (always a temptation when love is part of the calculation), but I would urge them not to worry. Most of us couldn't be Klingons for long. It's a tough job, best left to Klingons. Still, I can endorse Klingon appreciation with no reservations. That's something we Earthers can handle just fine. Our present is delight. Our future is invention—full of surprises as well as old pleasures, I trust.

How can we help but love the Klingons? In a weird way, while preserving their alien integrity absolutely, they give us ourselves, reverberated back to us from some backboard across the galaxy. Here they come, stronger, fiercer than we dare to be, challenging us to transcend our self-conceived limits (hasn't it always been a good strategy to "play" with a more accomplished opponent?). So come, my friends, and let us stir up Klingon love. Why not?

THE RETURN OF DENISE CROSBY

By Michael Scott

I spent some time recently watching most of the first season of *Star Trek: The Next Generation*. It proved pretty educational.

As many of you know, I took a liking to the Tasha Yar character from the beginning. I have had some of you tweak me about her, pointing out that Tasha was always losing her cool and breaking down when she was supposed to be the straight, professional security chief of the ship. Well, having gone back and reviewed those early episodes, I find that your memories, and mine as well, are quite selective. Viewing the development of Tasha Yar as a character from the perspective of time has revealed some very interesting points.

The original concept of Denise Crosby's character was one that Gene Roddenberry had attempted before; that of the highly placed, strong female character who can compete and hold her own with any of the male crew. From *Star Trek*'s earliest inception, Roddenberry tried to show this possibility, starting with the character of Number One, played be Majel Barrett in the first pilot. Studio and network executives felt that the audience wouldn't believe in a female second-in-command and asked that Number One be dropped. They also asked to have the guy with the pointed ears dropped, but Roddenberry managed to keep him on anyway.

As it turned out, *Star Trek* did very little for the

feminist cause. All female crew wore miniskirts and low necklines. When a female was a major character, she was easily seduced or was shown making errors in judgment that helped create the jeopardy of the episode. Grace Lee Whitney's character, Yeoman Janice Rand, had a relatively strong part as the captain's personal aide, but she was reduced to being a helpless female on more than one occasion and was soon dropped from the show rather than have her growing relationship with Kirk interfere with his other liaisons. Nichelle Nichols' character of Nyota Uhura was a landmark in television history: one of the first regular black characters in dramatic TV, and the first in science fiction. The fact that Uhura had to wear that miniskirt and basically act the part of the switchboard girl somehow hasn't kept Ms. Nichols from exploiting her character in the causes of feminism, racial equality, and space exploration.

The lack of strong female characters was brought to its final conclusion, ironically enough, in Star Trek's final episode ("Turnabout Intruder") when it was stated unequivocally that a woman could not serve as a starship captain.

The intervening years would be kinder to women in the Star Trek universe. Many of the animated episodes had strong female characters, including an instance where Lieutenant Uhura actually commanded a landing party, but the short story format (animated episodes were about twenty minutes long) allowed for little character development and the continuity was still rooted in the original series. It wasn't until the Star Trek movies that women of the future were shown in positions of strength and equality.

After that disastrous pronouncement about female starship captains in "Turnabout Intruder," it was nice to see Starfleet employing women as captains in Star Trek IV: The Voyage Home. The characters of Saavik, Chapel, Carol Marcus, Ilia, and Uhura helped to foster the impression that Star Trek was finally growing up.

Then came the arrival of *Star Trek: The Next Generation*.

In the original cast of nine major characters, three were women in positions of relative power. Ship's Counselor Deanna Troi held the position of the captain's closest advisor on the mental condition and well-being of the crew. Dr. Beverly Crusher was the ship's chief medical officer, with all the responsibility and power that position carries. And Lieutenant Natasha Yar was the ship's security officer and tactical officer, in charge of a large force of security personnel for the vast starship and controlling its main phasers and photon torpedo weapons, as well.

The Tasha Yar character was conceived as a troubled person, rescued as a young girl from a failed colony and brought into Starfleet to become a security specialist. She felt that she had to live up to her Starfleet rescuers' level of civilization and, in many ways, was as much a ward of Starfleet as Data the android. As such, Tasha Yar kept up a front of stern coolness and professionalism with little leeway from emotional entanglements. I say it was a front because she did lose her cool on more than one occasion and did show a healthy interest in the opposite sex.

As the first season of *The Next Generation* progressed, it became apparent that the writers either failed to pay much attention to Denise Crosby's character, or delighted in finding situations that challenged Yar's detachment past the breaking point. Q was able to easily break Tasha's professional front both times they met, getting her to lose her temper and react emotionally.

The very first regular episode, "The Naked Now," managed to show Tasha Yar longing for love and acceptance as a woman under the inhibition-releasing influence of the contamination. Once you've seen a character, who's supposed to be strong and unemotional, break down and drunkenly seduce an android, it's hard to later maintain belief in her strength. If you think that this should apply equally to the other characters in the episode, I would like to remind you of the cultural bias that makes us, man or woman, perceive women in a different light than men. We had no problem with Beverly Crusher trying to seduce Captain Picard, as she was supposed to be a relatively normal, emotional woman, but when Tasha Yar acted silly, it was hard to keep up that suspension of disbelief in later episodes. My statement is borne out in repeated conversations with Star Trek fans concerning their remembered perceptions of that first season.

Denise Crosby's portrayal of Tasha Yar wasn't helped a bit by the presence of Michael Dorn's much stronger character, Worf. As the first season progressed, it became apparent that Worf was the steadier of the two, the more interesting of the two, and the more *believable* of the two. Denise Crosby, reportedly, loved the idea of Tasha Yar and went to bat a number of times to get Tasha more lines and more presence in various episodes. Unfortunately, with such a large ensemble cast, Yar was often shown standing at her weapons console with little to do other than open hailing frequencies and raise shields. Denise Crosby saw the handwriting on the wall and approached Gene Roddenberry, asking to be written out of the show. In the episode "Skin of Evil," Lieutenant Tasha Yar is killed almost offhandedly by a malevolent entity, with nothing to show for her sacrifice. Ironically, in several prior episodes, Tasha Yar had some very strong participation in the plots, and even more ironically, her farewell speech at the end of "Skin of Evil" is the most memorable part of the episode.

Though Tasha Yar was dead and Denise Crosby no longer a regular on the show, the actress still felt a bond with Star Trek and her ill-used character. In the intervening period, Denise played the female lead in *Pet Semetary,* had an excellent small part in *Miracle Mile,* and was the introductory scorned woman in

Blake Edwards' comedy *Skin Deep.* However, Denise Crosby never forgot her role as Tasha Yar and began to try to find some way to return to the show.

That way was found in the third season episode, "Yesterday's Enterprise." The starship encounters a rift in space-time and Worf detects a ship emerging from it. As the ship emerges into normal space, everything subtly changes, and suddenly Lieutenant Tasha Yar is at the tactical station, reporting that the emerging ship is NCC-1701-C, the Ambassador-class starship *Enterprise,* lost in space and last seen twenty-two years previously near the Klingon outpost Narenda III. In that time, the Federation has been fighting a long, bloody war with the Klingon Empire and is now losing. The older *Enterprise* (with a female Captain Garrett) had answered a Klingon distress call and attempted to defend the outpost from a squadron of Romulan starships. The *Enterprise* had been overwhelmed and subjected to a massive barrage of photon torpedoes, which seem to have opened up the space-time rift through which the crippled starship escaped to the "present."

It seems that the time trip has caused an alternate reality where the Klingons fight the Federation rather than ally with it. Only Guinan senses the change, but she manages to convince Picard that the old *Enterprise* must be returned to its fight in the past in order to restore the correct timeline. However, Captain Garrett is killed in a Klingon attack, Guinan tells Tasha Yar that she dies uselessly in the other timeline, and Tasha asks to go with the older ship and die a more meaningful death. The *Enterprise*-C goes back through the rift as the *Enterprise*-D is about to be destroyed by the Klingons. When the older ship disappears, the correct timeline is restored with no hint of any ship having come out of the rift. But, twenty-two years in the past, NCC-1701-C emerges to fight the Romulan squadron, so impressing the Klingons with their sacrifice that they initiate the peace talks that eventually lead to the Klingon-Federation alliance.

Denise Crosby plays the part of Tasha Yar very well in this return. The Tasha we see is more stable and more mature than the one of the first season episodes. Of course, this is due to Denise Crosby (and the writers) reviewing her role from a long-range perspective and putting everything into this one-shot affair. From a continuity standpoint, we might imagine that this Tasha Yar's personal character has been honed by continuous war with the Klingon Empire and in her extremely responsible position as a battleship's chief tactical officer.

While this return of Tasha Yar was intended as a one-shot deal, it excited the imagination of those of us who liked the original character. One of my suggested scenarios involved the survival of Tasha Yar in the past. After all, she is a trained tactical officer. Perhaps her abilities were able to allow the *Enterprise*-C to prevail against the Romulans. Then you would have Tasha Yar in two places at once: as a child in her failed homeworld, and as a adult in Starfleet, in her own past. Would she be able to resist the temptation of trying to rescue herself from that colony? Or was she actually instrumental in getting herself rescued by others? Even so, where has Tasha Yar been all this time? Such speculation was fun and led to many good discussions with friends. But there was to be an even stranger twist to the story of Denise Crosby's involvement with Star Trek.

In the episode broadcast on June 2, 1991 (in Baton Rouge, at least; we understand that it was broadcast the prior week in other cities), Geordie LaForge is captured by Romulans and brainwashed. During this procedure, the Romulans take their orders from a female commander standing in the shadows. The voice of the Romulan Commander is unmistakably Denise Crosby's.

Of course, my poor brain was already speculating

like crazy. The best continuity explanation I have heard (and the one that I like a lot) is that this commander is Tasha Yar's daughter, born after her capture by the Romulans at the battle of Narenda III. If so, is she human or half-Romulan? Where is Tasha Yar herself? No wonder she didn't rescue her younger self. If this scenario is true, the crew of the *Enterprise* would have *no* idea about the time trip, and the concept of the commander being the daughter of Tasha Yar would be very confusing.

As this article goes to bed (June 17, 1991), it has been confirmed through BBS contacts that the Romulan Commander is Tasha Yar's daughter, presumably fathered by Lieutenant Castille, raised as a Romulan from survivors captured at the Narenda III massacre. The fourth season finale "Redemption" has a Romulan fleet under her command decloak and join the Klingon rebels. "Redemption" is to be a three-part episode with the second and third part being the opening episodes of the landmark fifth season. The story is supposedly going to end with Worf regaining his full status as a true Klingon and restoring his family's honor. Whether this story will end Denise Crosby's current involvement in Star Trek is a very good question. Her character is the product of a union from a time loop; an alternate reality that has only a temporary existence in the normal *Next Generation* universe. The Tasha Yar who was captured by the Romulans is not the same person who was killed by the "Exxon Valdez Creature," but she knew a Captain Picard, a Geordie LaForge, a Will Riker, and so on. This Tasha Yar came from a future that is different, but very similar in personnel and technology. This would certainly go a long way in explaining some of the Romulan behavior and capabilities. I know that "Redemption" is supposed to be a story about Worf and the Klingon civil war, but I will be sorely disappointed if some lip-service isn't paid to the story of Lieutenants Yar and Castille. Also, is Tasha's daughter wholly a loyal Romulan, or did Tasha give her some human heritage that she is drawing from, allowing her to play her own game? Perhaps the only one who can straighten out this mess is Guinan.

Tune in next season for more.

MORE ABOUT STAR TREK IN AUSTRIA

By Ingrid Schwaller

After reading Karin Embacher's article about Star Trek fandom in Austria in *Best of Trek #13,* I have finally decided (after much hesitation) to write about my own experiences with Star Trek in Austria.

First, a few remarks about what Star Trek means to me: Since I am basically a pessimist (obviously in contrast to many Star Trek fans), who does not really believe that mankind will be able to overcome the folly of the arms race and the threat of nuclear war, Star Trek provides me with the optimism I need so much at times. After all, it tells about a future that would be worth living for (the details of which have been analyzed time and again, and I do not want to discuss them here) and it gives a glimpse of a time after the nuclear age, thus implying that man is, indeed, able to act rationally in spite of all evidence to the contrary.

As Karin points out in her article, some of the original *Star Trek* episodes were first carried on Austrian television in 1973. At that time I was twelve years old, and I do not recall having read any advance announcement about a new science fiction series. I stumbled upon *Star Trek* somewhere in the middle of "The Ultimate Computer." I remember that I liked the new series, but I was much more impressed with its action-adventure aspect than with anything else. I kept watching the individual episodes more or less (rather less, I suppose) regularly, but when they were over, *Star Trek* again disappeared from my life.

The next thing I remember vividly is that I found a "complete" edition of the German translation of James Blish's *Star Trek* novel adaptations in a tobacconist's shop which also sold books. I put "complete" in quotes because, as I found out much later, the German version of the Blish books was compiled in an entirely different way, and even though it consisted of thirteen books, they did not include all episodes. At that time I had no idea about this, and even if I had known it, I could not have done anything to get the additional episodes because they were not available in German and I did not know enough English to read the original books.

Again there was a long "Star Trek-less" period, with an occasional rerun of already dubbed *Star Trek* episodes during vacations. In this connection, I think I have to point out that *Star Trek* has never been considered anything more than kid stuff in Austria (like any other science fiction series, no matter how serious it might be) and, except for the very first screening, it has always been scheduled either at 6 to 6:30 P.M., just before the "real" evening shows, or at some time in the afternoon, around 3 P.M. That is why most people consider Star Trek fans crazy, because they get excited about a "kids" show.

I do not think that there are many people in Austria who would freely admit to liking science fiction. Most of my friends consider science fiction as something one might read or watch just for recreation, but that is not read or watched by "serious" people. Actually, I am very proud of myself that I have persuaded one of my friends to read two or three Star Trek books and to come with me to see *Star Trek II: The Wrath of Khan.* I think she liked it, and she now understands better what I feel about this subject.

In 1979 the first six fotonovels were published in German. The sixth book carried an announcement for the publication of number seven, but this one and the subsequent fotonovels never turned up. I remember pestering the assistant in one of Vienna's bookstores to get me the books I still needed. Since neither he nor I knew that they had not been published in the first place, it took quite some time until I gave up the hope of finding them in Vienna.

The next summer I went to England on vacation, and there I found all the fotonovels I still needed. No question that I bought them immediately. This was actually the time when I became aware of the fact that there was so much material about Star Trek around that I had not read. In the meantime, my English had also improved sufficiently to read English books in the original. Thus, in the following years I acquired quite a number of Star Trek books during my travels to the United States and Great Britain, and I always tried to get books in Vienna, too.

Unfortunately, it is virtually impossible to order books from the United States and have them sent to Austria (at least, I have not managed to do that). I do not know why, but obviously U.S. publishing companies are not interested in business with private citizens abroad (and a bookseller told me that even bookstores have problems in this respect). Even though I tried to order books several times, I did not even receive an answer in spite of the international reply voucher I included every time.

The only time I ever got books directly from the States (via a Vienna bookstore) was when I ordered eight volumes of Alan Dean Foster's *Star Trek Logs*. After waiting for an interminable period, I finally received the entire bunch—in hardcover. It cost me about $180 at the current exchange rate. I will never forget my mother's shocked voice when she phoned me at work to tell me that I had received a package of books with a bill of $180. I think this incident finally confirmed her opinion that I am slightly crazy.

In the meantime, I have resorted to having my friends look through bookstores in English-speaking countries when they go there. I am afraid I am making myself rather unpopular, particularly when I ask them to get one of the rarer Star Trek books for me. I vividly remember that two years ago I asked a friend of mine to get *The Fate of the Phoenix* for me from the States and he had a terrible time finding it. I think he went to several bookstores across the States (he took a Greyhound bus from New York City to San Francisco) before he found one store that would order the book and send it to Austria. When he came back and told me about all the trouble he had gone to to get the book, I did not dare tell him that in the meantime I had finally bought it in Austria (oh, irony of fate!).

After getting *Best of Trek #2* in England some years ago, I tried to get the other *Best of Trek* books, too, but so far I have been able to get only #6, 8, 9, 10, and 13. This week I will try to order the others and, maybe, one day I will get them. Two bookshops in Vienna have now started to sell Star Trek novels published by Pocket Books. I am always looking forward to any new book on their stalls, because the novels are the only up-to-date Star Trek publications (except for a very occasional *Best of Trek*) that you can get here.

A German publishing company has now also started to publish German translations of some of Pocket Books' Star Trek novels, but they cannot be compared with the original versions. Most of the time when I read the German version I can hear the original English behind it. I certainly do not want to denigrate the work of the translators (after all, I am one myself, even though I do not do literary translations), but in the case of Star Trek, the German versions do not live up to the originals. As Karin points out, sometimes they are simply incorrect.

There is another thing, which might be a minor issue in the eyes of the publishers, but which jolts me every time I see a German Star Trek book: as far as I can see, the covers of the English originals relate to the story told by the book. The German versions, however, change the covers apparently at will. *The Web of the Romulans,* for instance, was published with the cover of *The Wounded Sky.*

Passing from the books to the original television episodes, I would like to add a few discrepancies between the English and the German versions to those already mentioned by Karin (I have not read the article by Charlotte Davis on Star Trek fandom in Germany in *Best of Trek #7,* so I do not know whether I repeat some of her observations here).

In almost all episodes, the term "warp" is changed to "sol" and sometimes speeds like "sol 15" are used (e.g., in "The Trouble With Tribbles").

In "Assignment: Earth," the German version calls Gary Seven "Gary Sevenrock."

In "Journey to Babel," Sarek says his blood type is "X-Y negative" instead of "T-negative." This discrepancy kept me in confusion for years, because it took quite some time until I found out what English-language publications were talking about when they mentioned T-negative. As Karin says, Amanda's name is changed to Emily for no apparent reason—in the credits she is still cited as "Amanda."

In "The Trouble With Tribbles," the Federation currency unit "credits" is changed to "Federation ducats."

In "Is There In Truth No Beauty," Miranda's first name is turned into "Marion."

In "The Savage Curtain," Zora, the female warrior, is turned into a male named "Zores." (Here I might add that "Zores" in German is a slang word for "trouble" and thus not totally inappropriate.)

In "Operation: Annihilate," Kirk's sister-in-law Aurelan is turned in "Aurelia."

These are some of the most glaring discrepancies—I am sure there are many more.

Over the past few months, SAT-1, a private FRG satellite TV station which can be received in Vienna via cable TV, carried about thirty *Star Trek* episodes that had never been broadcast in German, enabling me to watch episodes I had only read to date. I have now managed to see (and videotape) all but three of the original seventy-nine episodes and to read (and own, I might point out) 113 books, all in all. Of course, I also want to see the five Star Trek movies, and I am certainly looking forward to the sixth one. Unfortunately, it always takes some time until the movies come to Austrian cinemas since they have to be dubbed first. However, by reading the movie reviews in *Time* magazine, I try to find out when they are released in the United States and then get at least the novelizations as soon as possible.

This should have been a brief, concise article just giving you a few more details about Star Trek fandom in Austria, but as you can see, I ended up telling about my problems with regard to getting Star Trek material here in Austria.

PAYMENT IS USUALLY EXPENSIVE: THOUGHTS ON "THE JOURNEY TO BABEL"

By Karla Taylor

> Happy families are all alike: every unhappy family is unhappy in its own way.
>
> —Leo Tolstoy, *Anna Karenina*

The question of whether or not to admit the Coridans to the Federation must have been one of the most momentous controversies in years. Important enough to draw an ambassador out of retirement, perhaps against his better judgment. Important enough for a starship, no less, to be in charge of transporting the diplomatic parties to the conference, code-named with rueful irony, Babel.

In a way, this story was "Agatha Christie in Space," a classic "closed circle" mystery where a diverse group of people are confined to one place while a murderer stalks and long-buried conflicts come to the surface.

The passengers included Andorians, quiet and watchful, and harboring a snake in the grass; Tellarites, furry and ferocious, even the ambassador himself looking for a fight; and the Vulcans, in the person of Sarek, ambassador of long experience and immense reason. Accompanying him was his Terran wife, Amanda, and thereby hangs the tale.

Did she usually travel with him? Or did she only decide to go when they heard that the *Enterprise* was to be their host? One can imagine the conversation between Sarek and Amanda back home and aboard the shuttle to the starship. Amanda must have known the trip was going to be a strain, but hope springs eternal in the human breast.

Things were rather strained aboard the *Enterprise,* as well. Captain Kirk worried about juggling a bunch of antagonistic beings. Dr. McCoy grumbled about the uncomfortable dress uniforms. And what did they know? One expects that First Officer Spock would rather have been anywhere else in the universe at that moment. What were his, dare one say, feelings about the situation? Apprehension? Resignation? In *Star Trek*'s first season, Spock mentioned his parents several times, always in the past tense. The impression was that they were dead. Well, they must have seemed dead to Spock, who probably never expected to see either of them again, and putting all that behind him was surely a way to cope with his loss.

In "The Corbomite Maneuver," Spock saw the grim false face of Balok as reminiscent of his father. We discovered this "resemblance" in "Journey to Babel" to have been subjective on Spock's part. However, surely Sarek's stern countenance must have struck terror in the heart of an errant little boy, or a young man in the process of telling his father that he was signing up with Starfleet.

As anyone familiar with the story knows, Spock and his father Sarek had parted company eighteen years before when Spock decided to dedicate his life to Starfleet instead of the Science Academy on Vulcan. It was an impasse which neither seemed to want, or to be able, to break.

Sarek ignored his son during the introduction in the shuttle docking bay. Even Amanda had little chance to speak with him. Her conversation with Kirk, however, was illuminating for one point: Amanda considered the Vulcan way of life to be better than the human way. An extraordinary statement, considering what came later. But this was Amanda, wife of Sarek of Vulcan, speaking from the contentment of her life and the happiness she must have felt, having the two most important people in her life together at the same place.

To digress for a moment: the marriage of Sarek and Amanda seems to have been a completely accepted thing, therefore the Vulcans must not have known of the institution of morganatic marriage. This was a European custom in which royal princes could marry nonroyal ladies. The marriage was legal, and the children were legitimate. However, the wife did not rise to her husband's status, and the children could inherit nothing. It was, in practice, a system of coercion to keep princes from throwing away their futures by foolishly marrying their true loves. As usual, it was the children of morganatic marriages who suffered the most, caught somewhere between legitimacy and illegitimacy, legally acceptable but never "top drawer." We heard in "Amok Time" that Spock owned property on Vulcan, and certainly Sarek regarded Spock as his heir. Therefore, it seems Sarek and Amanda's marriage was fully accredited. One more historical item: history's most famous morganatic couple was Archduke Franz Ferdinand of Austria and Sophie Chotek, a mere impoverished duchess. While on a diplomatic tour in Bosnia, they were assassinated—which touched off World War I. The murderer's name, honestly, was *Gav* Princip.

The formal reception was complete with exotic food and scarcely disguised hostility. Kirk, to his credit, hovered like a hawk, ready to pounce at the first sign of trouble.

It was not long in coming. The Tellarite Gav forced an argument with Sarek, who didn't seem entirely averse to the prospect. His statement, "Tellarites do not argue for reasons; they simply argue," was obvi-

ously not meant to calm down Gav. Sarek must have
known how provoking those words would be to the
touchy Tellarite. This means war! Apparently Vulcans
and Tellarites got along like, well, cats and dogs.

One has to sympathize with Spock. There are few
social situations with more potential for horror than
having one's friends met one's family. Babel, indeed!
No one spoke the same language. Throughout the
story, Spock was the perfect Vulcan, obviously overcompensating for the fact that his human heritage was
standing before everyone in the person of his mother.

Later, Gav, who'd apparently been drinking too
much, renewed the argument with Sarek. Gav wanted
Coridan to stay out of the Federation so his people
could make use of it. Sarek was of the opinion that
Coridan should be under Federation protection, to
stop such marauding. These were fighting words to
Gav, who attacked Sarek. The Vulcan easily fended
him off, but Gav was still surly. "There will be payment for your slander, Sarek of Vulcan!" he warned
in his stilted, growling voice. "Payment is usually expensive," returned Sarek, the story's most premoni-
tionary statement.

Soon Gav was found murdered. His neck was broken, and Spock was not at all reluctant to point out
that his father was capable of the act. What was he
thinking of? Was it purely to offer pertinent information, or was Spock prompted, even subconsciously, by
a desire for revenge? Who's sorry now, Sarek of
Vulcan?

If so, he got more than he bargained for, because
when Sarek was questioned, he collapsed with a heart
attack. The story descended swiftly into nightmare.
McCoy said an operation was necessary. Spock would
have to give blood, and a dangerous new drug would
have to be used to speed up blood production. Then
Kirk was attacked by the real murderer, a smarmy
pseudo-Andorian named Thelev, and ended up in
sickbay himself. The *Enterprise* was attacked by an

anonymous ship. Spock decided his first duty was to the *Enterprise*. Another terrible impasse had been reached.

Some questions should be asked at this point. Why didn't Sarek tell his wife about his heart condition? Was it just that he knew, from long experience, how it would upset her? Or did he think that she would try to dissuade him from this one last mission, which would mean missing a chance to see his son? Sarek had a preliminary attack earlier, while in meditation along on the ship's observation deck. He refused to explain the need for this meditation, but one can easily imagine it consisted of sorting out the various stresses and problems of the day, and perhaps a stern self-order to stay in control and not betray his pain to anyone else, not even his wife.

Sarek was an interesting character. Joyce Tullock, in her article "The One Who Is Spock" (*Best of Trek #13*), pointed out that Spock's origins lie in old Hollywood movies. The character of Sarek, also, drew upon Hollywood's past. He combined the unearthly, possibly dangerous sexuality of Dracula; the eloquence, political idealism, and slightly amused calm of *Casablanca*'s Victor Laszlo; and the stubbornness and patriarchal imperiousness of Charles Foster Kane. Placed in a science fiction context, it was a fascinating combination.

But Sarek was also a deeply ironic character. He "disowned" his son for making an unusual life choice, but Sarek himself once made a choice that was far more nontraditional and momentous than anything Spock ever did. Was *Sarek* "overcompensating"? He must have faced considerable opposition when it became known that he'd chosen an Earth woman to be his wife. (One can imagine being called in for a conference with T'Pau.) Comments like, "She'll turn you into a human," might have led him to the determination, with all its far-reaching implications, that his son would *be a Vulcan*. Furthermore, Sarek seemed to have kept a curious sort of "double entry" set of books on his family. Some show of emotion was all right for his wife, the human, but not for his son, the Vulcan. Sarek smiled ever so slightly at Amanda when she told him she loved him; if Spock had ever in his childhood uttered those words, he would have been sent to his room without any supper. One can feel a considerable sympathy for Sarek's opposition to Spock's choice of career. He had something in common with someone he never met: Carol Marcus, who didn't raise her son to be a soldier, either. At the same time, we admire Spock for standing up to his father and taking control of his own life.

Sarek's blood may have been T-negative, but his personality was definitely Type A: the driven, "I can handle anything" sort of person. There are drawbacks to that. What if Sarek had fallen unconscious immediately? No one would have been able to give an accurate report of his medical history.

Another question: Why did Thelev attack Kirk? Wasn't that going a bit far? Murdering the Tellarite ambassador was one thing, but the very captain of the ship? Shouldn't the next step have been Shras, the Andorian ambassador (which would have boosted Thelev's position), or even, heaven forbid, Amanda? Also, when he had Kirk down, why didn't Thelev finish him off with a quick slash to the throat? The Orions, Thelev's real race, didn't send a very good agent provocateur. He didn't even get his suicide right.

In the middle of all this stood Amanda. What was she thinking and feeling? It's not enough to say that she was frightened, anxious, horrified. After eighteen long years, she had been presented with some glimmer of hope that her family would be together again. At least she could have hoped for a measure of understanding. Now her husband was dying, and her son was refusing to help him live. Amanda must have wondered what her life had been for, if it came down to this. So, of course, she went to her son's cabin.

He was expecting her. He had his array of weapons ready, armor carefully in place.

The scene between Amanda and Spock was perhaps the most traumatic ever in *Star Trek*. Gone was the wife who believed the Vulcan way to be superior to Earth's. Gone was the mother who spoke of childhood pets. Amanda, on the precipice, fell back on her human nature, pleading, weeping, arguing, finally threatening, all to save her husband's life. All to no avail. If she thought that argument would work, Spock believed Vulcan logic to take precedence. If she cried, he regarded her with a face of set stone. If she threatened, he forced himself to accept her threats, even the threat of life-long hatred. She struck him. He remained steadfast. Her son was finally and completely a stranger to her.

Did he imagine she would dredge up his childhood? Her "When you were five years old ..." speech was a chilling counterpart to the teddy bear tale at the reception.

Even if Spock had wished for some sort of retribution for the pain his father had put him through, he would never have wanted the kind of horror that had visited itself upon this troubled and sundered family. Still, motives are infinitely mixed. Part of him, not necessarily the human part, might have sneered in joy somewhere deep within him ("for years I was in his power, now his life is in *my* hands"). If so, then guilt must have followed as surely as day follows night.

Amanda, a woman who'd spent most of her life on Vulcan, knew very well what it meant to *be* a Vulcan. Yet when her son asked her (with scarcely disguised agony) how she could not understand what being a Vulcan meant, Amanda answered in near hysteria, "If this is what it means, I don't want to know!" She'd traveled down a long, thorny road since her statement to Kirk that the Vulcan way was "a better way than ours."

We can sense some of Amanda's own isolation

when she reminded Spock that "human" was "a dirty word." How many times had she bitten back angry words to the Vulcans around her, when they used the word "human" as we would say "inferior"? But she and her son were locked into a pattern that she couldn't break and he refused to abandon for mere personal reasons. Who's sorry now, Spock of Starfleet?

Many Star Trek fans seem to forget that Spock never did relent; he was tricked into cooperation by Kirk and McCoy. Of course, it can well be said that the trick was so transparent that Spock must have seen through it and accepted it anyway, because it was what he desperately wanted. But the fact remains that without the captain's and the doctor's ploy, Spock would have stayed on that bridge, experiencing a new agony in a life already full of agonies: Sarek would have died, and Amanda would have seen her entire life go to ruin in a few short hours. Good thing the captain and chief medical officer weren't above a little fancy footwork in a good cause.

A minor digression: Spock's blood is described as green, but even with a small amount of red human blood, that coppery green would turn near-black. Also, would it have been a sort of poetic justice if they'd pumped it whole into Sarek's body? Or would that have injured him, even killed him?

Furthermore, in the light of later knowledge, what were Sarek's plans concerning his *katra*? There were his two assistants, either of whom would have been a viable candidate. Under the circumstances, one doubts that Sarek would have entrusted his spirit to Spock. What about Amanda? He must have discussed the possibility with her, even though they would have assumed, with her shorter life span, that he would outlive her. Amanda could have taken her husband's spirit. She certainly would have been better prepared for the ordeal that McCoy ever was, and *he* survived.

This conjured up the chilling vision of Sarek speaking, from beyond death, to the son who let him die.

"Journey to Babel" was about getting even, and how seeking revenge can be more expensive for the seeker than for the object of their anger. Besides the internal conflicts of Spock's family, there was surely Gav, whose thoughts in the last moments of his life were no doubt concerned with how he'd get even with the Vulcan ambassador; and then there were the Orions. What did they have to be vengeful about? We don't know much about them, but maybe the ongoing trade (condoned by the Federation?) in green Orion slave women had something to do with it.

Later, Amanda had her wish: her family was reunited. She stood between her husband and her son (a not unfamiliar position, one suspects). Amanda asked Sarek to thank his son, and he replied that one does not thank logic; "Spock acted in the only logical way open to him." Did he, indeed? Apparently no one had yet told Sarek that his son had intended to stay on the bridge. Amanda had had enough logic for one day. She lost her temper, and her husband and son finally found something to talk about. Spock asked his father why he'd married Amanda. (He didn't know? One would think that Spock would have been apprised of the juicy details by other Vulcans from childhood on. Perhaps he wanted to understand Sarek's personal motives.) Amanda was obviously shocked, as if she was afraid her husband would tell the whole story then and there. Sarek's now-famous answer, "At the time, it seemed the logical thing to do," is one of *Star Trek*'s great lines: obscure enough to allow for much speculation, suggestive enough to allow for fantasy.

So, what happened on the rest of the journey?